House Mate

Leah Brunner

Leah Brunner Publishing

Copyright © 2021 by Leah Brunner

All rights reserved.

No portion of this book may be reproduced in any form without written permission from the publisher or author, except as permitted by U.S. copyright law.

To my mom. Thanks for fostering my love of writing and creating books early on. I know it was my goal to write children's books, but this is close enough, right?
Love you, Mom.

Trigger Warning

This work of fiction speaks vaguely of sexual assault and also includes themes of losing a spouse and working through grief.

Contents

Author's Note	VIII
Prologue	1
1. Sophie	7
2. Drew	15
3. Sophie	30
4. Drew	38
5. Sophie	42
6. Drew	47
7. Sophie	53
8. Drew	57
9. Sophie	64
10. Drew	69
11. Sophie	77
12. Drew	96
13. Sophie	103

14. Sophie	108
15. Sophie	124
16. Drew	128
17. Sophie	140
18. Drew	152
19. Sophie	161
20. Drew	169
21. Sophie	174
22. Drew	179
23. Sophie	185
24. Drew	190
25. Sophie	194
26. Drew	197
27. Sophie	204
28. Drew	210
29. Sophie	217
30. Drew	223
31. Sophie	233
32. Drew	244
33. Sophie	252
34. Drew	259
35. Sophie	267
Sophie	273

Thank you for reading!	279
Other Books by Leah	280
Stay in the loop!	281
Acknowledgments	282
About the Author	283

Author's Note

House Mate was formerly published as *A Love Uncontainable*. The story is still the same, but with a new look on the outside!

Prologue

Sophie

Rubbing the swell of my pregnant belly, I put away the last of the dishes from the dishwasher. The house is so quiet without my husband here that I can clearly hear the gentle taps of rain against my kitchen window, like little pins hitting a tin can. I take a moment to watch the beads of rain trickle down the kitchen window. The obscenely quiet house often causes my ears to ring, so the rain is a welcome and soothing sound.

I was gutted when my husband, Sam, told me he had to deploy to Afghanistan. He received deployment orders a week after we found out I was pregnant with our baby girl. It's hard to believe he's already been away for over five months now.

Five lonely months.

The pregnancy hormones are definitely adding to my emotional state. I think I'm managing pretty well on my own, though. Getting ready for the baby has kept me busy.

I never realized how much Sam helped around the house until he left. For almost half a year, I have cleaned the house, paid the bills, put together the baby's room, washed all the dishes, done the cooking and lawn care, and remembered to take the trash out each week.

Whew.

I'm just grateful for a healthy pregnancy and that I still have the energy to do it all.

And we're over halfway; only four more months until he'll be back.

I can't wait.

I finish up in the kitchen and grab a basket of laundry to fold. I balance it awkwardly on my hip, which is getting harder and harder with my growing belly.

I can't help but stop and peer into the nursery on my way to the master bedroom. It's coming along splendidly, and I have loved decorating it. There are large, pink paper roses on the wall above the dainty white crib. I've looked at wooden cutouts on Etsy to put with the roses, but since we haven't decided on our daughter's name yet, I've put off ordering.

Smiling to myself, I continue toward our room. I set the laundry basket on the bed and begin folding. I actually miss folding pieces of Sam's wardrobe. The small loads of laundry are yet another reminder that he's gone. Along with my lonely toothbrush in the toothbrush holder.

A sigh escapes from my chest as I continue folding piece after piece of maternity clothing. I turn on my heel to put the clothes away when I hear the doorbell ring.

My stomach does a little flip. Every time I hear the doorbell or see an unknown number pop up on my phone, I can't help but get a little nervous, wondering if Sam got hurt or something. I take a deep breath and remind myself that it's probably just an Amazon package. I ordered some baby items a few days ago.

Yes, that has to be it.

Once I reach the front door, I open it slowly and peek my head around the door. No one is there, so I glance down at the welcome mat. Sure enough, just an Amazon package. I release a breath, not even realizing that I had been holding it in.

I grab the small box and close the door behind me, heading toward the kitchen in search of some scissors. This must be the cute ruffly baby socks I ordered the other day. I grin as I find the scissors in the kitchen and begin cutting through the tape on the package. Pale pink comes into view when I pull the flaps open. Oh my gosh, they're even cuter in person. I'm about to pull them out of the box when my doorbell rings again.

The mailman probably forgot something. Waddling back toward the front door, I open it, expecting to see another package. My breath catches in my throat when I see two Army officers in their dress uniforms standing on my front stoop. One of the men looks to be in his mid-forties; he's taller and has kind blue eyes. The other is shorter and seems younger, probably in his twenties, with dark hair and tanned skin.

The older man looks at me, and then his eyes drop to my belly as he slowly removes his beret.

Deep down, I know why they're here, but I try to convince myself there's been some mistake.

Maybe the wrong house.

"Sophie Miller?" he asks hesitantly.

The breath leaves my lungs, and the blood drains from my face.

"Yes, I'm Sophie," I reply, barely above a whisper.

His eyebrows draw together and he looks at his feet before he brings his eyes back up to meet mine.

"I'm Lt. Colonel Harmon, and this is Captain Ortez. It's our deepest regret to inform you that your husband, Sergeant Samuel Miller, was killed in action yesterday while he aided in a mission near Kabul. I am incredibly sorry for your loss."

I stand there paralyzed by the sudden onslaught of emotions running through me. It's like my mind can't keep up with the words they said, making me incapable of understanding.

There's no way they have the correct house. I literally just spoke to Sam on the phone yesterday morning.

Closing my eyes, I breathe out a breathy laugh. "I'm sorry. I think you have the wrong house. I *just* spoke to my husband yesterday."

The younger officer takes a step toward me. "Ma'am, I know this news is difficult to hear. I'm so sorry. What can we do to help? Can we call someone for you?"

Something in my brain snaps. "No! You need to leave. You have the wrong house."

The other man steps forward this time. "Mrs. Miller, I had the honor of working alongside your husband. Sam was a truly amazing man and soldier." He pulls his beret off of his head and twists it between his hands. "He spoke of you often. His love for you was always apparent. And for your baby too."

My baby. Our baby. "No, no, no …"

I can't do this alone. I can't do this without Sam. He was supposed to be here with me, by my side, helping to raise our daughter.

My legs give out from underneath me, and I faintly recall the two men helping me inside and onto the sofa.

The older officer—I can't remember either of their names—asks me if there's a friend they can call for me.

I hand him my phone and the word "Sarah" comes out of my mouth.

I barely recognize my own voice. Sarah is my closest friend here at Fort Bragg and lives just a few houses down from me. He takes my phone and starts looking through my contacts. After finding Sarah's name, he taps on the screen to call her. I can hear her voice answer on the other end and he steps back outside to talk with her.

The younger one asks if Sam and I had talked about what to do in this scenario. I remember the folder in our top kitchen drawer that had Sam's will, my power of attorney, and his contingency plan inside. I tell him about the contingency folder in the kitchen drawer by the microwave. He walks from the living room to the kitchen to retrieve it.

A moment later, he strides back into the living room, folder in hand, and tries to hand it to me.

I push it away and tell him, "No, I don't want to look at it. Can you just read through the papers?"

He nods curtly. "Yes, ma'am. Whatever I can do to help."

Leaning forward from my seat on the couch, I put my face in my hands, trying to calm myself.

"Your friend is on her way," the older man says in a sympathetic voice.

I feel movement next to me. He must've sat on the couch. I keep my head in my hands and focus on breathing.

"Do you have anyone else you'd like us to call?" One of them asks.

My mind has become too fuzzy to distinguish one from the other now. I can't find my voice to answer him. My husband is gone. I can't believe it. Maybe I'll wake up tomorrow and realize this was just a nightmare.

I'm in a fog of complete shock.

Not knowing how much time has passed, I hear the front door open. I lift my head and see Sarah rushing towards me. Once she reaches me, she pulls me into her arms. Tears are streaming down her face.

Now that she's here with me, the officers stand and announce they're heading out but that they'll contact me tomorrow. I can barely register anything they're saying to me.

Now that Sarah is here, this all feels too real. She's sobbing and holding me, but I'm just numb.

"Sarah, I need to call my family."

She pulls back and nods. "Would you like me to call them for you?" She barely splutters the words out as her chin quivers.

I shake my head. Pulling out my phone, I dial my mom.

"Hey, sweetie!" she answers cheerfully.

I take a deep, shuddering breath. Telling my mom Sam was killed makes it seem concrete. Like it's not a horrible dream, but actually real life.

"Mom," I say, my voice thick with emotion. "Sam was killed in action. I don't want to do this alone ... please, can you come?"

She gasps in shock. "No, Sophie. What? I think I heard you wrong."

I gulp. "Sam is gone, Mom."

I hear a strangled sob over the phone. "Sophie, no." A few seconds pass. "I'll be there as soon as I can. I need to get a hold of your father, but he's in surgery."

"Okay. Just come as soon as you can."

Chapter 1

Sophie

Three Years Later

The humid summer breeze blows through my hair as I stand before my late husband's grave at the Fort Bragg Cemetery. Our nearly three-year-old daughter, Samantha, is holding my hand. This is the first time we've visited Sam's grave. Each year I've told myself I'd bring Samantha here, but I just couldn't bring myself to book the flights. I wanted to remember Sam alive and strong, full of life. I was worried this would ruin that.

The past three years have been overwhelming. Just the thought of seeing Sam's grave again made me shudder. I could barely manage getting through the end of my pregnancy and put a smile on my face for baby showers with the sadness I faced every day. It felt like darkness clouded my brain and I couldn't even think straight most days.

Until Samantha was born.

She was the sunshine I needed to make the fog clear from my mind. Taking care of her brought me joy and gave me the strength to get out of bed each day—and several times in the middle of the night. She gave me the courage to see a therapist and to work through my grief over losing Sam. Things aren't perfect, and I still struggle at times, but I've implemented everything my therapist suggested—except for taking

Samantha to visit Sam's grave. Deep down, I don't think I wanted to visit Sam until he could be proud of me, proud of how I'm doing.

Not that I would ever admit that out loud; it would sound ridiculous to anyone else.

But I've felt more like myself this year. Starting my new teaching job helped a lot; it's been a great outlet for me to have my own *thing*, outside of being a mom and a widow. So I knew this was the year I'd finally be ready to visit his grave. I'm finally ready to face this and get the closure I need.

Samantha is oblivious to the loss of the man she never met; instead; she's entranced by two blue jays nearby, watching them land on one of the crosses a few yards away from us.

"Hi Sam," I say as I sit in front of his tombstone.

"I can't believe it's been three years since you passed." I swallow and brush a blonde curl off of Samantha's forehead.

"Sorry it took me so long to bring Samantha to meet you. I've been back in Kansas with my family." It feels weird to talk to a stone cross, but I hope this message will get to him. Samantha smiles up at me. She's probably a little confused about why I'm speaking to an inanimate object.

"I named her after you. Samantha is her given name, but everyone calls her Sam … or Sammy girl." A smile forms on my lips, thinking of the endearing nickname my family has given her. "She's the best gift you could have ever given me."

I'm trying to be strong, but a lone tear escapes down my cheek.

"I miss you so much, Sam. But I remember the conversation we had before you left." I pause.

"Do you remember? You made me promise you I would move forward with my life if anything happened to you. So I started teaching last fall, third grade. I love it so much. I know you'd be proud of me. Samantha and I are still staying with my parents. They've been so great." A breathy chuckle escapes from my throat. "I mean, my mom is still pretty overbearing, but I'm grateful for their help."

Bending down on one knee, I pull Samantha into a hug and kiss her chubby cheek. "I know you'd want us to be happy. And I want to be happy again. I'm really trying, Sam." More tears run down my face. "I miss you so much it hurts. I will never stop loving you."

Unsure of what else to say, I open the backpack I brought, pull out a picnic blanket, and spread it out on the grass in front of Sam's grave while Samantha runs in and out of the stone crosses like she's in an obstacle course. I unpack our lunch and try to put our picnic together quickly before Samantha gets too crazy, but once she sees the cookies I brought, she stops and runs back toward me.

I can't help but smile at her. She's obsessed with food.

She's been the happiest, sweetest child ever. I wish she would have inherited Sam's brown hair and eyes, or even his olive complexion, but she looks just like me instead. With light-blonde curls and large blue eyes. My mom said my hair was curly when I was a baby too, but now it barely has any wave to it.

Running my fingers through her ringlets, I look back at the stone cross with the name "Samuel P. Miller " on it. I wonder if he can see us, or experience this moment with us somehow.

I hope he can.

Little Sam stuffs a cookie into her mouth, and I roll my eyes, thinking of what my mother would say if she were here. Mom is already trying to teach her to be more ladylike. I love my mom, but her tendency to be in control is just one of many reasons I need some more independence.

I don't know what I would've done without my parents' help these past few years, but going from living across the country with my husband to moving back into my parent's house has had its trials.

Samantha and I finish our little picnic and I gently lay my hand on Sam's cross and whisper, "Goodbye."

That evening, Samantha and I walk through the door at my parents' house in Wichita, Kansas, after a bumpy and miserable flight. I'm exhausted after wrestling my tantrum-throwing daughter during the flight. And ignoring the glaring businessman who was unfortunately seated next to us.

Mom and Dad have obviously been waiting for us, meeting me and Sam at the door with big grins on their faces. Little Sam lights up as soon as she sees her grandparents.

My parents' normally prim and proper demeanors completely change the closer they come to Samantha.

My dad crouches down and hugs her, then Mom squeezes her fingers together playfully, an odd mixture between crab claws and spirit fingers. "Tickle monster is coming to get my Sammy girl!"

They look ridiculous, but Samantha loves it and claps her hands together with glee and yells, "Gramma! Poppy!"

Samantha reaches eagerly for my mom and I am pretty much forgotten as they fawn over her. It doesn't bother me. I adore how much they love her. And honestly, I'm ready for a break after that flight.

"We missed you so much," Dad says in a soft voice to my daughter.

I chuckle. "It was only one night. You guys act like we were gone for a month."

After being a military spouse, one night apart from a loved one seems like a cakewalk.

Dad smiles at me. "I know, but the house was so quiet without you both. How did your trip go?"

Mom and Dad both look at me expectantly, awaiting my answer.

I shrug. "It was good? Kind of strange to talk to a white cross … but I feel better now. Like I can finally move forward."

"That's great, Soph," Mom says as she brushes a ringlet from Samantha's forehead.

Rounding the corner into the kitchen, I hear the familiar creak of the original hardwood floors. My parent's house is a grand Victorian-craftsman. They've updated the home and added on to it but kept most of the original finishes.

My dad inherited the house from his father, who inherited it from his father, who inherited it from his father. I'm sure someday my oldest brother, Madden will inherit the home. The Windell family obviously holds onto traditions and family heritage very strongly.

Grabbing some ice cream from the freezer and a spoon from a drawer in my mother's immaculate and organized kitchen, I open the lid to the ice cream and dip my spoon in.

Right before the ice cream hits my lips, my mom interrupts me. "Excuse me, young lady, we are not uncivilized barbarians here. You can get yourself a bowl."

And there it is. The mothering tone. Part of the reason I need to be on my own again. It's wonderful to have their help with Samantha, but I miss my independence with a passion.

I remove a porcelain bowl from the cabinet and scoop some of the cotton candy-flavored ice cream into it. I realize that's a childish flavor, but it's my absolute favorite. And I need something sweet after that stressful flight.

I swallow a bite of my ice cream before interrupting my parent's baby talk with my daughter.

"So … I think I'd like to find my own place."

They stop fussing over Samantha abruptly and slowly bring their faces up to look at me.

"Why would you want to do that?" Mom asks, the corners of her mouth turning down.

I shift on my feet. I've been dreading this conversation, knowing Mom and Dad wouldn't like it. "Mom, I'm thirty years old. I need my own space. I appreciate all your help with Samantha and you both for letting us stay here. But it's not a permanent solution."

Dad's expression turns serious. "Soph, being a single mom isn't easy. Why don't you just stay here and let us help? We love having you both here."

What I don't want to tell them is that Sam and I agreed we'd raise our kids independently, without the financial assistance of my parents or my trust fund. He wanted our kids to learn how to work hard and earn their own way in life. And after growing up around wealth, I wholeheartedly agreed.

Things are different now that Sam is gone. I'll use what I need to take care of Samantha and myself. But I still hold true to the idea of raising her to work hard and be independent.

And I can't very well do that while I'm living with my parents.

I know they won't understand this decision. They both came from money, and my father is very successful on top of that. They gave my brothers and me every advantage in life, and I'm grateful. But one of many things I loved about Sam was how down-to-earth and unpretentious he was. I loved his drive and work ethic and how he never looked down on anyone who had less than him.

I want our daughter to have those same values.

My parents always had such big dreams for my brothers and extremely high expectations. Not only to carry on the Windell family legacy, but to become just as successful as my father. But the expectations for me? Basically, just to marry a rich guy and become a trophy wife.

Growing up, all of my friends were unmotivated in school and life, knowing they had their trust funds as a backup plan.

When I met Sam, he opened my eyes to how hardworking and generous people can be. His motives in life were simply to serve his country and leave the world a better place in some small way. I loved the way he saw the world. His zest for life was such a contrast to the lackluster expectation of being some wealthy man's arm candy. And it's my greatest hope Samantha inherits her father's mentality.

My dad is incredibly career-focused, but it's not because work ethic is part of who he is. I think he works so hard because he feels the need to impress people and to fit into his and my mom's social circle.

My parents aren't bad people. I love them very much. I just want something different for my daughter.

Something not so stuffy and proper.

"It's much easier for me to watch Samantha when you live here." My mom states, interrupting my thoughts.

Taking a deep breath, I answer, "Heartland Academy offers full-time preschool. Samantha can start this year since she'll turn three. So, I won't need you to watch her anymore."

My mom's head jerks back slightly, like someone slapped her.

"I know you've enjoyed watching her, Mom. I'm sorry."

My parents always hated that I wanted to go into teaching. They told me that teachers are poor, and teaching was a waste of time. But I *adore* kids and love my job.

"Are you finally going to use your trust fund then? You couldn't possibly support yourself and Samantha on a teacher's salary." Dad states, not bothering to disguise his doubtfulness.

People support themselves on a teacher's salary all the time, but I will not start an argument with my father. "I'm just brainstorming. I'm not in a rush." I take another bite of ice cream.

Mom purses her lips. "Would you please take smaller bites? Your eating habits are probably the reason little Sam has such a grotesque appetite."

It's little comments like this that make me even more anxious to find my own place.

Chapter 2

Drew

"Alright, Drew. You're up," Ted Windell tells me before putting his club back into his golf bag.

It's the beginning of July and despite starting our game first thing in the morning, it's already hot as hell outside. I've got sweat dripping down my body and into places that just aren't appropriate to talk about.

Selecting my driver from my bag, I take my place to hit the ball. I've got everything lined up for the perfect swing when Brooks, Ted's youngest son, groans next to me.

"Whose idea was it to walk today? We should've taken a golf cart."

Someone releases a heavy sigh behind me. It's probably David. David is Ted's middle son, and he's way more serious than the other two.

"Shut up. Drew is trying to concentrate."

I take my swing and watch the ball go flying over the green. Not a bad shot, if I do say so myself. I'd never played golf in my life until Ted started inviting me to golf with him and his sons once a month. Ted is my coworker turned friend and mentor. I was honored to be included in their family golf sessions. And I fit right in since I'm about the same age as his oldest son, Madden. They're all incredible golfers, though. I've had to practice and hit the driving ranges frequently to even come close to their level of finesse when it comes to golfing, but eventually I got the hang of it.

"Great shot, Drew! You're getting better and better." Madden claps me on the back as he walks past me, carrying his golf bag.

The five of us make the sweaty trek toward our golf balls. "Thanks, man. When are you heading back to D.C.?"

"Our flight is tomorrow evening. There's a big event for Independence Day, and Odette isn't thrilled about it." He grimaces.

Madden is a congressman for the 4th district of Kansas, and his wife is *very* pregnant with their second child.

Brooks chuckles behind us. "Hopefully the D.C. humidity doesn't send her into early labor."

Madden shoots him a glare. "Don't even joke about that; she's already been having Braxton-Hicks contractions like crazy."

"Braxton's what?" Brooks asks, scrunching up his face.

David rolls his eyes. "Don't ask questions you don't want the answer to. I made the mistake last week of asking Madden what the heck a mucus plug is. Literally the biggest mistake of my life."

Ted and Madden burst out laughing as David walks ahead of the rest of us. Brooks just looks confused.

"Mucus?" Brooks makes a gagging sound. "That's it. I'm never impregnating a woman."

Just then, a golf cart drives past us. There are four blondes in it that look to be in their early twenties. A few of them seem to know Brooks and wave at him before whispering to each other and then giggling.

"Hey ladies!" Brooks waves back and winks at them.

It's no secret that Ted and Diane's four kids are abnormally easy on the eyes, but Brooks seems to be especially popular amongst the ladies. Madden, Sophie, and Brooks inherited their father's blonde hair and blue eyes, and then there's David. The dark and serious one in the family.

Madden and Ted shake their heads in unison at his flirtatious nature. I can't help but laugh. Brooks is just about the most likable person you'll ever meet. Ted and Madden walk ahead of us to catch up with David. Brooks throws a sweaty arm around my shoulders.

"Those old married guys are just jealous their prime is over. You and I can still play the field and have fun." He raises his eyebrows up and down.

I force a laugh as I pull away from his sweaty body heat.

"Yep, we get to have all the fun," I lie. I can't even remember the last time I went out with a woman.

Hours later, we finished our game and stride into the country club for a drink. It's blissfully cool as we walk through the large wooden doors and into the air conditioning.

Ted waves us toward the dining room. "Diane said she'd save us a table after her coffee group finished up."

"You mean gossip group?" Brooks mutters under his breath.

Ted scowls at him, then continues walking. We follow him through the extravagant clubhouse. Everything in this place is white and makes you feel like you can't touch a thing or you'll mess it up. I'd never intended on having a country club membership, but Ted talked me into it when I started golfing. And I do enjoy bringing my daughter, Penny, here to swim on the weekends.

A group of middle-aged women wearing short tennis skirts sway past us, ogling Brooks the entire time. I glance over at him just in time to see him wink at them.

I elbow him in the side, and he laughs. "Brooks, those women were like twenty years older than you."

He simply shrugs his shoulders.

Upon entering the dining room, I can hear classical music streaming through the speakers and see the properly set circular tables throughout the grand room, the kind of place settings that have an absurd amount of forks. But all I care about is that I'm finally in the cool air and I'm about to get a cold beer. The waiters always give me funny looks when I order beer, but I really couldn't care less.

Diane spots us from a table a few yards away. A lady I assume to be in her fifties is seated next to Diane. She's dressed like she's going to Ken and Barbie's cocktail party in some frilly-looking pink dress and pearls.

The woman stands as we walk up toward the table. "Well, if it isn't the Windell boys! Looking just as handsome as ever." She smiles at them but her face barely moves, telling me she's had a lot of work done to keep her face from wrinkling. Her eyes move to me and she looks me up and down with a wicked gleam in her eyes. "And who is *this* tall drink of water?"

"Lillibeth, good to see you. This is our good friend, Drew." Ted responds politely, but his voice sounds strained.

She pats Brooks' bicep before glancing back at me.

"Nice to meet you, Drew," she says in a salacious tone. "Such a fine-looking group of men."

Brooks smiles, but it looks tight and unnatural. There's an awkward pause. I'm sensing no one wants to strike up a conversation with Lillibeth. We all just want a cold drink and some lunch.

"Well ... I suppose I'll let you all get back to your family time." She removes her hand from Brooks' arm.

Once she walks out of earshot, Brooks grimaces and wipes at his arm where her hand was. "Gross, my arm is going to smell like her perfume forever."

David smirks at him. "Serves you right for flirting with every female who can breathe."

"I've never flirted with Mom's coffee group ladies. Blech." He shivers dramatically.

"Would you all sit down and stop the teasing? People are staring." Diane scolds and then schools her features back into a smile. She tucks a strand of her dark hair behind her ear and then smooths the tablecloth in front of her.

David got his dark hair from his mom, although hers is slightly lighter. Diane is a petite woman, but something about her dark hair, in contrast with the rest of the family, makes me take her more seriously. That and she has this menacing glance that makes you think she could actually freeze you with her piercing gaze if she wanted to.

Everyone takes a seat around the table and a waiter walks over. "Good afternoon, what can I get started for you all?"

We go around the circle, giving our lunch and drink orders until the waiter gets to Madden. "Just iced water for me." The waiter nods before leaving us. "I promised Odette I'd pick up lunch for us on the way home." He smiles to himself, like he can't wait to get back home to his wife.

David notices the empty seat between him and myself. "Where's Sophie today?"

Diane purses her lips, looking irritated by the reminder of Sophie's absence. "You know how stubborn she is about coming to the country club with me."

Ted shakes his head in dismay. "The girl is too stubborn for her own good sometimes. Apparently she wants to get her own place now."

"Really?" David asks. "I suppose that makes sense ... She *is* an adult. I'm sure she wants her own space."

Diane's eyes widen in annoyance as she glares daggers at David. "Our house is huge; she has *plenty* of space."

Madden interjects. "Of course, Mom. I think he just meant a home to call her own."

David gives Madden an appreciative glance, like he's silently thanking him for saving his butt.

Diane's steely gaze flicks to me. "Doesn't your adult sister live with you, Drew?"

"She does." I nod.

"See!" She throws her hands up. "Drew's sister is perfectly happy not having her own house, so I don't see why Sophie can't be."

"Well, if Emily ever wanted to move out, I wouldn't be against it. I want her to be happy, wherever that may be." I say before glancing around the table.

Diane looks like she wants to dive across the table and attack me, but all the guys have a look of admiration in their eyes … Or maybe it's shock that I offered an opinion that differed from Diane's.

A few days after our game of golf, it's the Fourth of July. My heart warms when my adorable six-year-old daughter sweeps into the living room, decked out in her patriotic dress and sparkly bows. I wasn't really sure about this whole fatherhood thing in the beginning, but now I can't imagine not having Penny around.

My sister, Emily, enters the room right behind her. Penny twirls to show off the dress Emily got for her. My sister and I smile at each other, barely able to handle the cuteness.

"Do you like my dress, Daddy?" Penny asks as she continues to twirl.

"I love it, Penny. You look so pretty."

"Thanks!" She grins and then skips out of the room and in the direction of her bedroom.

"Thanks for helping her get ready, Emily. Are you sure you don't want to come to the party with us?"

She smirks. "You know the Windell's annual Independence Day bash is totally not my scene."

I put my hands on my hips. "That's right, you're too cool for us," I say sarcastically.

She gives me an endearing smile. "I just want to binge Netflix on your flat screen while you're gone." She lifts her chin to motion towards my large TV mounted on the living room wall.

"Alright, suit yourself." I lift one shoulder in a shrug. "Not sure who's going to watch that TV if you ever move out."

She flinches at my comment. "About that. Do you have a minute to talk?"

My sister has been living with me since we moved to Kansas ten years ago after losing our parents. We were eager to get out of Seattle and the depressing rain and move onto greener pastures, literally.

When I finished medical school, I had two criteria in my surgical residency search: (1) somewhere sunny, and (2) somewhere with little to no traffic.

I haven't been back to Seattle since. We love it here.

"Of course, shoot."

"Well, now that I finally finished my MBA, I've been setting up interviews. And I went to one yesterday."

My eyebrows shoot up. I knew this was coming. She worked hard to get her master's online while nannying for me. And I knew she couldn't be my nanny forever.

"That's outstanding! How'd it go?"

"Actually, they called me yesterday evening and offered me a job!"

I pull her into a bear hug. "Congratulations, Emily, I'm so proud of you."

"Yeah, I know, thanks," she mumbles into my chest, squirming to release herself from the hug.

After a few seconds, I ask, "So, how long do I have to find a new nanny?"

She plays with her fingers, looking uncomfortable. "They want me to start in two weeks." She looks up at me briefly. "But I told them I'd need to talk to my current employer first."

I laugh a little at her referring to me as her current employer. "Don't feel bad, Em. I knew this day would come. I'll find someone to watch Penny."

She sighs. "Yeah, I know. But is two weeks enough time?"

I bite the inside of my cheek, knowing it's probably not enough time. But I don't want her to feel guilty about moving forward with her life. She's been through enough as it is.

"It'll be fine. And if I can't find anyone in two weeks, I have some vacation days saved up that I can use."

She gives my arm a pat since she's not big on physical affection. "Thanks, Drew, for everything. You really are the best brother a girl could ask for."

I wink. "Yeah, I know. I'm pretty great."

She rolls her eyes and stalks off.

I turn on my heel and walk down the hallway to the master bedroom. Penny's room is right next to mine, so I peek inside to see what she's doing. She's happily playing Barbies. Looks like they're also having a Fourth of July BBQ. Lucky dolls.

I continue to my room and close the door to get changed. I grab a hunter-green henley from my walk-in closet and discard my tattered Washington State University t-shirt into the hamper.

I always look forward to hanging out with the Windells. Ted is one of the most highly respected orthopedic surgeons in the Midwest, and I look up to him. I was really grateful when he took me under his wing at work and mentored me. But now we're friends, and that means even more. Especially since my parents are gone.

Kansas summers are hot and humid, so I forgo jeans and opt for some grey linen shorts instead. Normally I'd just throw on some sports shorts and a t-shirt, but the Windells are a little on the fancy side.

I slip on my leather sandals and stand in front of my floor-length mirror. My dark brown hair is messy, and my 5 o'clock shadow is showing, but I hate shaving on my days off. I shrug my shoulders, deciding I look good enough.

Hopefully, Diane won't mind my informal appearance too much.

―――⁂―――

After parking down the street from the Windell's home, I open Penny's door and she jumps down from her booster seat, making her pigtails sway. She grabs onto my large hand with her tiny one. She's got these little dimples on each knuckle that I find ridiculously adorable.

"Daddy, will there be sparklers?" she asks.

"Yeah, Pen. Dr. and Mrs. Windell said there will be."

She smiles so big both of her dimples show and jumps up and down. Kids are so easily entertained.

We make it to the Windell's front door and although I can hear the party booming in their large back yard, I ring the doorbell instead of letting myself in. Diane is nice, but I always find myself being a little extra formal around her.

Instead of Ted or Diane answering the door, it's their daughter, Sophie. She smiles brightly at me and then at Penny. "Penny, I love your dress! We're almost matching!"

Penny looks her up and down with a slightly judgmental look before nodding in agreement. "It's the same color as mine!"

They're both wearing navy-blue dresses, except Penny's is sparkly and fluffy, whereas Sophie's is form-fitting and ruched on the sides.

"I wish mine had a tutu attached like yours, though," Sophie says with a playful pout, and motions for us to step inside as we wait for Penny's response.

Penny shrugs. "Yeah, it would be better with a tutu."

Sophie bites the insides of her cheeks to keep from laughing. "You guys can head out back! The buffet is incredible this year." Sophie spins on her heel, making her long glossy blonde hair fan out behind her. She walks off toward the staircase that I'm assuming leads to the upstairs rooms.

I take Penny's hand and we make our way to the French doors that lead to the backyard.

Penny tugs on my hand and whispers, "Sophie's so pretty, Daddy."

I don't bother arguing with her. You'd have to be blind not to notice how incredibly beautiful Sophie is. She's also incredibly off-limits. So I just smile and tug Penny along.

Walking into the backyard, I feel my eyes almost bug out of my head. Diane is known for her amazing parties, but this is a whole new level of bougie.

There's a man on stilts dressed as Uncle Sam making balloon animals. Twinkling lights are strung from tall poles, making the yard look like it has a ceiling made of stars. They even hung patriotic bunting flags along all sides of their privacy fence, and Sophie was right. There's a gigantic buffet table with warming containers holding a myriad of BBQ selections. The smell makes my mouth water.

Ted and Diane spot us among the crowd of seventy-five or so partygoers. Ted waves us over to where he's talking to the new surgeon who just started at our office. I walk over with Penny.

"Drew! So glad you and Penny could make it." He tugs on one of her pigtails, making her giggle.

My new coworker, Dr. Pham, introduces her husband, "Dr. Reed, this is my husband, Archie."

She gestures to the man next to her, wearing a dress shirt and slacks. His forehead is dripping with sweat. They both have deep brown eyes and sleek black hair. There's an air of formality about them, just like the Windells.

I definitely feel underdressed standing in this circle.

Reaching my hand out, I shake Archie's sweaty palm. "Please, just call me Drew, and this is my daughter, Penny."

I look down at my side where Penny was, but she has already run off to get a balloon animal.

Dr. Pham smiles in her direction. "She's darling!"

Just then, Sophie joins our circle, standing next to me and holding her daughter. I can't help but smile at Samantha's cute little face. I wasn't so sure about becoming a dad, but now that I am one, I love kids.

Dr. Pham looks at Sophie and then back at me. "Oh, this must be your wife! You two make such a beautiful couple."

Sophie and I look at each other, our eyes wide. Diane bursts out laughing and Ted scoffs and says, "Ha! Don't be ridiculous. They're not married. This is my daughter, Sophie."

I glance at her, and her cheeks are flaming. Everyone chuckles awkwardly and Dr. Pham apologizes for her mistake. I'm left wondering why Ted and Diane would think the idea of their daughter being with me is so laughable. Of course, we're not together, and we never will be … but I *am* a successful surgeon.

My jaw twitches in annoyance at the thought of not being good enough. Maybe it's because I wore shorts.

Sophie shakes the hands of Dr. Pham and her husband. "Nice to meet you both! Mom, do you mind watching Samantha while I get some food?" Sophie sets Samantha down and she runs to her grandmother.

"I'd be happy to! Come here Sammy girl!" Diane smiles and reaches out to embrace her granddaughter.

Penny finally runs back over to me, a pink balloon pig in hand. "Daddy, I'm hungry."

The Windells are back in conversations with the Pham's, making it easy to duck out and take Penny to get some dinner.

"If you're so hungry, why don't you eat some of that pork you have there?" I wink at my daughter while gesturing to her pig balloon animal.

She raises one eyebrow and looks at me like I'm a complete moron. "People can't eat balloons, Daddy." She shakes her head and runs ahead of me toward the buffet table.

Look at me, making dad jokes. Not bad for someone who unexpectedly became a father not quite seven years ago.

After filling our plates with corn on the cob, ribs, and potato salad, Penny and I see two seats left on the patio. Consequently, it's the table Sophie and two of her brothers are sitting at.

"Drew! My man, have a seat!" Brooks gestures to the seat next to him, clapping me on the back once I'm seated.

David gives me a brief head nod. "Drew, good to see you."

He and Brooks couldn't have more opposite personalities, even if they tried.

"Where are Madden and Odette?" I ask, realizing Madden is the only sibling not in attendance.

David answers since Brooks is distracted by a girl seated at the table next to ours. "They had an event to attend in D.C."

"Oh, that's right. I remember him talking about that during our golf game."

Sophie laughs. "Yeah, Odette has been dreading it."

David smirks. "Odette definitely doesn't enjoy the spotlight as much as Madden does. But they'll be back in town in a few weeks." He shrugs.

"I can't wait for them to get home. I already miss Oliver!" Sophie says with a frown.

David rolls his eyes. "Yeah, so does Mom. Why do grandparents like their grandchildren so much more than they do their *actual* children?"

I laugh along with the three siblings to disguise the jealousy I feel over the Windell children having parents to spoil their own kids. My daughter will never have that.

Brooks turns his attention to Sophie. "Speaking of grandparents being obsessed with their grandchildren, Mom has been whining incessantly about you wanting to take Sammy away from her."

Sophie throws her head back in aggravation. "Ugh, nothing is private in this family, is it?"

Brooks speaks around a mouthful of potato salad, an act that would most likely warrant some harsh words from his mother. "What would be the fun in keeping things private?"

Sophie rolls her eyes. "I'm not taking Samantha away from anyone. I just want to have my own place again. I don't have to move out right away." She stirs the food around on her plate. "I'm just thinking about it."

"Why don't you just buy a place with your trust fund?" David asks, sitting back in his seat and crossing one foot over his knee.

She takes a deep breath and looks around the table nervously. I feel like I'm in the middle of a private family conversation, so I look down at my potato salad.

"Well, Sam and I agreed we'd raise our kids to be hardworking and independent ... and it's difficult to teach those qualities while living on a trust fund from your mommy and daddy."

I smile to myself, admiring her gumption. This is not your typical spoiled princess, apparently. I hadn't realized until this moment how strong-willed and independent Sophie is.

Brooks stops eating abruptly. "Now, those are fighting words. I have worked very hard at being incredibly handsome and smart to earn that trust fund," he deadpans.

"Smart? You really want to go there?" David heckles him, then turns his attention to Sophie. "I can respect you wanting to make your own way in life ... but it's okay to accept extra help. Especially when you suddenly became a single mom, Soph," he says gently, his eyes glazed with sympathy.

Sophie rests her chin on the back of her hand. "I know, and I *will* use my trust fund if I really need to ... But I'm thirty years old, David. I don't want to live with my parents any longer."

Brooks sits back in his seat now that he has licked his plate clean. "Well, that's understandable ... Heck, I'm only twenty-five and I wouldn't move back in with Mom and Dad in a million years."

"Seeing as you graduated from M.I.T. and have a successful business, I truly doubt you'll ever have to worry about that." Sophie sighs.

David looks deep in thought. "I'd tell you to buy the house next to mine, but the most annoying person just moved in."

"Bummer. What's so annoying about them?"

"What's *not* annoying about her? Her personality, her loud music, her plants that creep over onto my side of the fence ... oh and her cat."

Sophie rolls her eyes. "She can't be that bad."

"Debatable," David mutters under his breath.

My mind wanders from the conversation, and I reflect again on my conversation with Emily this morning. A thought pops into my head.

Before I can stop myself, I blurt, "So, I don't know if you'd be interested, but I converted my basement into an apartment."

I pause and take in their expressions. Brooks looks amused, Sophie looks interested, and David looks like he wants to punch me? Maybe he's still thinking about his neighbor's cat.

"Anyway, my sister has been living there while she was finishing her MBA. But she just got a new job, so she'll be moving out in a few weeks. The apartment has two bedrooms and a kitchenette. I had hoped to hire a new sitter and offer them the apartment. But if you wanted it, I'd give you a discount since I don't want some random person living down there."

They all quietly stare at me for a few seconds. Maybe I overstepped.

Finally, Sophie's face lights up. "That might be perfect, and I could definitely watch Penny for you! Is she going to Heartland again this year?"

"She is, and that would be awesome. I only need a sitter until school starts next month, and then after that, just after school ... and once in a while, for my on-call weekends. But if that would be too much, I totally understand. No pressure whatsoever." I look around the table, then down at Penny, who has finished her food and is playing in the grass near our table.

Sophie smiles. "I think this could work really well. I could even bring her home from school since I teach at Heartland."

David and Brooks look between us with annoyed, overprotective looks on their faces. I can only assume they're leery of their sister moving in with me, since they seem to believe I have a history of promiscuous behavior with women.

"Would you want to come over next weekend to check out the apartment, and we could chat about the details?"

She pulls out her phone, ignoring her brothers, who are currently giving me mild stink-eyes. "Yeah! What's your number, Drew? I'm not sure I have it. I can text you later to set up a day to come over."

I give her my number and excuse myself to get my daughter some sparklers.

Chapter 3
Sophie

A week after my parent's Independence Day party, I'm driving over to Drew's house. He doesn't live too far from my parents, probably ten minutes away, in a contemporary subdivision.

I park in his driveway and am surprised by the size of the home and the classic design. My brothers hang out with Drew all the time, but this is my first time seeing his place.

I pictured him living in an urban loft downtown, but this house screams "family man."

I find myself wondering what happened to Penny's mom, and how Drew feels about being a single dad—he has clearly embraced that role though.

Now that I think of it, I've never heard anyone mention Penny's mother.

Shifting my car into park, I steady myself. I'm more nervous than I thought I'd be. Drew seems super laid-back and cool, but it's definitely nerve-wracking to think of being alone with just him and Penny. Anytime I've been around him, my entire family has been present.

Walking to the front door, I notice he's done some landscaping. At least, I'm assuming he's done it himself. It's not pristinely perfect, like the landscaping my parents hire out. Instead, it's cute and a little messy.

There are bricks lining the walkway, and the flower beds are filled with a plethora of colorful plants. I'm no gardening expert, but it looks like there are at least some hostas and zinnias.

I'm smiling at the cute little flower beds when I hear the front door open up.

"Sophie!" Penny exclaims as she runs toward me.

"Well, hey there, Penny."

"Do you love the garden me and my daddy planted?" Her eyes are wide with satisfaction.

"I love it!" I look up and see Drew standing a few feet behind her, looking a little sheepish.

"Daddy let me pick all the flowers."

"You did an excellent job. It's like a rainbow garden."

Drew chuckles. "Pretty sure she chose one of every color ... at least." He grins. "Let's get Miss Sophie inside, Penny. It's hot out here."

The three of us walk inside, Drew's calm demeanor making me feel at ease. I don't know why I was ever nervous. Drew is practically part of the Windell family. He and Penny come over for every holiday, though it's true that I don't really know him on a personal level like my brothers do. I guess I should've joined them for their golf games over the past few years.

Once inside, I take a quick look around his home. It's an open floor plan, with a large kitchen and an island with a white and grey marble countertop. Beautiful gold pendant lights hang above the island, and gold bar stools are pushed up to the bar. The entire main area has the same dark wood floors and brushed gold fixtures throughout. It's very stylish. I find myself, once again, surprised by him.

Perhaps his sister helped him design the place. It's not a feminine space; it's just more polished than what I had pictured in my mind.

"Your house is beautiful," I say as I continue to look around the main area.

"Aunt Emily made it pretty," Penny says matter-of-factly.

"It's true," Drew says without shame. "When the house was being built, I couldn't have cared less about all the tiny details, so my sister helped a lot. I probably would've just made everything brown." He shrugs. "Penny, why don't you go find Aunt Em while I show Sophie the apartment?"

"Okay, Daddy!" She bounces down the hallway in search of her aunt.

I laugh. "So your sister has lived here to help with Penny? You guys must be close."

He smiles fondly. "We are, despite me being seven years older. When we lost my parents, we were all each other had left, you know?"

"I'm sorry. That's awful you guys lost your parents so young."

One edge of his mouth twitches, like he's not sure whether to smile or frown. "Thank you, and it's okay. I know you're no stranger to loss. I'm sorry about your husband too."

My eyes blur with tears, but I swallow slowly, urging them away. "Thank you. I'm ready to move forward and have my own life again, you know? Without my parents hovering all day, every day." I smirk.

Drew lifts one eyebrow. "Yeah, your parents are great. But they can be pretty intense, huh?"

"Um, yeah. I love them to death, but I gotta have some space." I breathe out a half laugh, half scoff that sounds super awkward.

Drew clears his throat. "Well, like I told you before, I turned my basement into an apartment for my sister. But she wants to move into her own place with some friends. Since I'm on call at least one weekend a month, I figured I'd always use the apartment for a nanny, but now that Penny's in school, I don't think that's really necessary." He crosses his arms, unknowingly drawing attention to his broad chest and impressive biceps. "And if you were interested in babysitting Penny during my on-call weekends, I would deduct more off the rent, of course."

Quickly, I pry my eyes away from his muscles, telling myself I should think of Drew like a brother ... or maybe a really, really distant cousin ... once removed.

I've never really looked at Drew, like really *looked* at him. I haven't noticed any men since Sam died. These past few years have honestly been a total blur for me. I've tried to be present for Samantha, but it's been difficult to keep my sadness at bay.

"Yeah, that sounds great. I hardly ever have weekend plans." The truth is, I'd be grateful to babysit on the weekends. Weekends have been so lonely. That's when everyone is on dates, or going out with their spouse. Which means I'm usually just home hanging out with Samantha.

"Okay, great." He smiles. "Let me show you the apartment."

I follow him to the hallway off of the kitchen and he unlocks a door that leads downstairs. We walk down the stairway and the tidy apartment comes into view.

There's a small hallway at the bottom of the steps that leads toward the kitchen and living room.

I'm instantly pleased that this isn't a dark and dank basement. There's several recessed windows that bring lots of natural light into the space. The walls are painted a robin's egg blue, and the grey carpet looks new. The space smells clean, with a hint of citrus. There's a cute wall collage with a map and some artwork featuring famous landmarks from around the world.

It's a really pretty apartment; I could definitely see little Sam and I living here comfortably. Drew continues the tour and shows me the kitchenette attached to the living space. There's a microwave, a fridge, and a small, two-burner stove top.

"I didn't put a full kitchen in here, thinking just my sister would be using it. You'd obviously be welcome to use anything in the main house, if you felt comfortable with that."

I chuckle. "That's not a big deal. I hate cooking, anyway."

Drew laughs and gestures back toward the small hallway where the bedrooms must be. First, he shows me the full bathroom and then the two bedrooms. One bedroom has a queen bed and modern grey dresser, and the other room is empty.

"This is perfect. You did a great job with this apartment, Drew."

His cheeks color just a bit, although it's hard to tell against his tanned skin. His hazel eyes meet mine, looking more brown than green today against his black t-shirt.

I hear the door at the end of the hallway jiggle and Penny bursts through, a dark-haired woman trailing behind her. They look so much alike, my breath catches. This must be Emily.

Penny giggles. "Boo! I wanted to scare you guys." She looks up at me. "Betcha didn't know what that door went to."

The woman behind her speaks up, "I'm so sorry, I reminded her not to use this door anymore, and she snuck away from me."

"Sorry, I never bolted that door when Emily lived down here." He stuffs his hands into his pockets. "Oh, this is Emily, by the way. My sister."

"Hey, Emily, great to meet you!"

"You too," she says quietly. "This little squirt has told me all about your family." Emily smiles down at her niece, then cups her hand around her mouth to whisper to me, "I think she has a bit of a crush on your brother, Brooks."

I roll my eyes, but then laugh. "Don't tell him that. He's already conceited enough as it is."

We laugh, then Emily shuffles Penny back through the door and up the stairs.

Drew crosses his arms again over his totally average, totally unattractive pec muscles. "So anyway, Emily has already moved her stuff out, so you'd be free to move in whenever, if you wanted to."

"I think this would be perfect for me and Samantha. Could we move in this weekend? I gotta give my parents a few days to adjust to the idea." I grimace.

"That would work. I'm off that day so I could help out." One side of his mouth pulls upward. "I've been sweating trying to find a trustworthy sitter, so this works out for me too."

"Well then, this will be great for both of us! See you Saturday then?"

"See you Saturday." He smiles.

I walk inside my parents' house, excited about my newfound independence and the idea of moving forward with my life.

I know Sam would be proud of me.

But I'm also dreading this conversation with my parents about Drew's apartment. When I left to go to his house, I had just told them I was getting a pedicure. I shouldn't have lied, but I didn't think all of this would come together so quickly.

Mom walks around the corner from the kitchen into the living room with little Sam running along behind her.

"Hey, Sammy girl!" I get down on my knees so I can hug Samantha.

She squeals with glee and reaches for me. "Mommy!"

"How was your pedicure, sweetheart?" My mom asks.

"Well, actually, I sort of found an apartment."

Mom's jaw drops slightly, then she snaps it shut. "Already? Where?"

I pause, hesitant to tell her we'll be moving out this weekend. "Drew converted his basement into an apartment.

His sister was living there, but she just moved out."

"Ted! Get in here!" She bellows.

"Coming!" Dad yells from the dining room.

I drop my chin to my chest. Here goes.

He rounds the corner. "What do my favorite ladies need?" Dad says affectionately, coming up behind mom and wrapping his arms around her waist.

I'm not sure I'll ever get used to seeing them all googly eyed like this. When I was growing up, their relationship was rocky, to say the least. Dad worked way too much. But, apparently, having grandchildren has bonded them, and Dad has cut way back on his workload. He's even talking about retiring early. Their newfound "honeymoon phase" is just one more thing on my list of reasons to get the heck out of here.

We share a bedroom wall. Enough said.

"So, I'm going to rent Drew's basement apartment."

Dad blinks rapidly. "Excuse me?"

"Yeah!" I smile, trying to stay positive. "It has two bedrooms. It's super cute."

They both look at me with horrified expressions. I pick Samantha up and settle her on my hip.

Dad's face goes bright red. I swear I can see steam coming out of his ears. "You're going to *live* with Drew?"

"Calm down. The apartment I'll be renting is completely separate from the house. It has its own entrance and everything. And It's even closer to Heartland Academy than your house, so my commute will be shorter. It's perfect, so I'd appreciate it if you could be more supportive."

My dad drags his hand down his face in frustration. "Hon, you know I love Drew. He's somewhat of a son to me. But Penny was conceived from a one-night stand. Not only that, but in all the years I've known him, he's never even had a serious relationship. Which makes one think he's only into casual flings, does it not? I don't want you to live with a man who has a scandalous past."

I'm taken aback for a second. I don't know Drew as well as my dad does, but he does not even remotely seem like the type of person who would be careless with women and have random flings. Although, I guess he could've been like that years ago. Sowing his wild oats and whatnot.

"Dad, thanks for looking out for me, but that was forever ago. He's obviously grown up a lot since then. You know him; he has good character."

"Seven years isn't *that* long." Mom says pointedly, putting her hands on her hips.

"You're right. Drew and I are just going to ignore both of our daughters and have a wild and passionate affair with each other in his basement," I say with a dramatic eye roll.

"Sophie! Don't even joke about that," Mom says with an indignant huff.

"I appreciate you both making sure Sam and I are taken care of, but I trust Drew, and I'm really excited about this. So I'm moving into the apartment this weekend."

And with that, I turn and walk upstairs to my bedroom with Samantha still on my hip.

"Sophie Danielle Windell, this conversation is not over!" Dad says in his deep, booming voice.

"My last name is Miller, and this conversation *is* most definitely over."

Chapter 4

Drew

That evening, I'm relaxing, minding my business … when a knock comes from my front door. Emily is sitting on the other side of the loveseat and we quickly exchange a puzzled look before I get up to answer the door.

Looking through the peephole, I see Ted Windell. I gulp and look back at Emily. She puts her hands up, silently asking who it is.

"It's Ted, Sophie's dad," I whisper.

Emily bares her teeth in a grimace, then gets up and heads back to the guest room where she's been staying ever since I told her Sophie was coming over to look at the apartment.

I stand up straight and open the door to a very perturbed looking Ted Windell.

"Ted! To what do I owe this surprise?"

His jaw twitches. "I think you already know."

I step to the side and gesture for him to come into the house. He steps cautiously through the doorway, then looks back at me.

"If this is about Sophie…" I quickly say, "you know how much I respect your family. I don't have any ill intentions here. At the Independence Day party she mentioned wanting her own place, and since my sister is moving out, I told her about the basement apartment."

"I don't like this one bit," he grits out, the vein in his forehead looking as if it might burst.

"You *know* me, Ted. Not only do I look up to you, but I trust you. I hope you feel the same way about me." I shrug.

"I *do* trust you. If I needed a knee replacement surgery, you'd be the first person I'd call. Or if I needed help moving furniture, or wanted to grab coffee with a friend." He shakes his head and looks down at his feet before looking back up. "But this is my *only* daughter, Drew. She's been through a lot."

"I know she has, and I was just trying to help. I'm sorry if I overstepped, but she's an adult. Can't she make her own decisions?"

His fists clench at his sides again. "That's easy for you to say. Just wait until Penny is an adult."

I nod my head. "That's fair." I suck in a deep breath, then blow it out slowly. "Can I show you the apartment? Maybe then you'd feel better."

"Yeah, I'd like to see it," he says, slightly calmer now, but the vein in his forehead is still showing.

Having already bolted the door at the bottom of the stairs from inside the apartment, we walk back outside and around to the side of the house with the separate entrance. I open the door and flip the light on, Ted following closely behind.

He walks around the living area, taking in every detail. Then he moves to the kitchenette and then down the short hallway. He opens both bedroom doors and looks inside before his eyes land on the door at the end of the hallway. He eyes the deadbolt I installed this afternoon.

"Okay, I feel a little better now." His shoulders relax. "This is a great little space. I can actually picture her and Samantha here ... and the deadbolt is a nice touch," he says with a glint of humor in his eyes.

"I'd never do anything to harm Sophie, or anyone in your family for that matter."

He releases a heavy sigh. "I know. I'm not sure what came over me ... it's just that you're single and have a past. My mind got a little carried away."

I flinch at his comment. All I want is his trust and respect.

"Well, Sophie will be safe here."

He slaps me on the shoulder good-naturedly, then turns to walk back outside.

I lock the apartment, then follow him back to his vehicle parked in the driveway. Ted opens his car door and is about to step inside, but turns to me at the last second.

"Oh, and Drew?"

"Yes?"

"Please don't tell Sophie I came over here," He says, looking abashed.

"Never." I smile.

Walking back toward my house, I'm hit with the realization that this fabricated story about my so-called one-night-stand causes people to question my character. Even seven years after the fact.

Of course Ted wouldn't want his daughter renting the apartment in my basement. He thinks I have casual flings with women, that I throw caution to the wind where women are concerned.

Having not had any serious relationships since Penny was born, I've never really had to deal with the repercussions of this lie. This story I created to hide the truth. But the embarrassment of the situation is really hitting me after my conversation with Ted.

Fact is, I'm a conscientious and caring person. I'm careful and trustworthy. But the people I respect won't see me that way, not entirely anyway.

And unless the truth comes out, that won't change. But the truth *can't* come out. Because I made a promise.

Chapter 5
Sophie

Saturday morning, Brooks and David come over to help Dad and I get everything moved over to Drew's house—er, my apartment. Dad seems to be taking things much better now, but Mom is still stewing over us moving out. I think she's grateful to have the morning alone with Samantha. Right now they're snuggled up on the couch reading books.

Thankfully, Brooks has a pickup to haul the larger items. I got rid of a lot when I moved back here with my parents, but I kept some of the furniture Sam and I had picked out when we were married. Like the little armoire we found at an antique shop, his beloved guitar, and the large jewelry box he gave me as a wedding gift.

Between Brooks' pickup and my little Subaru Outback, we can get it all in one trip. When we arrive at Drew's, he meets us in the driveway to help carry everything.

His muscles strain against his t-shirt with every box he lifts. I squeeze my eyes shut, trying to will the thoughts of his arms out of my mind.

Why am I even noticing his arms? My brothers and even my dad have muscles. What's different about Drew's? Besides the fact that his muscles are bigger, and his skin is more bronzed. Oh, and he's *not* related to me.

Once everything is moved in and the furniture is placed where I want it, my brothers look around. Dad doesn't seem interested in looking at the place, which I find a little odd.

"This is a great space! Well done, Drew, didn't realize you were so handy," Brooks says as he leans against the corner of the hallway.

David stands next to Brooks and crosses his arms. "Don't think I won't be checking that deadbolt every time I come over here."

David gives Drew a pointed look, like he's trying to use his body language to communicate that if he doesn't keep a professional distance from me, he's a dead man.

"David!" I gasp, shocked that he would think Drew and I might partake in some kind of inappropriate activities.

Drew just chuckles. "It's alright. It's a brother's job to look out for his sister. I understand that."

"Good," David says seriously.

Ugh, David is always so stone-faced. He really needs to loosen up. Maybe not as much as Brooks, but a little.

I clap my hands together. "Alrighty, well, thank you all very much for your help. I think I've got it from here."

"You're kicking us out already? I see how it is." Brooks grins.

"I'm just ready to get the place set up, and I want to make it homey before Mom and Dad bring Samantha over tomorrow morning." I smile at Dad, grateful they agreed to keep her for the night. Not that it took much coercing.

Dad shoos Brooks and David towards the door. "Okay, let's leave her be."

David stands his ground. "I'm not leaving you two here alone."

Drew pushes himself off of the kitchen counter he was resting against, and walks out the door. The rest of them quickly follow. I roll my eyes at how ridiculous David is being.

"Thanks again, guys!" I wave and close the door and lock it before any of them change their minds. It's been way too long since I had any alone time, and I've really been looking forward to it.

I turn around and rest my back against the front door, breathing in a sigh of relief. It's so quiet. So peaceful. So private.

Just what me and Samantha need.

It doesn't take long for me to turn on my favorite album from The Head and the Heart, and get busy unpacking and decorating.

My jewelry box fits perfectly in my room next to the nightstand, and the armoire looks lovely in the living area. Sam's guitar is on display next to the armoire. It was his most precious belonging, and although I can't play the guitar, I just cannot bring myself to get rid of it. I can practically hear the sound of his fingers strumming the guitar just by looking at it. I used to love it when he played and our house was filled with the melodies he created.

Most of our household items were sold or packed away in boxes years ago. My heart lurches as I pull out each framed photo of me and Sam. I study each once as I unpack them. One of them is us at the Outer Banks, our arms wrapped around each other, bright smiles etching our faces. We were truly happy. My hands shake and I draw in an unsteady breath as I unpack another photo. This one was taken during our last hike together. We're in the Blue Ridge Mountains, standing side by side, sweat making our faces glisten in the sunlight. This was the last photo we took together. Once again, my heart wrenches inside of my chest and my eyes prickle with tears.

Finding new trails to hike was one of our favorite things to do together. Hiking can be a painstaking task, but once you get to the final destination and see the breathtaking scenery around you, all the work is worth it.

Which makes hiking a lot like marriage. All the work and communication is completely worth it when you get to fall into bed each night next to your favorite human.

But that's what makes losing that person even more difficult.

I set the photo of us on top of the armoire with some other framed pictures of me and Samantha and my family. I hold another one of Sam and me hiking and study it for a few minutes, tears filling my eyes once more, but I choke them back. My heart wants to display every photo I have of my husband, but this new endeavor is about moving forward, *not* dwelling in the past. So I choose my favorite photos and pack the others away.

Hours later, my stomach rumbles and I glance at the time on my phone. Wow, I've been unpacking these boxes and marinating in memories of Sam for *five* hours. Now it's half-past six and I'm famished. I haven't even made it to the store for groceries yet. I guess I should've stocked the fridge before unpacking. This goes to show it's been a while since I had my own house.

Just as I'm about to search for my purse to go grab some fast food, a knock comes from the front door. I walk across the room to answer it, a little too excited to have my first houseguest.

Drew is on the other side of the door. His hair is wet and tousled like he just got out of the shower and barely ran a towel through it. He smells like a mixture of Old Spice shower gel and handsome surgeon. I didn't realize that it was even a smell until just now.

After standing there silently smelling him for way too long, I notice he's holding a plate of food. I feel my cheeks heat at how awkward I'm being. I barely even noticed the man for the past three years, and now my nose suddenly thinks he's the best smelling man in the universe. Ugh.

He smirks at my expression. "Hey, you've been down here for a while, I thought you might be hungry."

My stomach growls loudly. "Wow, sorry about that. Apparently I *am* just a little hungry." I let out a tense laugh, and he hands me the food.

"Well, I better get back to the main house before David's spidey-senses go off and he finds out I'm down here." He points his thumb over his shoulder, his eyes twinkling mischievously. "Enjoy my very mediocre grilling skills." He grins before turning to walk away.

"Thank you!" I yell after him, and he turns back quickly to give me a brief salute.

Closing the door, I make my way toward the kitchen for a fork and dig into the grilled chicken, mashed potatoes and caprese salad. I'm impressed by how delicious it is, Drew majorly undersold his cooking skills. Then again, he hasn't had the displeasure of tasting *my* cooking.

Chapter 6

Drew

Once I'm back in the main house, Emily enters the kitchen from the hallway. She lifts one eyebrow and puts her hands on her hips.

"And where were you just now, young man?"

"I'm older than you, *little* sister. And I just took her some dinner," I say as I load the dishwasher.

"Really? So if an old lady who looked like what's-his-face from *Mrs. Doubtfire* moved into the basement apartment, you would've taken her dinner too?"

"Of course I would. I'm a very nice guy."

"Right." She smirks and takes a seat on the bar stool.

Typical annoying little sister, I just wanted to check on Sophie and make sure she was doing okay. And besides, anytime I'm tempted to think of how beautiful she is, I just remind myself of the intimidating vein that pops up on Ted's forehead when he gets angry.

I glare at her. "Stop, Em. I'm not interested in Sophie like that. Plus, I'm like six years older than her. And her dad would kill me."

She wrinkles her nose. "True. That would be awkward. Not to mention you're now her landlord. But seriously, you're getting old. You should really consider settling down, or at least dating."

"No one will want to be with me now that I'm a decrepit old man." I pretend to smack my toothless gums together.

"I said old, not elderly."

I laugh. "Well, actually … a nurse asked me on a date the other day. She's probably around my age."

Her mouth drops. "Like a nurse you work with?"

"She doesn't work in the surgical unit; she works in radiology. She comes upstairs after her shifts sometimes to chat with her friends."

"Nice! So are you going to go out with her?"

"I think so. We exchanged numbers. And I really need to put myself out there if I don't want to be single forever."

"Good for you, bro." Emily slides off the bar stool and walks to my side to slap me on the back. "Glad you finally said yes to one of the dozens of nurses who has asked you out."

Rolling my eyes, I respond, "You know I can't date someone I work with directly. Been there, done that," I scoff. "And when they ask me out, it makes things super uncomfortable."

Emily chuckles. "Oh, poor you. It must be so difficult to be a handsome surgeon."

"Hilarious."

"No, really, wouldn't life be so much easier if you were just a little uglier and a little less successful?" She's doing a terrible job hiding her sarcasm.

I squirt some detergent in the dishwasher and turn it on, then clack my old man gums at my sister once again before walking back to my bedroom.

—ele—

Between my office hours, surgeries, and being called in to work twice this week, it has flown by.

This is why I hardly ever date. By the time the weekend rolls around, I'm exhausted. All I want to do is curl up on the couch with my daughter, watching whatever Disney movie she picks out.

Last time it was *Brave*, the one where the crazy, red-haired princess turns her poor mom into a bear.

But I do want to get married. I want Penny to have a mom, and I definitely want her to grow up with siblings. I'm already thirty-six years old. It's about time I make dating more of a priority.

I'd always wished I had more siblings. My parents wanted more kids, but it took them a long time to get pregnant with my sister.

Penny is turning seven in a few weeks, which means I need to get a move on it if I don't want her to have siblings ten years younger than her. That's probably something I should keep to myself and not bring up on my date tonight.

I run my fingers through my damp hair, trying to achieve that perfect tousled look the ladies seem to love so much. Walking into my closet, I look around like I actually have any date-worthy clothing. Hopefully Mariah doesn't mind casual-Drew. Surely, anything is an improvement from the scrubs she always sees me in.

After donning a pair of dark jeans, some sneakers and a navy blue v-neck, I open my bedroom door and walk down the hallway. I can hear a soft voice singing. It sounds like it's coming from the living room.

I creep quietly into the main area to see what the girls are doing. Emily is braiding Penny's freshly washed hair into two intricate braids that start at her forehead and go back to the nape of her neck. Penny is smiling as Emily sings *Lavender's Blue*.

My heart warms at the sight of them. I can't believe next week Emily won't be living here anymore. Who's going to do all the girly things with Penny? I don't know the first thing about braiding.

Clearing my throat to announce my entrance, I walk into the living room to join them.

"Daddy!" Penny jumps up and runs into my arms.

"Hey, munchkin," I say, giving her a squeeze. "How was your day?"

"Amazing! We did finger painting, went to the library, and made cookies!"

I look over her head at Emily, who's grinning as Penny relays her day.

"Sounds like Aunt Em is pretty fun."

"The funnest!" Penny wiggles down and runs back to her aunt.

Emily hoists her up into her arms. They've grown so close over the last seven years.

"Okay, shoo! You're going to be late for your date. Penny and I have a popcorn and movie night to start." Emily gives me a shove toward the garage door.

"Okay, okay." I put my hands up and chuckle. "See you gals later." I wave to Emily and then place a kiss on Penny's cheek as I pass by her on the way to the garage, which is connected to the kitchen.

Thankfully, I remembered to take my vehicle through the car wash on my way home from work. My classic 1974 Ford Bronco doesn't tend to impress the ladies. But she's my prized possession. Restoring her to all her former glory was the greatest achievement of my life … besides Penny and my doctorate, of course.

The few women I've taken on dates in the baby blue Bronco haven't seemed too thrilled. If only they knew it's the most expensive thing I own. But most women don't seem to know much about cars, at least not the classics. And they have certain … expectations when it comes to doctors.

Like all doctors are supposed to wear ties for fun and drive BMWs. Ugh, no thanks, talk about boring.

I try to relax while I drive to Mariah's house to pick her up by listening to Yo-Yo Ma's first album. It was my mom's favorite and I always listen to it when I need to get out of my own head.

Dates always go the same way for me:

1. They're excited I'm a surgeon.
2. They don't appreciate my choice in vehicles.
3. They're disappointed I'm a single father.

Penny is my whole world, and if the woman I'm dating can't see how amazing it could be to have her in her life, I'm not even remotely interested in going on a second date with them.

Mariah and I don't work together directly, but she has worked with the other nurses in the surgical unit enough that she knows I have a daughter. Therefore, I'm hoping tonight goes well. Or at least better than my other dates have.

I pull up to a cute little house across town. It's small but well-maintained, with pale yellow siding, white shutters, and wooden flower boxes under each window. I double-check the house number by the door to make sure this is Mariah's place. After releasing a slow breath through my mouth, I exit the Bronco and walk up the tidy sidewalk to knock on her front door.

A minute later, she answers with a bright smile. She's a pretty girl, probably just a few years younger than me. She has dark brown eyes and hair—reminding me a bit of Emily.

"Drew, great to see you." She gestures for me to come inside.

"You too, you look nice." I smile and stick my hands in my front pockets.

She looks down at her floral sundress. "Oh, thank you! So do you." She gives my chest and arms an appreciative glance, then looks away awkwardly.

Mariah and I drive to my favorite taco truck near the Wichita River and eat in the picnic area they have set up. I never start out with a fancy date. The last thing I need is a woman who expects a constant myriad of fancy dinners and charity galas.

Nope, I need someone who's willing to get messy and be adventurous. Someone fun, and hopefully someone who loves tacos.

And let's be honest: who could possibly trust a person who doesn't like tacos?

The picnic area has a great view of the river, and the overhead bulb-lights give it a magical feel. Penny and I come here often and then walk along the river walk.

After eating, Mariah and I walked along the river for a while chatting before the evening came to an end and I took her home.

She was easy to talk to, and with both of us being in the medical field, the conversation flowed easily. Mariah seemed to enjoy herself, and she devoured those tacos. So that's a good sign.

This was definitely the best date I've had in a long time, but I'm not sure I felt that "spark." It's frustrating that every time Sophie—my tenant *and* babysitter—walks into a room, my body is on high-alert. But when I'm with a woman who's totally appropriate for me to date … nothing.

Perhaps one date isn't enough to feel a spark. Maybe I'll feel it on the second date?

Chapter 7
Sophie

It's been a week of living in freedom in my own place. Walking around the house in just my underwear and a t-shirt. No pants, no bra.

This. Is. The. Life.

At least until Samantha is old enough to be embarrassed by me.

We have settled nicely into our little apartment. It's been a calm and quiet week. I've worked on lesson plans for this upcoming school year during Sam's naps and we've simply enjoyed our alone time. Just the two of us. It's our first weekend here together and Samantha is sleeping in. Of course, I still woke up early, as usual. That's the thing no one tells you about having kids; your body resets, so even when they sleep in, you cannot.

After scrolling through TikTok on my phone way longer than I'd like to admit, I finally make myself get out of bed and start a pot of coffee.

I make sure my phone's volume is up before pouring myself a mug of the hot steaming liquid.

Drew gave me a schedule of his on-call weekends, and this is one of them. And when Drew's on call, *I'm* on call.

Eyeing my black coffee, I wrinkle my nose. I wasn't lying about being a terrible cook, and yes, I consider brewing coffee cooking.

I doctor my bitter, too-dark coffee up with plenty of sugar and caramel macchiato creamer. It's drinkable now, but not necessarily enjoyable. Coffee creamer and sandwich supplies are basically the only items I stocked my little fridge with.

Finishing my mug, I make a face at my coffee-making skills. The thought pops into my head that I need to find a man who makes good coffee. Then I remember the thought that popped into my head last week about dating. I worry my bottom lip as I think about making a dating profile. Would it be so scary to just sign up on a dating website and see what happens? I mean, I don't even have to respond to anyone who messages me. I can choose to ignore them if I decide it's too soon.

I walk back to my room, grab my iPad from its charging port, and make my way back to my little kitchen table. With a deep breath, I square my shoulders and begin researching the best dating websites.

As I type the first dating website into the search bar, my heart clenches. This is the first time I've entertained the idea of a relationship since Sam died. Sam and I met soon after I graduated highschool and connected instantly. We were together for six years. The thought of finding someone else not only feels impossible, but like I'm being unfaithful to Sam.

I couldn't possibly find anyone who *gets* me like he did. Surely that kind of love only happens once in a lifetime. And if that's true, why even bother dating?

But do I want Samantha to grow up without a father figure? I mean, sure, she's got plenty of uncles and my dad is super involved in her life ... but it's not that same as having a daddy. Ugh, why is this so hard?

If I want to find love again—if it's even possible—my mind needs to be emotionally prepared for it. And I just don't think

I'm there yet.

The realization of how much healing my heart still needs brings on a steady stream of tears. I slam my fist down on the small dining table, feeling incredibly frustrated by how far I still have to go. For weeks or even months, I'll feel so normal, like there's fire and energy pumping through my veins. I will go out and enjoy life, taking Samantha to parks, hanging out with family. Living my life.

But then, sometimes out of nowhere, it feels like the grief takes over again. And that fire in my veins is replaced by cold, hard sadness. Two steps backward all over again.

Maybe I should've left all those photos of me and Sam tucked away in their box.

Even the thought of Samantha having her first day of preschool without her daddy being there, or basically anytime we hit a milestone that Sam should've been here for, the grief comes back like a tidal wave. That's the thing about trauma; once you feel like you're safely back on land after treading water and managing not to drown, you get pulled right back out into the rough waters to do it all over again.

I just want to feel like myself. I'm so tired of treading water.

I want to be happy again.

I backspace my search and end up searching for articles about grieving the loss of a spouse. As I'm scrolling, a page stands out to me: *WonderfulWidowsSupportGroup.com*. Noticing it's listed in Wichita, Kansas, I click on the link. Their page has a photo of two older ladies with white hair. Their skin is wrinkled, but their eyes and smiles are bright. They each have an arm draped around the other. I read the paragraph of information under the photo:

"Gerda and Bernice are sisters who began Wonderful Widows after both losing their husbands within a year of each other. They took comfort in having the other to talk to and work through their grief with. They began this support

group so other women can also have a place to connect with other widows who are working through their grief."

This is exactly what I need, to talk to other women who have lost a spouse. Some days I feel like no one really understands what I'm going through, and I'm tired of feeling alone in this. I know my family has tried so hard to help, and I love them for it. But I think meeting with other widows could be really helpful.

I make myself another cup of the disgusting sludge I brewed and choke it down while I sign up for the Wonderful Widows group.

"Momma?" I hear Samantha's sweet little voice stream down the hallway, and I grin.

She always wakes up so happy. It's the best part of my day. I walk down the short hallway to her room and she beams at me, her eyes twinkling when I peek my head in the doorway.

"Good morning, Sammy girl." Tears fill my eyes again, unexpectedly. I choke them back to be strong for my daughter. She eyes me curiously, possibly sensing that something is wrong but not knowing how to communicate it. Kids are way more perceptive than we give them credit for.

Chapter 8
Drew

Sitting at the breakfast table, just me and Penny, feels strange. Like when you take down all the Christmas decorations once the holiday is over and the house feels bare.

Emily has almost always been here to eat with us, but this morning she left early, excited to do some shopping for her new place. It's nice to see her making friends and becoming her own person. It's going to be difficult for us when Emily moves out this week, but she's excited to move in with her two closest friends. And I'm happy for her.

But she's lived with me for so long, it's difficult to think about her leaving. My eyeballs have been reacting all week like someone is cutting onions. Since losing my parents, it's just been the two of us. We confided in each other and grew so close during the last ten years. Part of me feels more like her father than her brother. This must be what a parent experiences when their first child is moving out.

And then there's Penny, who will miss Emily terribly. She's had her here nearly every day of her life. Seeing her just once or twice a week will be an adjustment for everyone.

"Daddy, where's Aunt Em?" Penny asks, interrupting my thoughts, then taking another bite of her scrambled eggs.

I look up from adding butter and jam to my toast to Penny's sweet face. "It's quiet this morning, huh?"

She wrinkles her nose. "Yeah."

"Aunt Em is shopping and running errands. You'll have to settle for just me today, I'm afraid."

She releases a heavy sigh. "Alright," Penny says, finishing her last bite of eggs.

"There's something I wanted to talk to you about actually. You know how Aunt Em has always stayed with us?"

She takes a sip of her orange juice. "Yeah?"

"Well, she has a new job, so she'll be moving in with a few of her friends and starting her own adventure," I say in the most upbeat tone I can manage.

She shrugs. "I know. She told me."

"She did?" I keep my facial expression neutral, not sure whether I feel relieved or annoyed that Emily talked to her about this without me.

"Yeah, but she said she'll still see me every week! And bring me chocolate chip cookies." She beams.

I laugh. "Okay, well I'm happy you're alright with the change."

"And Miss Sophie is going to stay with me when you're at work, right? I really like her."

I smile at her. "Yep, that's right. I want you to be a good girl for her, okay?"

She gives me a side-eye. "I always am, Dad."

After breakfast, Penny and I go out to the garage and she rides her bike in the large driveway while I work out in the garage gym. It's nothing fancy, just a squat rack, pull-up bar, and weight bench. Penny and I love to be outside, especially when it doesn't feel like an oven.

I'm about to finish up my workout regimen when I hear my phone ping with a text. Picking up the phone, I glance at the screen and see a text from Mariah. I guess she's not one to do the whole wait forty-eight hours before any contact rule.

Mariah: Hey Drew! I really enjoyed last night. When are you free again? I have a date idea ...

I smile, appreciating her forwardness, and type out a response.

Drew: Hey! I had a great time, too. I'm on call this weekend, but free next weekend. What do you have in mind?

Mariah: How about Friday night at seven? It's a surprise.

Tilting my head to the side, I read her text again. I can't remember the last time a woman asked me out and planned the date herself. Actually, I'm pretty sure that's never happened.

Drew: Sounds like a plan, looking forward to it.

And just like that I have a second date. I rest my hands on my hips and take in my reflection in the mirrored wall I installed behind the squat rack. I puff out my chest and do my best Superman pose.

"What are you doing?" Penny asks from behind me.

I spin on my heel to look at her, not realizing she was watching me. "Uh, nothing."

Her mouth twists as she studies me. "You were standing the way superheroes do."

"Well, surgeons are basically superheroes."

"Right," she scoffs, then continues riding her bike.

Kids. They keep you humble, that's for sure.

***

Stepping out of the hot shower, steam billows around me. I'm not a tedious man, and I don't require many of the finer things in life ... but I installed a large shower in my master bathroom, complete with two waterfall shower heads. I'm taking advantage of an extra long and relaxing shower while Penny is watching her tablet. Screen time for the win.

There's just something incredibly relaxing about the steam and the sound of water hitting the tiles. It must be soothing to me after growing up in Seattle. I especially enjoy it after being on my feet all day performing surgeries. But it works just as well after a rigorous workout.

I can tell the heat and humidity of the Kansas summer has increased outside because the steam from the shower isn't dissipating. Wrapping a towel around my waist, I open my bathroom window to let the bathroom air out.

A glimmer of gold catches my eye and I squint through the steam. Sophie is outside in the large backyard, watching Samantha climb on the little play structure.

Samantha is adorable, but that's not what catches my attention. It's Sophie's wide smile, gleaming brightly through her full lips.

She's always smiling. Even when her eyes look sad, the smile remains firmly in place. I don't know how she stays so positive. I'm no stranger to loss, but losing your young husband while you're pregnant with his child? I don't know how she manages to smile at all after experiencing something like that.

She's wearing a pink sundress with little straps tied at her shoulders. The dress shows off her willowy form and endless legs. Sophie is slim, with dainty wrists and long golden hair. It's usually up in a bun or ponytail, but today it blows softly in the wind, catching the light like a thousand pieces of broken glass.

Samantha is a tiny miniature of Sophie and smiles all the time, just like her mom. I continue watching as Samantha slides down the slide a little too quickly and lands on her bottom with a thud. Samantha looks stunned, and Sophie runs to her side to make sure she's okay. Samantha bursts into giggles, making Sophie laugh too. Her laughter is loud and joyful and exuberant. I could listen to that sound all day.

I'm mesmerized by the sight of them.

"Daddy! The battery on my iPad is dead!" Penny yells, while banging her fist on my bathroom door.

How a fist that tiny can cause such a ruckus is beyond me, but it's loud enough to draw Sophie's attention to the open bathroom window ... where I'm standing and staring at her ... in nothing but a towel ... like a total creep.

I quickly shoot her the most natural smile I can muster up, then wave like a buffoon.

She has a quizzical expression on her face but waves back at me. I turn from the window and walk to unlock the bathroom door, shaking my head at how weird it was for me to watch Sophie and Samantha through the window. Here she is having a completely innocent interaction with her daughter, and I can't pry my eyes away from her just because she's wearing a sundress.

What the hell is wrong with me?

The next day, I am called into work early. Dr. Pham has some kind of stomach bug so, naturally, the on-call surgeon steps in. Which is me this weekend. Physicians aren't great about taking sick days. Usually we just hook ourselves up to some I.V. fluids and carry on about our days. But I don't suppose anyone wants a surgeon with a stomach bug cutting them open. I know I wouldn't.

I'm disappointed I can't take Penny to the park today, our Sunday ritual. But I'm also relieved to get away after my awkward window fiasco yesterday.

Sophie is my mentor's daughter *and* my daughter's sitter. She's so off-limits I definitely shouldn't be noticing her full mouth or her gorgeous flowing hair.

Which would be a lot easier if she wasn't in my yard wearing a sundress with her hair down.

I bet her hair smells incredible … like the ocean at sunrise.

STOP, YOU BIG CREEP.

I smack my palm to my forehead. What has gotten into me lately? This is ridiculous. I've been around Sophie dozens of times before she moved into the basement apartment and never thought about her like this.

As I pull on my black scrubs, I remind myself over and over that I should think of her more like a sister. But I know that's impossible.

But you know who's *not* off limits? Mariah—who I have a date with in five days. She's beautiful and completely appropriate girlfriend material. We work in the same field, but not together. It's perfect. She's easy to talk to, down to earth.

And so far gives me no flutters in my stomach or sparks in my chest.

We've only had one date, though. After Friday, I'll probably feel all the sparks. And if not, then at least that's less drama in my life, right?

I arrive at work and am surprised to find Ted there. He's looking over the C.T. scans for today's patients and smiles when I enter the room.

"Drew!" He claps me on the back, then re-crosses his arms to examine the images once more.

"Good morning, Ted." My voice is shaky, making me sound nervous. Which I am, although I'm not sure why. Thinking Ted's daughter is gorgeous doesn't make me a bad person, it makes me human.

"I had to run in to check on a patient. Looks like you have a full workload today." He points to the scans in front of us.

"Looks that way," I agree.

"So how are things going with Sophie?"

My back stiffens. "What do you mean? Nothing's going on," I say defensively.

Ted angles his head and looks at me with a confused expression. "Calm down, son. I just meant how was her first week in the apartment?"

A relieved laugh escaped my mouth. "Right, ha. Sorry, I didn't sleep well. As far as I know they're settling in. She hasn't mentioned any issues."

Ted nods. "Glad to hear it. Diane mentioned Sophie is excited to watch Penny for you. She's always loved kids. I figured she'd have a dozen of them herself." His lips turn down slightly, which makes me wonder if he's thinking she may never have more children since she lost her husband.

"Well, Penny adores her, and she's a pretty tough judge of character," I say, trying to lighten the mood.

He laughs. "We sure miss having them at the house."

"I bet," I say honestly, remembering the sound of Sophie's laughter. I'd miss that sound too.

"Alright, well I'm heading back home. Good luck today." He takes one last look at the scans and grimaces.

I smirk and wave at him as he exits the imaging room.

Chapter 9
Sophie

It's a hot, sunny day in Wichita, Kansas.

Would I have preferred to stay inside in the air conditioning? Yes.

Does Penny care that it's hotter than Hades outside? No.

So here we are at the park. I have Sam in her stroller while Penny plays happily on the playground equipment with the other children. Looking around, I can see all the other adults here look just as miserable as I feel.

Drew seriously does this *every* Sunday? The vision of Drew chasing Penny around the park happily sends a shiver through me, despite the heat.

Since yesterday, thoughts of Drew send an unwanted jolt through my body, bringing a flush to my cheeks. He has never looked at me like he did yesterday from the window. And in *nothing* but a towel. I mean, sure, it was a little awkward … but the man's perfectly sculpted chest was something to behold.

Drew is undoubtedly a handsome man, but I don't understand this sudden attraction. Maybe it's just the close proximity. Or maybe it's all in my head.

I need to make myself go to the widow support group I found. I saw a therapist regularly the year after losing Sam—

and that was a tremendous help with working through my grief—but I wonder if talking to other women who have experienced the loss of a spouse is the piece that I'm missing. Perhaps they might even have some insight for me on my strange new feelings for Drew ... and the spark of electricity that is always followed by a pang of guilt in my gut.

I look down at my left hand and where my wedding ring used to be. A year after finally taking it off, my hand still feels strange without it. And thinking of another man still feels completely inappropriate. Even though I'm single, it's difficult to think of myself as unattached after years of being happily married.

But I *have* to work through these feelings if I want to move forward.

My thoughts are interrupted by Penny yelling, "Miss Sophie! Watch this!"

I watch as she slides down the slide on her side instead of on her back. I believe I'm supposed to be thoroughly impressed by her sliding skills.

"Wow, impressive!" I grin at her.

After two hours of sweating my tuchus off, I convince the girls to head back to the house. The wonderfully air-conditioned house.

Walking in through the front door, we're greeted with a soothing blast of cool air. The girls run down the hallway to Penny's room, where all of her toys are located.

"Hey girls," I holler down the hallway. "I'm going to run downstairs and grab some stuff."

"Okay!" They yell back at the same time.

Drew eats super healthy, which is probably why he looks like a Greek god. But I need sugar to survive. Which means I need to bring my own snacks when I'm upstairs. I hurry down the stairs and grab my caramel macchiato creamer and a bag of Sour Patch Kids, then run back upstairs.

Drew made a full pot of coffee this morning, but hardly drank any of it. Even though it's cold now, I'm thankful for the caffeine. Once I nuke it in the microwave and add some creamer, it's perfection. And paired with some candy, I have the snack of my dreams.

I glance at the clock. It's time for lunch already.

Hm, what to do for lunch? I remember seeing a teapot in the cabinet with the coffee mugs. The girls would love a tea party. I grin to myself; the girls will be so excited. Opening up the cabinet again, I rummage around and find the teapot. After filling it with warm water from the sink, I search for tea bags. Drew, of course, has a collection of herbal teas from some health food store. I grab one of the tea bags and steep it in the teapot.

Next up: sandwiches.

I find some bread in the fridge. It's some kind of fancy sprouted bread that doesn't feel very soft, but hopefully the girls won't care if I cut the sandwiches into little shapes.

Keeping it simple with just turkey and cheese, I cut the sandwiches into little triangles and arrange them nicely on a plate. I'm not sure if they have any teacups, but I bet Penny would know.

I walk down the hallway and peek in at the girls. They're playing with Penny's dollhouse, and Penny is directing Samantha on how to play. Samantha doesn't mind, she just goes along with it. The best thing about watching Penny is that she and Samantha entertain each other so well.

I knock on the door frame. "Hey Penny, do you guys have any teacups?"

She stands and claps her hands together. "Oh my gosh, are we having a tea party?"

I wink. "Maaaaybe."

"Let me show you where Daddy keeps them! We have tea parties a lot."

I hold on to the doorframe a little tighter, trying not to melt into a puddle at the image of Drew hosting a tea party for his daughter.

Penny runs down the hallway into the kitchen, and I follow her, little Sam trailing behind us. Penny pulls open a cabinet and pulls out three white teacups and matching saucers, and then ducks back into the cabinet and digs around. She comes back up with her arms loaded up with a floral tablecloth and a little vase filled with silk flowers and carries it all to the dining table.

"Your dad got all of this for tea parties?" I ask, my voice sounding higher than usual.

"Yep!" She grins. "Oh wait! We almost forgot the dress-up clothes." She gestures for us to follow her back down the hallway to her room.

Samantha and I follow her back to her room and she opens the trunk at the end of her bed. It's full of princess dresses, but there's also a black bowtie and a top hat. Penny sets those off to the side.

"We don't need the top hat and bowtie—those are my daddy's."

I swallow the lump that has formed in my throat. How can Drew be affecting me this way when he isn't even here?

Penny hands me a pink silk scarf and some elbow-length gloves. Then she finds a princess dress for Samantha and another one for herself. The girls throw them on over their play clothes. They look darling.

"Okay! I think we're ready," Penny announces. We head back into the dining room and Penny gets the table ready for our tea party while I grab the teapot and sandwiches from the kitchen.

With the table cloth, vase with flowers, dress-up clothes, and tea set, it's actually a pretty fancy-looking tea party. I grab my phone out of my back pocket and try to unlock it before realizing I have gloves on. I remove one and get my camera app up.

"Okay, girls… smile!" I tell them.

The girls grin and lean into each other. After I snap a picture, I pull it up to make sure it looks okay. It's so cute. I pull up Drew's contact and send it to him.

Sophie: Having a tea party :) I'm really looking forward to seeing you in your top hat soon.

I snicker to myself, but I have an inkling the man looks damn good in a top hat.

Chapter 10

Drew

Moving day has arrived and my little sister is moving out. For the first time in my adult life, I won't be looking after her. And I'm freaking terrified of all the things that could happen to her. Emily has been through so much in her life already. If I could, I'd wrap her in bubble wrap and hide her in her room forever. That probably sounds creepy, but after the sudden loss of our parents, I never want to see her hurting again.

I requested the day off when she told me several weeks ago she'd be moving out. I was hoping I wouldn't get emotional, but there's not a chance this big cry baby isn't going to shed any tears. And besides, no one will ever know, anyway.

Yep, I'm a crier. It helps me to just let everything out instead of attempting to bottle it up.

I got a dozen donuts and made a full pot of coffee. I like coffee well enough, but I noticed Sophie drank the rest of the pot I made on Sunday. Unless Penny suddenly acquired a taste for coffee, Sophie sure can put it back. Sophie came upstairs this morning to keep an eye on Penny while I help Emily move, and she brought caramel macchiato creamer with her. Between the coffee creamer and the candy wrappers I found in the garbage bin last night, I'm fairly certain she's addicted to sugar.

Emily comes down the hallway from the guest room and eyes the donuts and coffee skeptically. Neither she nor I like donuts, but Sophie obviously has a major sweet tooth. And Emily definitely takes notice of my thoughtfulness.

"Donuts, huh?" She leans against the counter and crosses her arms.

I shrug. "Donuts are a moving staple."

"You hate donuts," she says with a challenging tone.

"Who hates donuts?!" Sophie asks, walking from the living room into the kitchen with a mouthful of a pink sprinkled donut. "These are amazing."

Emily looks at me pointedly, then walks toward the front door where we stacked all the boxes last night. She grabs one and gives me one last stare before taking it outside to load it into my Bronco. I grab a box and follow her.

Emily hoists the heavy box into the back of my Bronco and turns to look at me, her brows drawn together in annoyance. "Drew, what are you doing?"

Glaring back at her briefly, I set the heavy box I'm carrying on the tailgate. "Helping you move. What does it look like I'm doing?"

She rolls her eyes. "Don't play dumb. I meant with Sophie."

My head jerks back in surprise. "I'm not doing anything with Sophie."

"Your eyes never leave her the entire time she's in the same room as you."

I rub my thumb and index finger on my temples as I compose my anger. "You're being ridiculous, Em. It probably seems like I'm looking at her because Penny follows her around like a puppy."

"Ha! You're delusional. She's still grieving the loss of her husband. You and I both know how long it takes to heal after a loss like that." I open my mouth to interrupt her, but she puts her hands up to stop me. "I just don't want to see you get hurt,

Drew. You've taken care of me and Penny so well, and I want you to find someone who can take care of *you* for once."

"I appreciate that, but you have nothing to worry about. I wouldn't want to risk my relationship with Ted, or make things awkward with Sophie by acting on this ... attraction." My cheeks heat. This is the last thing I want to talk to my little sister about.

"So you admit you're attracted to her?" Emily smirks, then turns on her heel.

"Have you *seen* her?"

She rolls her eyes and walks back inside to grab another box.

I follow her back into the house to find Sophie playing Barbies with the girls on the living room floor. I smile to myself and turn to grab another box, but meet the intense gaze of my sister, who just caught me grinning stupidly at Sophie and the girls.

"Stop that," I mouth.

"Stop what?" She whispers.

We both grab another box and stomp back outside.

"Okay, enough with the attitude." I pin her with a serious look. "Hey, you still have the pepper spray I got you, right?" I ask her.

"So you're just going to change the subject abruptly, huh?" She smirks. "Yes, it's always with me. I promise."

"I'm nervous about you living with two women. There's no one there to protect you, Em." I slide the box into the trunk with the others.

"I know, but we'll be careful. The house we're renting has a security system." She pauses, looking down at her feet. "I have to move on, Drew. I can't stay with Penny forever. You know that. It's too hard for me. She's *your* daughter," she whispers with tears in her eyes.

Deep down, I know some space will be good for all of us, but being separated just feels wrong. "I just want you to be safe. And you know you can see Penny whenever you want."

"Thank you. That means a lot to me." She smiles, but her eyes are full of sadness.

After loading all of her boxes in our vehicles, we drive to the house she's renting across town with her friends. The neighborhood looks safe and clean, and there's a security system just like she said.

It's time for me to let go.

Once everything is unloaded, I step back and look at the empty trunk space in my Bronco. My eyes burn with tears and I try to shake them away.

Emily walks outside to say goodbye but stops in her tracks when she takes in my somber expression.

"Don't cry, Drew," she groans. "You're going to make *me* cry."

"Sorry, Em." I swipe a tear away with the back of my hand.

She attempts to sling her arm around my shoulders, but I'm almost a foot taller than her. She inherited my mom's petite stature. "I'm only twenty minutes away, and I'll see you Saturday for dinner, okay?"

I sniff. "I know, I know. It's just not going to be the same."

She takes a deep breath. "I don't say this enough, but I appreciate everything you've done for me. I know it wasn't easy for you to finish school and do your residency while making sure I was taken care of, but you did it. You were my inspiration to finish my MBA, no matter what life threw at me," Emily says, her voice thick with emotion. "I love you so much."

"I love you too, baby sister." I pull her into a hug, and she reluctantly pats me on the back a few times before pulling away.

"Alright, enough of the water works. Get out of here," she says playfully with a wink, making me chuckle.

Friday evening, I arrive home from work, excited about my date with Mariah, or at least hopeful the evening will go well. After showering, I pull on a dark blue t-shirt and some khaki shorts. Mariah said to dress casually, and I'm hoping this isn't too casual.

Mariah insisted on picking me up, obviously excited to surprise me. I've contemplated all week whether or not to introduce her to Penny, and I've finally come to the conclusion that I might as well. It's just an introduction, and if children freak Mariah out for some reason, I'd rather find out now.

Sophie agreed to watch Penny tonight, and Penny is thrilled to spend the evening with her and Samantha.

I squirt a drop of gel into my hands and run my fingers through my thick hair. I'm not really a gel guy, but I want to look good for my date tonight.

After giving myself a spritz of cologne, I walk back out into the main room where Sophie is serving chicken nuggets and macaroni and cheese to two very excited little girls. Sophie definitely wasn't lying about her cooking abilities. She seems to be the queen of the microwave. I've thought about teaching her how to make a few simple meals, but I don't want to come across condescending. Knowing how her mom can be, I definitely wouldn't want her to think I believe her to be incompetent.

I walk up behind Penny and kiss the top of her head. Sophie sits down next to the girls at the table and grins.

"Wow, you smell good," she says, then clamps her mouth shut. Her eyes are wide like she's surprised she said the words out loud.

I glance at her curiously, amused by the pink twinge on her cheeks.

"I mean, better than usual," she continues, trying unsuccessfully to explain herself. "It's a special scent, like cologne, you know? Not that I keep track of your smells." She clamps her mouth shut again, getting redder in the face by the second.

"Right, I knew what you meant. Thanks," I say, my lips pulling up into a smirk, silently flattered she noticed my cologne, and approves. Shaking the thought, I clear my throat. "Hopefully Mariah likes it."

As if summoned, the doorbell rings. I can only assume Mariah is on the other side.

I walk across the room and open the front door, and Mariah grins up at me, looking lovely with her dark hair up in a high ponytail and her tan arms and legs on display in her cut-off shorts and tank top.

"Mariah, come on in." I grin. "You look great."

"Thank you, so do you." She laughs nervously.

Glancing behind me, I see Sophie and Penny watching us. "Come on in, let me introduce you to the most important person in my life."

Mariah smiles and follows me into the room.

"This is my daughter, Penny," I tell Mariah as Penny jumps down from her seat.

"Hey." Penny extends a greasy chicken nugget hand, and Mariah clasps it without skipping a beat.

"Very nice to meet you, Penny," Mariah says, pumping her little hand a few times.

"You too, I guess." Penny quirks her mouth, taking in Mariah's shorts. "How come your pants have holes in them? Are you homeless?"

My jaw drops. "Penny!"

Mariah guffaws with laughter. "She's fine," she says, placing her hand on my arm, then focuses back on Penny. "I'm not homeless, but I probably need some new shorts, huh?"

Penny nods. "Yeah, you should go shopping."

I shake my head at her blunt honesty.

Mariah glances up at Sophie and extends her hand. "You must be Drew's sister! I'm Mariah."

Sophie stands from her seat and shakes Mariah's hand gently with her small, delicate hand.

"Hey, great to meet you. I'm Sophie, actually. I'm just the babysitter." She smiles.

Mariah's eyebrows raise slightly as she takes Sophie in. She smooths her facial expression quickly and offers Sophie a smile.

"Nice to meet you."

I breathe a quiet breath of relief. I can only imagine how she could have reacted to the fact that I have a gorgeous babysitter—who also lives in my basement. But that's a story for another day.

Sophie gets up from the table and puts her hands on Penny's shoulders. "You two take off for your date. We're baking cinnamon rolls tonight." Her lips pull up in a smile.

I quirk a brow. "You're baking?"

"Don't worry, they're *Pillsbury,* from a can." She winks and makes a shooing motion with her hand. "Go have fun!"

We say our goodbyes and walk outside to Mariah's car. I squeeze into her tiny two-door car, feeling like my knees are up to my chin. I'll definitely insist on driving next time. Not all vehicles are compatible with my six foot four frame.

Mariah drives across town and we sit in amicable silence for a few minutes. Being a single dad, I rarely get to be the passenger. It's funny how you notice different things when you're riding than you do driving. I never noticed how striking the Kansas sunsets are in the evening, or that you can see the reflection of them in the Wichita River.

"So, how long has Sophie been your sitter?" Mariah asks abruptly, pulling me from my thoughts.

An awkward cough escapes my mouth. "Oh, Sophie? Just a few weeks." I pause, but continue when Mariah remains quiet. "She's Dr. Windell's daughter, actually. They're like family to me."

"Oh, no way! Dr. Windell seems nice."

I nod. "They're a great family."

Thankfully, that seems to be the end of that conversation.

Mariah pulls onto a bustling street downtown and finds a parking spot in the parking garage. As we walk back out onto the main road, I notice cones blocking off one entire brick side street and it's lined with classic cars.

"The car show!" I grin at her, surprised by her thoughtfulness. "This is incredible! I've always wanted to come."

"I noticed your Bronco and figured you must like old cars." She grins.

My heart warms at her thoughtfulness. I look up and down the street and my eyes widen. "Is that a 1967 Shelby?!"

She laughs, and I grab onto her hand and pull her towards the shiny, red sports car—hoping the physical contact will magically bring about the infamous spark I need to feel with any woman I want to date.

Chapter 11
Sophie

After baking cinnamon rolls and playing dress up, I put the girls to bed. I think Penny had a great evening. There are girly girls—and then there's Penny who's on a whole other level. Possibly the girliest girl I've ever met.

She's fabulous.

It was fun to have a little girls' night. Growing up with three brothers and no sisters, I didn't have many evenings spent watching princess movies and painting my nails.

But I want Samantha to enjoy all the girly things, and I know Penny will be more than happy to help me out in that department.

The girls are asleep, and Drew is still on his date. I savor the quiet house for a moment before turning Netflix on and finding something to watch. Odette has been insisting I watch this new historical drama, *Bridgerton*. And since I don't have a TV downstairs, this is my chance. Grabbing a fluffy blanket, I curl up and make myself comfy.

Several hours later, I've binged half of the first season of *Bridgerton*. I've discovered this is not your ordinary period drama; it's definitely more risqué than anything on *Masterpiece Classic*. My mother would never allow any shows like this in her home, no way. If my mom ever let us watch television, it was a documentary or something educational.

I'm immersed in watching a passionate scene between the duke and duchess when I hear the distinct sound of someone clearing their throat behind me.

I whip my head around to find Drew standing there with an amused look on his face.

"Um, watcha watching there?" He asks, his deep voice laced with mischief.

I whirl my head back around to the TV where the Duke of Hastings is about to lift the duchess's skirt over her head. With a gasp, I reach for the remote, accidentally knocking it onto the floor.

"Sorry!" Jumping up from the couch, I retrieve the remote again and press the pause button. "It's just a historical drama," I try to say nonchalantly, but it comes out in a squeak.

"Really?" Drew angles his head toward the TV.

I glance up and see that I've paused Bridgerton in the worst possible spot. I quickly turn the TV off.

"The Duke of Hastings, huh?" Drew asks in a mocking tone.

I quirk an eyebrow at him. "You've watched it?"

"No," he chuckles. "But all the ladies at work talk about it."

"It's not the most wholesome show, but I got sucked in." I attempt to disguise my humiliation with a laugh—unsuccessfully.

He puts his hands on his hips. "I have a feeling Diane Windell would not approve of you watching Bridgerton."

I mirror his stance by putting my hands on my hips and glare back at him, suddenly feeling annoyed instead of embarrassed.

"Well, seeing as I am a 30-year-old adult human, my mother doesn't get to dictate what I do with my time."

He throws his head back and laughs. It's a rich, husky sound that makes me feel warm all over. Really wish I could stay annoyed with him.

"Anyway, how was your date?" I ask, ready to change the subject.

One side of his mouth pulls up into a smile. "Pretty good, actually."

He looks surprised while he says it, like he hadn't expected the date to go well.

"Nice," I say, wondering if I will ever feel ready to date. Maybe that's part of this whole moving forward process.

I clear my throat. "Well, I'm going to head to bed. I'll let you have your television back."

"You're fine, I'm going to sleep too."

"Oh, right, goodnight then."

"Goodnight, Sophie."

The next evening, I drive over to my brother Madden and his wife's apartment. His wife, Odette, and I became quick friends after their precipitous marriage. My brother somehow convinced Odette to marry him to help his chances of getting elected to Congress… and the only people who were surprised when they fell in love with each other for *real* were Madden and Odette. My brother is now a congressman for the 4th district of Kansas, so they're out of town a lot, and I miss them dreadfully.

Pulling up to their luxury apartment complex downtown, I park in one of the designated parking spots. Samantha and I walk inside hand in hand and take the elevator up to the top floor. We enter the small hallway that leads to Madden and Odette's penthouse apartment. It's not as fancy as something New York City would have, but it's a great space. The hallway has marble floors, dark textured walls, and brass door handles and wall sconces. It has a 1920s feel that I love. If they didn't have such a cool apartment, they'd probably buy a house in the suburbs. Especially now that they're expecting their second child.

I knock on the door and my very pregnant, very sweaty sister-in-law opens it after a minute passes.

"Hey Soph, come on in," she pants, wiping her brow with one corner of the apron she's wearing.

We give each other a quick embrace, which is hilariously awkward with her large, round belly.

"Oh my gosh, I missed you guys! How are you?" I ask with hesitation, glancing at her disheveled appearance. Before she can answer, my adorable nephew, Oliver, barrels into me and Samantha.

"Olly!" Samantha exclaims, then they happily run off to play in the living room.

Odette walks toward the kitchen, but glances over her shoulder at me briefly. "Thank goodness Samantha's here to keep him company. He's been so bored. I'm at the stage of pregnancy where I'm exhausted, but can't sleep. Am boiling hot, but can't seem to cool off. And I'm extremely grouchy, but can't have a glass of wine to relax."

I chuckle to myself, remembering the misery of the third trimester. As I follow her into the kitchen, I take in their apartment. It's been over a month since I've been here.

The entire apartment has the same marble floors as the hallway outside and elevator, but the kitchen changes into a herringbone pattern. It's modern with a subway tile backsplash and stainless steel appliances, but has the lovely brass trimmings that make the apartment look more glamorous than others I've seen.

Trying to suppress a smile, I bite the insides of my cheeks. "I'm sorry, the last trimester isn't much fun—"

I'm cut off as my oldest brother stomps into the kitchen.

"What are you doing on your feet?" He demands, his hands on his hips.

Odette doesn't even bother to look at him, but answers, "I'm just putting together a charcuterie board. Don't get all misogynistic on me."

"How come when a doctor tells you to stay off your feet he's not a misogynist, but if your husband says it, it is?" Madden asks in an annoyed tone.

She lifts the tray off the countertop to carry it to the living room, but after a few steps, Madden gently takes the tray from her and carries it the rest of the way to the coffee table.

Finally, he turns to me. "Hey Soph. Sorry to ignore you, just trying to keep my wife—" he glares at Odette. "—from going into preterm labor."

I pat him on the shoulder as he walks by me. "That's okay, someone's gotta keep Odette in line."

"Hey!" Odette protests.

Samantha rushes over to Madden's side.

"Uncle Maddy!" She squeals as he grabs her and throws her into the air then sets her back down on the ground.

"I missed you, Sammy girl," He says as he ruffles her curls.

"Samantha, Aunt Odette needs a hug too!" Odette says, pretending to pout.

Samantha grins and runs over to pounce on her, but Madden catches her just in time.

"The doctor said to stay off your feet as much as possible *and* not to lift over twenty pounds."

"You're being ridiculous." She rolls her eyes and pulls Samantha into a hug.

I wrinkle my nose at her. "Samantha is well over twenty pounds…"

Odette groans before slumping down onto the large leather sectional.

Taking a seat next to her, I pat her knee. "Only two more months."

Madden tickles Sam, pulling high-pitched giggles from her. "Thank goodness. I can't for the life of me get her to follow the doctor's orders."

Odette ignores him and turns to me. "I love your brother dearly, but he's suffocating me."

Madden shakes his head from side to side in sarcastic dismay, then takes a seat on the other side of Odette.

Samantha looks at Odette's belly with wide-eyed curiosity.

"There's a baby in there?" she asks in awe.

"Yes, sweetie. In a few more months, you'll have another cousin," Odette tells her with a grin.

Samantha places a kiss on Odette's belly, then scurries off to find Oliver.

Odette looks down at the small drool spot left on her apron and bursts into tears. "That was the sweetest thing I've ever seen," she cries.

I look at my brother and wrinkle my nose, as if silently saying, "I feel for you, bro."

One side of his mouth pulls up in a smirk before he wraps an arm around his wife and kisses her temple. Madden and Odette have the sweetest relationship, even though their marriage started off as a farce.

Watching them gives me a wistful feeling... maybe I can find love again someday.

"How are things going, Soph?" Madden asks in his deep voice.

Settling back into the couch, I think for a moment before responding, "Really good, actually. I love having my own space again. Mom and Dad take Samantha once a week so I can have a break, and I found a support group for widows. I'm going tomorrow for the first time."

Madden stops filling his small plate with charcuterie and meets my gaze. "That's great. Although we all know the real reason you moved out is so you can bring guys home."

"Oh brother, ignore him." Odette says before shooting a glare at my brother. "How's babysitting for Drew?" Her question seems innocent, but there's a twinkle in her eyes telling me it's not.

Ignoring her suggestive expression, I answer, "He's super chill and Penny is awesome. I was worried Drew would be similar to Dad—you know, super uptight. But he's been great, and he's a really involved father."

"Drew's an awesome guy. I'm happy it's been a good fit ... despite David's concerns." Madden smirks and takes a bite of a cracker covered with brie and fig jam.

I roll my eyes dramatically. "Oh my gosh, David is ridiculous. I'm surprised he hasn't randomly stopped by yet to check up on me."

Madden swallows his bite with a chuckle. "Oh, he will."

"We really need to find a girlfriend for him so he'll chill out."

Odette rubs her hands together like she's plotting something. "Oh yes, let's! He needs someone that will make him a little ... messier. Not so formal and put-together."

Madden contemplates for a moment. "Hmm ... what's the complete opposite of a certified public accountant?"

"Someone committing tax fraud?" I answer, and we all bust up laughing at the idea.

"Okay, maybe not *that* opposite," Madden adds once he's stopped cackling.

Madden finishes his charcuterie plate, then turns to me. "Oh hey, I was wondering if you could keep an eye on Odette for me. I have to go back to D.C. next week and she's not allowed to travel anymore with all the contractions she's been having."

"Yeah, of course," I say without hesitation. "Drop her off whenever, and I'll watch her."

Odette protests, "I'm sitting right here!"

Madden and I smirk at each other. She's too fun to mess with sometimes.

The next morning, I drop Samantha off at my parent's house. Mom and Dad are delighted to spend the day with her. Mom has literally texted me about it every day this week. My parents weren't the most affectionate and present parents when my brothers and I were kids; it's like they're making up for it now with their grandchildren. I think they see it as a second chance for their marriage and their relationships with their kids and grandkids. If only they would've figured things out thirty years sooner.

After dropping her off, I drive over to the coffee shop where the Wonderful Widows support group meets. The name of the group is strange, but hopefully that's a sign of a good sense of humor, and not that they're insane.

The group reserves a private room twice a month for their meetings. I'm relieved it's small and private, but I have no clue what else to expect.

I walk into the coffee shop, and the scent of coffee and pastries instantly soothes my nerves. I wish I didn't have such a sweet tooth, but also... YOLO and all that.

The building is old, probably built in the Victorian era. It has high ceilings with an intricate scroll design engraved on it. The hardwood floor creaks beneath me, making me wonder if they're the original floors. It's a beautiful building.

After looking over the menu, I decide to stick with my favorite, a caramel macchiato. I walk toward the large wooden coffee counter and give the barista my order. As I'm waiting for my coffee, I notice a sign for Wonderful Widows with an arrow indicating they meet down the hallway behind me.

Once I have my drink in hand, I follow the arrow down the long hallway, towards the back of the building. I come to a door and hear voices on the other side. Slowly, I push the door open and peek my head inside. All the talking stops and the women stare at me curiously. There are five women sitting in a circle of comfy armchairs. Their ages probably range from thirty to eighty.

"Are you Sophie?" One of the older ladies asks in a sweet voice.

I step inside the room and gently close the door behind me. "Yes, is this Wonderful Widows?"

"That would be us!" She says with a smile, her blue eyes glinting with kindness. "Ladies, let's welcome our newest member, Sophie."

Everyone says hello and I take the open seat in the circle. "Hey, everyone," I mutter shyly.

I'm not usually shy, but these women are looking at me like they can see through me and straight into my soul. It's probably just knowing they've lost their spouse just as I have, but we all instantly have an unspoken understanding of each other. There's no hiding from them, and that's the scary part.

"It's okay to be nervous, pumpkin. Why don't we go around and introduce ourselves?" She pauses. "I'm Bernice, I lost my husband ten years ago, and this is my sister, Gerda." She gestures to the older woman next to her.

They both have the same white, back-combed hairstyle, making me wonder if they go to the salon together. "We both lost our husbands within a year of each other and decided to start this group together to help other widows have a safe space to talk about the struggles of losing someone dear to you."

Bernice looks at Gerda expectantly, waiting for her to introduce herself. "Well, you already introduced me! What am I supposed to say now?" Gerda says in a cantankerous voice.

"Oh, stop your fussing. I was just explaining how we started the group!"

Gerda smirks. "Alright fine, you bossy thing. I'm Gerda, the *younger* sister." She bats her seemingly non-existent eyelashes at her sister.

Bernice rolls her eyes. "I'm only one year older than you."

"Still older," Gerda replies in a mischievous tone.

The young blonde woman next to Gerda clears her throat. "I'm Ashley. I lost my husband four years ago. I have two children, six and eight. And I recently got engaged," she adds with a blush.

"And boy howdy, is he easy on the eyes!" Gerda whistles.

Bernice fans herself dramatically. "Oh, he really is!"

Ashley shakes her head. "You two, can't you at least *try* to behave yourselves when we have a newbie?"

The woman sitting next to Ashley laughs at their antics. She has sleek, dark brown hair pulled back in a ponytail. She has a youthful appearance, but the fine lines around her eyes make me think she must be older than she seems at first glance—maybe forty?

"Hey, I'm Lisa. My husband passed away eight years ago. I'm a nurse at Woodford Medical Center. My late husband and I never had children, but I do have three cats that I adore."

Bernice mutters what sounds like, "crazy cat lady," between coughs.

"Yep! I *am* a crazy cat lady, and proud of it!" Lisa unzips her hoodie, revealing a t-shirt that has a photo of her cats on it, making us all giggle.

The fifth woman seems more reserved than the others. She also seems to be the youngest. With dark hair pulled up in a bun on top of her head, a few loose curls resting on her nape and forehead, she's strikingly beautiful. She looks up at me with her big, brown eyes and smiles.

"I'm Evie. I lost my husband six months ago." Her voice wavers, but she continues, "I have a little boy named Dalton.

He's four." She grins, showing obvious adoration for her child. "I teach english at Foxwood High School."

Everyone's attention returns to me, awaiting my introduction. Having just taken a big sip of my macchiato, I gulp it down quickly.

"It's really great to meet you all." I lick my lips, thinking of what I want to say. "I'm Sophie, my husband was killed in action in Afghanistan a little over three years ago." I pause for a second, hearing their audible gasps around the circle. "I have a little girl named Samantha. She's three years old now. Last year, I started teaching third grade, and I recently moved out of my parent's house."

"We're so sorry for your loss, Sophie." Bernice says gently. The rest of the women nod in agreement.

"Thank you, and I'm sorry for your losses as well," I say with genuine empathy, glancing around the circle at the women surrounding me.

"So what led you to find our group, dear?" Gerda asks.

"Well, actually ... I thought I was ready to date, or I thought I *should* be I guess. So, I got online to create a dating profile, and I sort of had a breakdown about it." Furrowing my brow, I contemplate what to say next. "I felt like that was a sign I wasn't done grieving, so I Googled support groups instead."

Bernice, who's sitting next to me, pats my shoulder. "We've all been there, sweetheart. It's difficult to put yourself out there again."

Evie, the shy one on my other side, nods her head. "I think you're so strong for even entertaining the idea of dating again. I definitely haven't gotten to that point yet, but I hope I will, eventually."

After exhaling a deep breath, I respond, "Thank you, ladies. That makes me feel a little better."

"So you live on your own now with your daughter?" Lisa asks.

"Yes, actually a family friend of ours offered me the apartment in his basement. He works for the same orthopedic surgery group as my father, and we kind of adopted him and his daughter into the family. I watch his daughter for him when he's on-call." I smile at the ladies. "It's been so nice to have my own space again, and I feel safe knowing Drew's right upstairs."

"That's wonderful!" Lisa says with a smile.

Ashley nods. "Sounds like the perfect situation for you! I lived with my parents after losing my husband too, and I completely understand how strange that can be."

I nod my head enthusiastically. "It's so weird. I'm glad they were willing to help though."

"So, how young is this surgeon exactly?" Gerda waggles her eyebrows.

I chuckle awkwardly. "Umm, I think he's like mid to late thirties?"

Gerda brings her hand to her chin in contemplation. "A little young, but I could make it work."

Bernice slaps her shoulder playfully. "Oh, stop! You already have a *friend*," she says, using air quotes on the word "friend."

"Can a woman ever have too many friends?" Gerda quips back.

"Yes! I, however, don't have a special friend. Is this surgeon handsome?" Bernice winks at me playfully.

The women in the circle giggle and wait for me to answer.

Hearing the pairing of the words Drew and handsome in the same sentence brings a deep and unexpected blush to my chest and face. I feel burning hot and set down my macchiato.

Gerda erupts into laughter. "Well, I'd say that blush is answer enough for us."

Lisa gives Gerda a stern glance. "Oh, leave the poor girl alone."

Gerda looks besmirched. "You're right. I'm sorry Sophie. Bernice and I get a little rowdy sometimes."

Bernice whips her white back-combed head to look at her sister. "I do not! It's all you!"

The rest of the ladies shake their heads at the two sisters with bemused expressions on their faces.

I have a feeling I'll fit in here just fine.

When I arrive back home that afternoon, I go to the main house and meet Drew in his kitchen. Since Penny is spending the day with Emily and Sam is at my parent's, he offered to teach me how to cook a few simple meals. And learning how to cook from someone besides my mother didn't sound so bad. I'm a little nervous he's going to teach me how to make ridiculous meals like calamari and crepes.

Those are the kinds of meals my mother taught me to make —er, *tried* to teach me to make. Her fancy meals were so intimidating, I never felt comfortable attempting to make them on my own.

Drew has a big grin on his face and classical music is playing from the kitchen's Bluetooth speaker. He's surrounded by supplies, ranging from flour and salt, to cuts of meat. He's even wearing a white canvas apron.

I shake my head from side to side in amusement, but slowly, a smile spreads across my face. Goodness, the man is adorable. I never imagined adorable would be an adjective I'd use to describe this masculine, confident man.

But he *is* adorable.

I stand next to him, feeling eclipsed by his tall form. My dad and brothers are tall, but Drew has to be several inches taller than all of them. He's also more brawny, with a thickly muscled chest and arms. The man obviously makes good use of his garage gym.

This is the first time Drew and I have been alone in the house, but it feels oddly normal. For weeks now, we've seen each other in passing but we're never alone. The girls are always around. But still, it doesn't feel that strange to be here in the kitchen with him.

Drew holds out a white apron that matches his own and gestures for me to take it.

I raise one eyebrow sardonically. "Really? Matching aprons?"

He shrugs one of his broad shoulders. "I had a second one lying around."

I slide the apron strap over my head and feel something scratch on my neck. Bringing my hand up to discover what the problem is, I clutch the price tag still attached and pull it off.

I smirk at Drew, and he wrinkles his nose.

"Okay, you got me. I bought you one yesterday." He chuckles.

Unsure what to think about him buying me an apron that matches his, I change the subject. "So, what are we making today?"

He rubs his large hands together. "Well, first, I want to teach you how to use the grill. It's pretty easy, and doesn't heat up the house."

I grimace. "You're trusting me with an open flame?"

"You'll be fine. I'm just showing you some basics."

Before getting started on the meat, he takes me to the back patio and instructs me on how to turn on the propane and get the grill heating up.

When we step back into the house, he opens up a package of chicken breasts.

"Grilling chicken is super easy and also pretty healthy. You can basically choose any flavor you want to add to it: honey-mustard, lemon pepper, BBQ, whatever you feel like."

Drew lines up the sauces and lets me choose. He's standing close enough to me that when I reach out to select the BBQ sauce, my arm brushes against his. My heart rate speeds up at the touch, but he doesn't seem affected at all. He hands me a silicone brush to coat the chicken, like his skin touching my skin is no big deal at all. I inhale a quick breath and brush the chicken in BBQ sauce.

Once that's done, we chop some red potatoes, season them, and toss them into the air fryer, then chop and steam a few heads of broccoli.

Once everything is cooked, we have a small, but delicious-smelling feast before us. And if I'm being honest, it was all really simple to make.

We sit together at the dining room table and devour the delicious lunch we created. Drew lets out a small moan, obviously enjoying the meal. But the sound does something funny to my insides.

"See? That wasn't so hard." He gestures to his plate. "Protein, carbohydrate, vegetable. Easy peasy."

Grateful he's not moaning anymore, I answer quickly, "Yeah, it actually *was* really simple. My mom always made cooking seem really complicated—but she can make *anything* seem complicated."

Drew eyes me with a contemplative expression. "Yeah? Aren't you close with your mom, though?"

"I mean, I love my mom, and I don't know what I would've done without her help these past few years."

I look down at my plate and think about what I want to say before continuing. "Growing up, I took the ballet classes and French lessons, but it just wasn't *me*. The path I chose wasn't what they wanted… marrying a soldier, getting a degree in education. I know my parents just want me to be happy, but they think a privileged lifestyle will give me that. Money has never been my motivation in life." I smile wistfully. "My mom has never understood my desire to do things differently than they did, and that can be frustrating."

I glance back up at Drew to find him watching me intently. He's looking into my eyes like he can see straight through to my soul, like he somehow understands me in a way my parents never have. Several seconds pass, but he doesn't look away.

His gaze becomes too much for me to handle, so I try to lighten up our conversation. "One time, my mom tried to show me how to make flan. It was a disaster."

Drew blinks a few times, making me wonder if he was just as affected by our eye contact as I was.

He smiles and responds, "You know I love your parents, but your mom is intense."

One side of my mouth pulls up in a smile. "She definitely can be."

"So, did Sam do most of the cooking then?"

I smile. "Yeah, when he was home, he did. He loved to cook."

Drew nods. "My mom loved cooking, too. She's the one who taught me. I've converted a lot of her recipes into healthier options." He smiles to himself, obviously enjoying the memories of his mother.

"Can I ask you a personal question?"

Drew's gaze meets mine again. "Of course, shoot."

"What happened to your parents? My dad mentioned they passed a while back."

He sits back in his chair and takes a deep breath. "They were in a head-on collision with a semi truck. They were both killed instantly. I was barely twenty-three and Emily wasn't even out of high school yet."

He looks off into space, his eyes filled with pain like he's remembering back to that day.

"I'm so sorry. That must've been awful."

"Thank you." His eyes come back to meet mine.

I bite my bottom lip and hesitate for a moment. "After losing them, how long did it take you to feel normal again?"

His hand comes up to rub his chin as he thinks about the question. "The thing about a loss like that is you're never normal again." He pauses and moves the food around his plate with his fork. "I think you get used to the new person you become after grief changes you, you know? You eventually become comfortable with who you are again, even though you're not the same person you once were."

I nod, taking in his words. "That makes sense. I've never heard anyone put it that way before."

He glances up at me, his hazel eyes looking into mine. At this moment, I feel like we understand each other in a new way. We understand what it's like to grieve and how that changes you. I feel seen by him in a way I've never felt before with anyone else.

Drew and I finish our meal in silence.

"So, there's one more thing I want to show you, and it's slightly more complicated, but I think you'll like it."

My shoulders slump. "Oh no, what is it?"

"Quiche." He pauses, taking in my terrified expression. "The crust can be a learning curve, but the rest is easy. I swear. The best part is we can stick it in the refrigerator and it'll be all ready to cook for breakfast tomorrow. It's important to start the day with protein."

"You look like you eat a lot of protein," I mutter before I realize I'm saying it out loud.

He looks at me with a bemused expression.

"Really? Why do you say that?" His voice is serious, but there's a wicked glimmer in his eyes.

I look down at my hands and begin to stammer. "Umm, I mean, you know... ha. You have muscles and stuff."

"And stuff?" He asks, his eyes sparkling with hidden laughter.

"So let's make that quiche!" I blurt a little too loudly while clapping my hands together.

"Perfect! Glad you're so excited about it." He stands from his seat and walks back into the kitchen. I follow behind him, feeling stupid for commenting on his muscles.

Drew pulls out the crust recipe and patiently walks me through the instructions. Once we have all the dry ingredients mixed together, he points to the softened butter and tells me to cut it into the dry ingredients.

"Cut it in?" I look up at him. "What does that even mean?"

"Grab two knives and scissor them like this." He crisscrosses the knives.

"Umm, okay." I cross the knives and cut the butter into the mixture effortlessly, turning it into a lumpy dough.

"Perfect! Now pull the dough out and knead it with your hands."

I do what he says and am surprised how enjoyable the kneading process is. "This is surprisingly cathartic."

"I told you you'd like it," He says as he grabs the rolling pin and sprinkles a handful of flour on the countertop. "Now that the dough is smooth, roll it out into a 12-inch circle."

"Alright, that seems easy enough."

I take the rolling pin from him, accidentally making our fingers brush. A crackle pulses through my body. It reminds me of the feeling you get when you put pop rocks on your tongue and they snap and pop.

And just from a finger brush. I really need to get out more.

I begin the motion of rolling out the dough, but I'm not quite tall enough to put enough pressure on the firm ball of dough.

Noticing my struggle, Drew comes up behind me, his deep voice sending a vibration through body. "Try pounding the dough down with the rolling pin."

I can hardly think with him standing so close, but attempt to flatten the dough once more. He puts each of his large hands on top of mine on the rolling pin handles and effortlessly helps me put enough pressure on the dough to flatten it completely.

Which makes me wonder what else those strong hands are capable of.

I can feel his chest brushing against my back, making me feel hot all over. I'm not sure I've ever blushed harder than I am right now. I close my eyes briefly and remind myself this is Drew, a close family friend, Penny's dad, MY LANDLORD.

He continues helping me like this for a few minutes until the dough is in a large, flat circle. The amount of close contact with Drew has turned my limbs into limp noodles and my brain into mush. I listen quietly as he tells me how to place the crust into the pie pan and pour in the egg mixture.

All I can think about is how I want to stick my head into the freezer to cool down, but looking at the clock has the same effect.

"Oh, my gosh! I didn't realize how late it was!"

Drew pulls back and looks at the clock on the microwave. "Oh wow, you're right. Em will be back with Penny soon."

"I need to pick up Samantha." I practically run out of the kitchen to grab my keys and purse by the door.

"Bye Drew! Thanks for the heated lessons." My eyes nearly bug out of my head, realizing my mistaken words. "I mean, cooking lessons!"

Chapter 12
Drew

I've kept my distance from Sophie for the past week, which is difficult when she literally lives in my basement and watches my child.

Cooking with her last weekend was honestly … thrilling.

That's the problem. Spending time with my babysitter isn't supposed to be thrilling. It's supposed to be friendly, amicable, all business. Thrilling is not an adjective that is allowed in the context of my relationship with Sophie.

I want to have those feelings when I'm with Mariah. She's perfect for me. She took me to a freaking car show for crying out loud. Not to mention she's beautiful and funny and uncomplicated.

And nothing. I feel nothing.

Last weekend as Mariah and I were leaving the car show, I invited her to Penny's birthday party. I thought it would give us one more chance to connect and see how she is with Penny. But now I'm regretting it.

The last thing I want to do is lead her on. I just genuinely wanted to see if the chemistry between us could grow. Surely it's not instantaneous for everyone.

I thought about texting her to cancel after me and Sophie's my sexy rolling-pin fiasco. How is that even a thing? But she had already texted me saying she found the perfect gift for Penny and was so excited about coming to the party today.

Ugh, I'm in way over my head here.

I keep finding myself looking over my shoulder to see if Sophie's nearby, and when she's not, I feel a pang of disappointment. I don't want to feel this way. I don't want to be constantly aware of her presence. I don't *want* to want her.

I don't know how to get rid of this feeling. Maybe David was right. I mean, what red-blooded man wouldn't be sucked down this rabbit hole with a woman as beautiful as Sophie basically living in his house.

I swirl the last bit of frosting onto Penny's bright pink cake. Strawberry cake with strawberry frosting, her favorite.

Taking a deep breath, I remind myself to just focus on Penny and not worry about the rest. Today is all about her.

Hearing a pitter-patter on the wood floors, I jerk my head up from where I'm frosting the cake and see little Sam running into the kitchen. Sophie is on her heels with a bright smile on her gorgeous face. Looking at her feels like a punch to the gut. Everything about her is like sunshine in the midst of a storm.

I look back down at Samantha to distract myself from Sophie.

"Need any help with the party preparations?" Sophie asks sweetly.

Her voice is soothing, like one of those harps that angels probably play in heaven.

I take her in briefly. She's wearing another freaking sundress. Does she have to do that? This one is blue, the color of my Bronco. If it wasn't my favorite color before, it is now.

"I'm almost ready, but thanks for the offer." My voice comes out weak, much like a puppy's whimper.

"Alright," she replies quietly, rubbing the sides of her arms awkwardly.

"Are you cold?" I ask before I can take it back. Sophie Miller's temperature is none of my business.

"A little, but I'll be fine. I'm always cold." She shrugs. "Junk food warms me up, so I'll be fine after eating my weight in birthday cake."

I chuckle. "You and your junk food. You need protein, remember?"

She blushes at my comment. Perhaps thinking about Saturday affects her the same way it does me.

"I actually did enjoy grilling the other day, even though my chicken breasts turned out more dry than yours."

I close my eyes and think about the vein in Ted Windell's forehead. I really wish she wouldn't say the words *my* and *breasts* in the same sentence.

I swallow hard and huff out a strangled sounding laugh. "Ha, they weren't so bad. They were... you know... tender."

Damn it, Drew. Why are you the way that you are?

Sophie looks pleased at my compliment. "Oh, thanks! Glad they tasted okay."

She spins on her heel to chase Samantha down the hallway before she can see my pained expression.

Once the Windell's and Emily arrive for Penny's party, the house is alive with people and conversations. The Windell's are a pretty lively bunch, except for David, who thankfully seems to like me again.

The dining table is lined with a festive pink tablecloth and a sprinkling of rainbow confetti. I even splurged for a balloon bouquet this year. Seven seems like a big deal. Emily is quiet. I wonder if it's difficult for her to see Penny getting older.

The doorbell rings and I rush to answer it, knowing Mariah will be on the other side. Maybe today will be the day sparks will fly between us. Who knows?

Opening the door, I look at Mariah admirably. She really is lovely. Tanned skin, chocolate colored eyes, long eyelashes, beautiful smile. Heck, she's even wearing a sundress. It's a dark red color that looks magnificent against her bronzed skin. And yet, my idiotic brain has decided that she'll remain permanently in the friend zone.

"Hey!" I give her a quick side hug as she steps inside.

"Hey Drew, thanks again for inviting me."

"Of course, glad you could make it," I say, ushering her into the dining area where everyone has gathered. "Hey everyone, this is Mariah. She works at the hospital. Ted, you've probably seen her around?"

Ted steps forward and shakes her hand. "Yes, you look familiar. Nice to meet you, Mariah." He smiles and puts his hand on the small of Diane's back. "This is my wife, Diane."

Once everyone has said hello and introduced themselves, Penny tugs on the hem of my shirt.

"Daddy! Is it time for presents yet?" She whisper-yells, making everyone laugh under their breath.

"Let's eat dinner and do cake first, okay?" I lift her up and kiss her cheek.

She wrinkles her nose. "Alright, I guess."

Mariah sidles up next to us. "Penny, how old are you now?" she asks with bright eyes, trying to win Penny over.

Penny looks at her with one eyebrow raised. She slowly turns her head to look at the giant balloon bouquet behind us with a balloon number seven at the center. Slowly, she brings her head back to meet Mariah's gaze.

Mariah smiles at her with a besmirched expression. "Oh right, seven."

"Yep." Penny pops the "p" extra loud.

I set Penny down in front of me and get down on my hunches so we're at eye level. "Penny, you will be nice to *all* of our guests, or you won't be opening any of those presents."

She looks down at her feet before responding, "Yes, sir." Then she runs off to her aunt Emily.

"It's really fine, Drew. She doesn't know me yet." Mariah states.

She's trying to be nice, but the *yet* she added at the end of her sentence makes me feel a pang of guilt. I have to end things with her, and soon.

"Thanks for understanding. She can be harsh. But we're working on it." I gesture toward the kitchen where I've laid out a make-your-own hamburger buffet.

Once everyone is finished with their dinner, I bring the cake out and set it in front of Penny. Her eyes go wide with excitement and she claps her hands together.

"Cake time!" Penny announces loudly, making everyone laugh.

I poke the number seven candle into the top of the cake and realize I don't have a lighter.

"Oh! I hid the lighters, let me grab it," Sophie says as she heads into the kitchen.

I follow closely behind, wondering why on earth she hid the lighters.

"Penny was a little too curious about the lighters the other day. She was giving me major kleptomaniac vibes, so I hid them on top of the fridge," she explains, seeming to have read my mind.

I shake my head from side to side with a chuckle. "Why am I not surprised?"

Sophie smirks, then climbs on top of the kitchen counter. "I put it right up here on top of the refrigerator."

Before I can stop her, she's standing on the very messy countertop. "Soph, please get down and just let me grab the lighter. I'm much taller than you."

"It'll be fine." She waves me off.

Sophie grabs the lighter from the top of the fridge, but as she's about to come down from the countertop, her foot catches a slippery Ziploc baggie. Almost as if in slow motion she shrieks, and falls backward.

I catch her swiftly in my arms, with one arm behind her back and the other under her knees. Like a knight in shining armor. Her arms slide around my neck instinctively, and she looks stunned.

Our eyes meet and it's like we're locked in this moment together. I've never held her, but she feels so good in my arms. Her blue eyes are even brighter up close, with a thick black rim around the edges. Her chest is heaving as she inhales deeply from the shock of falling.

"Did you find the lighter?" Penny yells from the dining room table, pulling us from our trance.

We both blink rapidly before noticing that everyone in the dining room is staring at us in silence. Ted and David have scowls on their faces. Madden and Brooks just look amused. Odette has hearts in her eyes, or maybe tears? Emily looks smug, and Mariah looks extremely uncomfortable.

Crap, crap, crap. Could this be any more awkward?

"Um, Drew? You can put me down." Sophie whispers, her eyes shifting back and forth.

Yes, apparently it can.

I quickly release her legs, so they drop back down to the floor. But she must not have anticipated the urgency with which I released her legs, because she stumbles back into my chest.

I grab her by the waist to make sure she's balanced herself on the floor before letting go. "Are you okay?"

A high-pitched laugh stumbles from her mouth. It sounds strained and awkward. "I'm fine, ha! Crisis averted."

We saunter back to the dining room, and I light the candle on Penny's cake. Everyone sings "Happy Birthday," and Penny's giant grin seems to distract our guests from the kitchen incident.

After Penny has opened all of her gifts and thanked everyone, I feel a tap on my shoulder.

"Drew, I'm gonna head out." I turn around to see Mariah standing there. She looks down at her feet and avoids eye contact with me.

"Right, let me walk you out."

Silently, we walk to Mariah's car and linger for a few seconds before she speaks, "So, I don't think it's a good idea for us to see each other anymore."

I comb my hand through my hair. "I'm sorry about the Sophie thing in there."

She opens her mouth to say something, but closes it and hesitates. She thinks for a moment longer. "With our jobs, we know better than anyone that life is short. If you and Sophie have feelings for each other, you should pursue that."

My face flames with embarrassment. "Mariah, there's nothing going on between me and Soph—"

Mariah cuts me off. "I know, I know. I'm just saying... you didn't need a lighter to light that candle when there are enough sparks between you and Sophie to light this entire city on fire. And I have zero interest in dating a man who has the hots for someone else." She smiles gently.

I huff out an uncomfortable laugh, my cheeks still aflame.

"I understand." I nod and give her a quick hug.

Mariah opens her car door and slides inside. "Bye, Drew."

"Bye Mariah."

As I watch her drive away, I can't help but wonder how a beautiful, level-headed woman like her has remained single all this time. I truly wish nothing but the best for her. And I'm relieved she handled this awkward encounter so graciously.

Chapter 13
Sophie

"So, this is it!" I spin around in my small living room.

Madden and Odette stayed behind after Penny's birthday party. Madden stayed upstairs to hang out with Drew, but Odette wanted to check out my apartment.

I glance back at her to see what she thinks of the place, but she's just staring at me with a smirk on her face.

"What?"

Odette crosses his arms over her enormous belly. "What's going on with you and Drew?"

Heat rushes to my face. "What? Nothing!"

"He caught you in the kitchen earlier like you guys were doing a routine from *Dirty Dancing*," Odette retorts with a laugh.

I bring my palm to my forehead, then drag it down my face in frustration.

"There is seriously nothing going on between Drew and me. He caught me when I fell, like anyone would have. And he's basically my boss slash landlord."

Odette raises an eyebrow. "A super handsome, super young boss… with super big muscles."

"Not sure Madden would be too happy to hear you talking about Drew's muscles."

She shrugs. "What? It's true."

Baffled, I shake my head at her. "You're being ridiculous. Sure, Drew is *decent* looking. But that doesn't mean there's anything going on. And honestly, I'm not ready for any kind of romantic relationship yet. I'm still working through things emotionally."

She looks at me with sympathy in their eyes.

"Okay, I'll drop it. Why don't we finish the apartment tour?" Odette says as she waddles toward me, then loops her arm through mine.

"But when you are ready to date? Drew wouldn't be a terrible choice—" She stops short when I glare at her. She raises her hands in defense. "I'll stop! Sheesh."

We continue down the short hallway, and I show her the bedrooms. She chuckles when she sees the door with the deadbolt which leads upstairs.

"Is this the infamous deadbolt I've heard so much about?"

I roll my eyes. "Yep. Will you please make David aware that it was locked when I gave you the tour?"

"Will do."

Odette sees the photo of Sam on my dresser as we pass by my room. "Oh, hey, how was your widow support group?"

"Wonderful Widows?" I smile. "It was pretty great, actually. Definitely an odd assortment of women, but it felt so good to be around other people who have gone through the same thing as me." I pause as we walk back into the living room. "Seeing a therapist has helped, of course. But talking to other women who lost a spouse was helpful in a completely different way. It felt very comforting."

Odette tears up and pulls me into a hug. Or at least she tries to. She can't pull me very close with her big belly in the way.

"Oh, Sophie, I'm so happy to hear that."

"Aw, Odette. You must be exhausted from standing so much today. I better get you back upstairs so Madden can get you home."

Her face twists in annoyance, and she opens her mouth to argue. But she stops short and yawns instead. "You're probably right."

We laugh together and head back upstairs.

Later that night, I'm trying to put Samantha to bed, but I can't find her favorite blanket anywhere. She will not stop crying. I've tried everything from singing to acting out her favorite story. I know her blanket must be upstairs (the one place I haven't searched), but I was crossing my fingers she'd fall asleep and I could avoid Drew until Monday.

My stomach is still doing funny little flips from remembering the feel of his arms around me. I know he was just catching me to keep me from hurting myself. But he felt so strong and safe, and he smelled so manly. That musky man smell with a hint of cinnamon.

It's getting harder and harder to ignore my attraction to him. I don't know if it's just Drew himself, or the fact that we see each other so much.

If I wasn't helping with Penny, would I have ever even noticed how his skin has a slightly spicy scent? Or that his chin always has a 5 o'clock shadow, even after he's just shaved?

Being romantically involved with Drew would be complicated, not just because I babysit for him and rent this apartment, but because he's a close friend of the family. What if we were together and then things ended badly?

Not only that, but Sam and I agreed to raise Samantha to be independent, and not reliant on my parent's money or a trust fund. We wanted her to have a normal childhood, free from the expectations of my parents' social circle. And Drew is an orthopedic surgeon, just like my father. Penny will most likely have everything handed to her, like me and my brothers did.

Although, Drew seems way different from my parents; Penny has a list of chores to complete before she gets her tablet. Small chores, but still, more than I had when I was a kid. Drew has done a great job with her, actually.

I shake the thought. Why am I even thinking about this??

Before I can psych myself out, I shoot Drew a text.

Sophie: Hey! I think I left Samantha's blankie upstairs. Do you mind if I come up and look for it?

Drew: Of course not, come on up.

Sophie: K! Be right there.

Pulling Samantha from her bed, she stops screaming for a second before she starts crying again.

With a groan, I snuggle her to my chest and tiptoe up the stairs to the main part of the house. I'm trying my best to be quiet since I know Penny is fast asleep, but Sam isn't making it easy.

Drew meets me at the door with a look of concern. "I thought I heard crying. Someone needs their special blankie, huh?" He says to Samantha in a sad voice. "Here, let me take her while you look for the blanket."

I'm about to protest when Samantha reaches for Drew. He scoops her out of my arms and she instantly cuddles into his broad chest. I must look baffled, standing there with a slack jaw.

"I got this," Drew says, laying his cheek on top of Samantha's head. "I kind of miss Penny being this small." He smiles fondly.

My heart squeezes at the sight of them. There is nothing as sexy as a big, solid man cuddling a small child. It can't be beat. It's probably scientifically proven.

I force myself to turn away from them and begin my search for the missing blanket. After scouring the main rooms for a good ten minutes, I take a moment to think. If I were three … where would I hide my blankie?

Suddenly, it comes to me. The Tupperware drawer. She loves playing with all the colorful lids. I open the drawer in the kitchen, and sure enough, there's her soft pink blankie.

Stifling a yawn, I grab it from the drawer and head back toward Drew and Samantha. I find them in the dark hallway next to the basement steps. Drew is slowly swaying. As I get closer, I can hear him quietly humming a lullaby. My chest tightens at how sweet they look.

"Found it," I whisper, causing him to turn around slowly.

Samantha is sound asleep.

He grins, looking very proud of himself. "You want me to lay her down so she doesn't wake up?"

"That would be great, actually," I say, trying to withhold another yawn.

I follow Drew down the stairs and into Samantha's room. He gently lays her down, then runs his large hand over her blonde curls before stepping out of the room. I kiss her chubby cheek then cover her with her blankie before backing out of the room and quietly closing the door behind me.

Drew is waiting at the bottom of the steps. "Glad you found the blanket."

"Ugh, me too. Thanks for putting her to sleep. I didn't think she was ever going to calm down."

He shrugs. "No problem. Let me know if you ever need help, I'm just one floor away."

"Thanks, I appreciate it." I attempt to smile but a yawn finally escapes from my mouth. Pretending not to be wildly attracted to my landlord is tiring.

Drew chuckles. "Goodnight, Soph."

"Goodnight."

Chapter 14
Sophie

The following Saturday I attend my second Wonderful Widow's meeting. I'm eager to hear their thoughts on my attraction to Drew, along with the guilt I'm dealing with. They're the only ones I'm comfortable talking to about this, the only ones who will truly understand.

I walk back to the meeting room with my caramel macchiato in hand and say hello to all the ladies.

"Sophie!" Gerda hugs me. "I'm so glad you came back, and we didn't scare you off."

I chuckle. "There's no way you could scare me off, you should meet my family."

She throws her head back with a laugh. "Oh, I like you Sophie. You've got spunk."

We all take a seat in the circle of chairs and Bernice turns her attention to me. "Sophie, why don't you start? What's been happening with you the past few weeks?"

I nervously play with my hands in front of me. "Well, I've been busy babysitting my landlord's daughter, Penny. She's a blast, and my daughter loves playing with her. Then in my basically nonexistent spare time, I've been working on lesson plans since school starts next week."

Bernice nods. "Your landlord is also a family friend?"

"Yes." I smile. "Drew. And speaking of Drew... I actually was hoping to get some advice from you all." I gulp down the lump in my throat. Talking about this with them means I can't be in denial about my attraction to him any longer. And being in denial feels much safer than admitting my feelings.

Bernice looks over at Gerda with a knowing smile. "Of course, what's on your mind, sweetheart?"

I clear my throat and glance around the room. Everyone is waiting for me to continue.

"Well, after I moved into the basement apartment and started watching Penny, I noticed myself getting nervous around Drew, which is new. I have been around him a lot since he and Penny come to most of our family holidays, and I never felt uncomfortable around him. He just fits in so well with my brothers, I sort of looked at him like another big brother figure, you know?" I pause and take a sip of my coffee.

"Ahh." Bernice nods like she's putting the pieces together already.

"So, I tried to ignore this new feeling I had around him, chalking it up to being the newness of the situation and living on my own again. But the more time I spend with him, the worse it gets. And I'm realizing it's not nervousness, but butterflies. I'm feeling a strong attraction to him." I inhale a deep breath and glance around the room.

Everyone is still listening intently, so I tread on. "When he's around, I feel happy and warm, but as soon as I'm alone again, the feeling of shame takes over. I think I'm ashamed to move on. It feels like I'm being unfaithful to my husband." I shake my head. "I mean, late husband."

The ladies nod and hum in understanding.

Ashley, the one who recently got engaged, responds first. "I felt like that when I first met my fiance, Mike. The guilt I had over my feelings for him tore me apart. I could hardly eat or sleep. But then I realized something." She pauses and gives me a warm smile. "My late husband doesn't need me anymore. There's nothing I can do to make him happy or sad because he's gone. But my guilt was hurting Mike, who was alive and present in my life. Mike needed me and he was patiently waiting for me to allow myself to love him. I had to choose to let myself love him, and I had to remind myself that it didn't take away from the love I experienced with my late husband. It's okay to experience a completely new love with another person. I can't say that what you're feeling for Drew is love, but I'm just saying it's okay to allow yourself to have feelings for another person."

Gerda nods in agreement. "Well said, Ashley. And we're so happy for you and Mike, sweetie."

"Thanks, Gerda," Ashley says with a grin.

"What you're feeling is completely normal. I think we all had those same thoughts when our brains were ready to move forward, but our hearts weren't quite there yet," Bernice says gently.

I slowly nod. "That makes sense. And Ashley, what you said about experiencing a new love reminds me of something Drew said the other day. He lost his parents ten years ago, and I asked him when he felt normal again, and he told me you never go back to your old self after a loss like that. But you *do* become comfortable with the new person you become. Maybe that's how a second love is, too? I don't know that Drew will be my second love, but I mean, whoever it ends up being." I shrug.

Lisa, the one with three cats, arches an eyebrow, and slumps back in her chair. "A handsome surgeon who understands grief? Girl. You better lock that one down. Whenever you feel ready and everything." She winks.

I laugh. "Well, Drew is actually seeing someone. And she's really great, so I don't want to get in the way of that."

She grimaces. "Ah, that makes things awkward."

"Right?" I smirk. "But maybe my heart is trying to tell me I'm ready to love again? Whoever that may be." I release a wistful sigh. "Thanks for letting me talk this out, ladies. Honestly, I already feel lighter getting this off my chest."

Evie, who's sitting next to me, looks at me with her beautiful brown eyes, then pulls me into a side hug. "That's what we're here for, Sophie."

After my support group meeting, I head back to my apartment and get caught up on cleaning and laundry. Since my parents are kind enough to keep Samantha on Saturdays, it gives me time to breathe and get the things done I can't do with a toddler around.

Once the apartment is sparkling and all the laundry is folded and put away, I check my phone to see what time it is. I probably need to leave soon to get Samantha. Seeing I have a missed text from my mom, I open it and read it quickly, worried something happened to Samantha.

Mom: Hey, could you wear something nice when you come get Sammy girl? We have something to discuss with you. *smiley face emoji*

Hm, that's strange. It doesn't seem like anything urgent, seeing as she put a smiley face in the message. I look down at the running shorts and sweaty t-shirt I've been cleaning in all day and decide to change. But only because I feel gross, and *not* because my mom asked me to.

Throwing on a cool cotton dress and sandals, I walk to the bathroom and freshen up my deodorant and pull my hair back into a neat ponytail. Looking at myself in the bathroom mirror, I shrug and say to myself, "This is as good as it's going to get."

Thirty minutes after reading Mom's text, I'm pulling into my parent's driveway. I have no clue what she wants to discuss, but I haven't seen them much lately anyway, besides dropping Samantha off. Although we have our disagreements, I do love them and enjoy hanging out with them. Especially now that we have some space from each other.

Walking inside the house, I greet my mother in the entryway. She peruses my plain grey, jersey-cotton dress and frowns.

"*That's* what you're wearing?" She brings her hand to her chest like she's having chest pain.

I thought it was cute and casual, but apparently I was mistaken. "What's wrong with this? It's a dress. It's cute."

Dad must hear our conversation because he walks into the entry way with Samantha on his heels. "Oh sweetie, you look great!"

"You can't be serious, Ted." Mom looks at him with her mouth slightly open in offense.

Dad looks befuddled, clearly not realizing what he did wrong.

Hmm. Okay, this is already getting weird. "So, what did you guys want to discuss?"

"Well, we actually arranged a special surprise for you this evening. Since we'll have Samantha, anyway." The oven timer dings from the kitchen and she turns abruptly and walks toward the kitchen.

I look at my dad and throw my hands up. The universal sign for *what the heck is going on?*

He opens his mouth to speak, but Samantha interrupts him.

"Mommy! We made cookies!"

"That's great, sweetie! Let's go see if they're done."

I take her hand and we walk into the kitchen, where my mom is removing the cookie trays from the oven. Dad strides over to her side, and they share a strange look. Mom's eyes are wide and Dad's are narrowed in a glare.

"So, what are these surprise plans you made for me without knowing if I was even free this evening?" I ask, feeling confused... and also a little terrified.

Mom laughs and removes her oven mitts. "Oh Sophie, you've been such a homebody lately we assumed you'd probably be free."

I put my hands on my hips. "That didn't answer my question."

Dad clears his throat. He doesn't seem as confident with whatever scheme they've planned as my mother is. "Well, you see... I made a new acquaintance at the country club. Someone new in town who needs a Wichita native to show them around a bit. I thought you could go to dinner with them and, you know, make a new friend."

I look between my parents, who are looking guiltier by the second. "Okay. What's her name?"

My father looks at his feet. "Um... *his* name is Bradley."

My nostrils flare of their own accord, so that invisible, angry steam can blow through.

"You arranged a *blind date* for me without my consent?"

"Don't be silly. It doesn't have to be a date. Just two young, attractive, single people enjoying all that our lovely city has to offer," Mom says with a flourish of her hand.

"Yeah, Mom. That's called a date." I roll my eyes. "A *blind* date."

"Well, if it makes you feel any better, I can assure you Bradley is a very handsome and incredibly successful man. So nothing to be worried about."

I shake my head from side to side. This is a whole new level of control-freak—even for my mom.

"I'm not even sure I'm ready to date, Mom! I'm not going."

"It was all your mother's idea," Dad blurts.

"Ted!" Mom yells while glaring at him.

"Listen," Dad continues, ignoring Mom's death glare. "It's *one* dinner. Maybe it'll be a good test to see how you feel about dating? And if it's awful, or too difficult emotionally, then you never have to see the man again. You don't hang out at the country club, anyway."

I think for a moment, taking in my father's words and my conversation with my support group earlier. Maybe it would be better for me to be forced on a random date with someone I've never met to rip off the proverbial band aid. But do I want to give my mother the upper hand here and make her think she can hoodwink me into her deceptive plans?

Absolutely not.

"I'm leaving," I say matter-of-factly. "Come on, Samantha, pick up your toys. We're heading home."

"Sophie! Don't be ridiculous." My mom whisper-yells from behind me as I walk toward the front door.

Ignoring her, I yank the front door open.

"Please try to hurry, Sam!" I call out before turning and coming face to face with an attractive man standing on my parent's front steps.

He smiles, showing off his perfectly white teeth.

"You must be Sophie? I've heard so much about you." He's holding a bouquet of flowers and extends them to me. "These are for you."

I gulp, suddenly feeling bad for the man. He's innocent in all of this, and here he's just being perfectly kind and polite.

"Thank you. You're Bradley?"

"Yes, Bradley Vanderven. Nice to meet you."

He reaches his hand out for what I assume is a handshake. His mannerisms seem stiff and formal, but then again, he probably feels nervous. I reach out to shake his hand, but instead he takes my hand in his, turns it over, and places a kiss on it. Wow, that was weird.

Bradley looks behind me and smiles, releasing my hand. "Mrs. Windell, lovely to see you again."

Oh, that's right, my mother is standing right behind me, watching this entire encounter.

"You as well! Sophie is *so* excited for your date."

Slowly, I turn to face my mom and find her grinning like the Cheshire Cat. I glare at her so she knows I'm not amused and then turn my gaze back to Bradley. "Bradley, do you mind if I speak with my mother privately for a moment?"

His expression looks apprehensive, but he nods. "Of course."

I close the front door, leaving Bradley on the front steps and my mother's jaw drops. "Sophie, where are your manners?"

Rolling my eyes, I respond, "Listen, I will go on this stupid date. But only because I feel bad for you finagling this poor man into taking me out. I will *not* go on a second date, and you will never set me up on a blind date again."

She purses her lips. "*Fine*. But can you at least try to be a lady tonight and not order something ridiculous like a margarita?"

"Yes, I'll pretend to be the debutant you've always wanted me to be." I bat my eyelashes. "Please tell Samantha I'll be back in a few hours to pick her up?"

"I will, don't worry. Now you have a good time!" She pushes me toward the door, then disappears into the kitchen.

I take a slow, deep breath before opening the door again. Bradley is leaning against the front porch, his legs crossed at his ankles. He's a tall man with dark, glossy hair. It's obviously been gelled into submission. He's wearing grey trousers with a black leather belt and a white dress shirt rolled up to his elbows. His oxford shoes match his belt. I definitely look casual compared to him. He has deep brown eyes and his hair has some grey at the temples. He's a nice looking man, obviously older than me, but probably not more than ten years. I'd guess he's around forty.

He glances up at me through his dark lashes. "Are you ready now, milady?"

I want to cringe at his use of *milady*, but stop myself and force a smile instead. Who does this guy think he is, a viscount from a romance novel?

"I made reservations for dinner. I had to pull some strings to get one so last minute. But I made it happen." He puffs out his chest like he's very impressed with himself.

Unsure how to respond to that, I reply, "Wow. Must be a popular place."

"Shall we?" He gestures toward his black Mercedes in the driveway.

We walk toward his car, and he opens the door for me. I slide onto the leather seat and he closes the door. In the four seconds it takes for him to walk around to the driver's side, I realize how awkward this car ride is going to be. I don't know anything about this guy.

After opening his own door, he slides in and immediately looks at himself in the rearview mirror. He smooths his already perfectly smooth hair with one hand and then starts the car. He backs out of the driveway and we begin our descent to the restaurant. Based on my experience so far with Bradley, I'm worried my mother was right and I'm way underdressed for this place.

He glances at me from the driver's seat. "You're even more stunning than the picture your dad showed me."

Oh my gosh, Dad showed him a photo of me? That's so weird. Definitely bringing this up to my dad later.

"Oh, thank you. I didn't even know you existed until about fifteen minutes ago," I say, hoping to be funny, but it comes out way more harsh than I wanted it to.

"Really? Your parents didn't mention our date?" He quirks his head to the side.

"Nope."

"Oh, we set this up weeks ago, so I figured they'd told you."

Weeks ago? I bite the insides of my cheeks to keep my face neutral. "Ha, they're so funny. Must've wanted it to be a surprise."

He preens, looking pleased by that response. Like he's so special my parents saved him for me as a surprise present. "Your dad is great. I've enjoyed golfing with him. Do you play?"

"Golf?" a laugh bubbles out of my throat before I remember my manners. "Sorry, no I do not. That's more of my dad and brother's thing."

"Ahh, I see." His voice sounds disappointed. "I've never seen you at the country club before."

"The country club is a bit stuffy for me," I say, without thinking. Ugh, I keep saying the wrong thing. "I mean, it's lovely. If you enjoy golfing and tennis."

"Right." He says, his jaw twitching like he's annoyed.

Thankfully, my parent's house isn't too far from the restaurant and ten minutes later we're walking inside. I didn't even realize this place was here, but I can see why it books up quickly. The atmosphere is quiet and romantic, much to my dismay. A pianist plays soft music from a grand piano. In the center of the restaurant, there's a bar with leather bar stools. Incandescent spheres hang from all different lengths from the ceiling, keeping the area dim for ambiance, but not too dark. Artwork made from different colors of blown glass hangs from the tall ceiling above the bar.

Bradley places his hand on the small of my back as he guides me toward the hostess booth. It's an intimate gesture—one that is entirely unwelcome.

"The restaurant is lovely," I admit. "Let's hope the food is as amazing as the design." I joke, trying to keep things light, but he doesn't laugh.

"The food here is impeccable, I assure you. It's a five-star restaurant." He responds sharply.

Before I can say anything else, the hostess arrives and takes us to our table.

We're seated in a quiet corner of the restaurant. There's a white tablecloth, blush-colored cloth napkins, and a small votive candle in the center. Bradley pulls my chair out for me before taking his seat across from me. We open our menus and peruse the choices silently for a few minutes.

The waiter approaches our table with a kind smile. He's dressed in black pants, a black button-up shirt, and a white tie, just like the other servers.

"Good evening, welcome to L'aMour. May I start you off with a bottle of wine?"

"Yes, please. Sophie, what kind of wine do you prefer?" He asks, which is nice of him. He struck me as the type to order for me without caring what I actually like.

I bite my bottom lip. "Umm, actually I only like sweet wines, like moscato."

Our waiter's eyebrows crease in a judgemental expression before remembering his manners and smoothing his features back into a smile. "Ma'am, we have a selection of some of the finest wines from France, Italy, and Napa Valley. Could I perhaps make a recommendation?"

Bradley is staring at me. He doesn't look amused, but more irritated. He turns his attention back to the waiter. "A recommendation would be great."

Ha! I was right. He *is* the type to order without caring what his date wants.

The waiter looks between me and Bradley, then makes his recommendation. Some cabernet that's apparently oaky with a hint of strawberry. But I know it's just going to taste like any other dry red wine.

I unconsciously screw up my face at his recommendation, not knowing Bradley is watching me.

"What's wrong with cabernet?" He asks, his chin jutting forward like he's challenging me.

"What's *right* with cabernet?" I mutter under my breath. "Nothing, the cabernet sounds great." I fake a smile.

Bradley smiles at my response, but I'm pretty sure he thinks I'm an uncultured swine.

The waiter returns with a bottle of cabernet. I recognize the expensive bottle as one of my parents' favorites. He pours two glasses for us without spilling a drop.

"I'll let you enjoy your wine and be back momentarily to check on you." He does a little bow and then leaves.

I take a sip of wine. Bleck, this tastes nothing like strawberries. Bradley is watching me to see my reaction. "Mmm. That's great ... I can definitely taste the oak."

He nods, looking satisfied, then swirls his glass and inhales the scent of the wine. I have to hold back a laugh. He looks ridiculous. Like he thinks he's a sommelier or something.

He takes a sip and swishes it around inside his mouth as if it's mouthwash.

"Mmm, you're right. I detect the oak as well."

I smile and take another tiny sip to keep from laughing at him.

"So, you're in education?" Bradley asks, setting his wine glass down.

"Yes, I'm an elementary teacher. What do you do?" I return the question.

He smirks. "I'm the CEO of Midwest Credit Union. I used to be CFO at one of our branches in Kansas City, but was promoted and moved here."

"Oh, wow, I'm sure that keeps you busy."

He nods. "It does, which is why I had to schedule this date a few weeks in advance. My schedule fills up rather quickly."

I get the impression that he thinks I should feel honored to be on this date with him.

"I bet," I reply before taking another sip of the disgusting cabernet.

The waiter comes back to our table and takes our orders. Bradley orders something that sounds fancy and pronounces it correctly—or at least he says it with enough confidence I believe it to be pronounced correctly.

I keep it simple by ordering chicken alfredo. Honestly, I've yet to find a place that makes alfredo as good as Olive Garden, but we'll see what this place can cook up.

"How are you liking Wichita so far?"

He rolls his lips together while he thinks. "Since we're from Kansas City, we're used to the luxuries of a bigger city. But Wichita isn't so bad."

"We?" I ask.

"Oh, yes. I have a son. He's nine." He smiles genuinely for the first time all evening. "Smartest kid you'll ever meet; the apple doesn't fall far."

Okay, I thought he was actually being sweet until he tacked on that last part. "I love kids. I have a daughter. She's three."

"Three is a fun age," He pauses. "Your father mentioned you lost your husband. I'm sorry for your loss." He seems genuinely sympathetic in the way he says it.

"Thank you. I appreciate that. It was several years ago, but it's still difficult." I run my finger along my wine glass. "What about you? Were you married before?"

"Yes, my wife and I divorced years ago." He says it nonchalantly, like it's no big deal. "Sometimes it takes a few tries to find the right one, you know?" He shrugs.

I take another sip of wine to avoid saying something I'll regret. Marriage is something I take very seriously. I don't understand how he can have such a flippant attitude about it. I'm not so naive that I think every marriage is perfect, but if I ever get married again, I want to be 100% sure that myself and the man I'm marrying are willing to give it our all, no matter what life throws at us.

Our waiter brings our food out, and it smells delicious. I'm relieved to have a break in our conversation, and also that the portions aren't tiny European sizes, because I'm starving. I dig into my Alfredo and sauces dribble down my chin as I slurp up the noodles. There's just no graceful way to eat chicken Alfredo. I probably should've taken that into consideration before ordering.

"Mmmm." I swallow and wipe my mouth with my cloth napkin. "This is even better than Olive Garden's alfredo."

Bradley bursts out laughing. This is the first time I've heard the man really laugh. "You like the Olive Garden?"

"Who doesn't?" I answer before taking another big bite.

He doesn't answer, but shakes his head in dismay.

We continue eating our food and making small talk. I even managed to drink about half of my glass of wine. Yay for me.

The waiter appears at our table asking if we'd like dessert. Bradley looks at me expectantly, waiting to see what I say.

"I'm actually pretty full, so no thank you." I give the waiter a gracious smile.

"Same here, thanks." Bradley says with a nod and our waiter.

After paying the bill, we walk back outside to Bradley's Mercedes. The sun is setting, and the weather has finally cooled down. We get in the car and Bradley drives me back to my parent's house.

When we arrive, he walks me to the front door. I look up at him to thank him for dinner and my eyes widen when I see his eyes are closed and he's leaning towards me with his lips puckered. I swivel my head at the last second, so his lips land on my cheek.

He stands up straight, his bottom lip slightly sticking out in a pout.

"Could I get your number? Then we can set up our own dates without help from your parents."

"Oh, um. Actually, with school starting, I don't think I'll have time. But thank you so much for dinner," I reply with a strained smile.

His eyebrows furrow, and he straightens his spine. His body language indicates his irritation. He's probably not the kind of guy who hears the word *no* very often.

"You're welcome." He grits out, his teeth bared in what's probably meant to look like a smile.

I give him one last friendly smile before opening the front door and ducking inside. I tiptoe over to the window and peek through the curtain to make sure he leaves. He's already walking back toward his car. He glances back toward the house once he reaches his Mercedes and he has a scowl on his face.

As I watch him drive away, I put my hand to my chest and breathe a sigh of relief.

"What on earth are you doing?" My mother asks from behind me, making me jump and scream.

"Mom! Don't creep up on me like that. You scared me to death."

She places her fists on her hips indignantly. "You're the one being creepy, peeking out the window." She relaxes and grins at me. "So, how was your date?"

"It was fine, Mom." I withhold the eye roll I want to release so badly. "Dinner was delicious."

She rubs her hands together. "Wonderful! When's your next date?"

"We're not going out again. I already told you this was a onetime thing."

"But, Sophie!" She starts.

I put my hands up, warning her to stop talking. "Even though you set this date up without my permission, I went. So don't push me." I walk off, leaving her in the entryway.

"Samantha?" I call as I walk through the house and into the living room, where I can hear cartoons playing on the television.

She's curled up next to my dad. My parents would've never let us watch cartoons all evening growing up. I'm glad they've relaxed so much now that they're grandparents.

"Hey, Sammy girl," I say as I enter the room.

She spots me and stands to jump up and down on the sofa. "Mommy! You're back!"

"Let's get home so I can get you to bed, okay?" I pick her up from the couch.

She wraps her arms around my neck. Her eyes look sleepy, but she still protests, "I don't wanna go."

Dad stands and rubs her back to console her. "It's okay, you'll come see us again next Saturday."

Dad smiles at me, and I'm glad he doesn't ask me about the date. It wasn't *awful*, but there was just no chemistry between me and Bradley. And we have nothing in common, besides both of us being single parents.

I'm sure there's a stunning woman out there who loves money and sniffing wine, who's meant to be Bradley's next wife. But *I* am not that woman.

Chapter 15
Sophie

The following Monday, I spend the entire day getting my classroom ready for the first day of school, which is tomorrow. Mom was thrilled to watch Samantha again today. My nerves are buzzing with excitement. I know this is only my second year of teaching, but I just love the first day of school. Meeting my new class of third graders tonight at meet-the-teacher night is what I live for. The second grade teacher, Mrs. Hartley, told me it's a great class of kids.

Once I'm finished decorating and arranging the desks, I run back home to change and get ready before all the students and their parents arrive at Heartland Academy this evening. Being a private school, we have a pretty strict dress code. Teachers are expected to wear business-casual attire, but tonight I'm wearing my favorite sundress. Since it's not an official school day, the headmaster won't say anything about it. I smooth my freshly washed hair with my flat iron and put on a little makeup so I look professional. I don't like to wear heavy makeup, but I add some bronzer to my cheeks and a few coats of mascara to my lashes. Taking in my reflection in the bathroom mirror, I decide to put a cardigan over my sundress and slip on my leather sandals. There we go: casual but still professional.

An hour later, I'm back at the school awaiting my students and their parents. Tonight, kids get to see their new classrooms and meet their teachers. It's nice to meet the parents too and have faces to go with names.

Throughout the evening, I check off my students I have met and only have a few who haven't shown up yet. There are twenty-one third graders this year: sixteen girls and only five boys. A lot of the kids look familiar since they were here last year in Mrs. Hartley's classroom, which is right next to mine. Once in a while, there's a lull of visitors and I peep in next door to the fourth grade room to say hello to my students from last year.

Gosh this is exciting, I love these kids already.

After several hours, the meet-and-greet is wrapping up. I glance at my class list and notice one of my students never showed up. Hmm, they must have forgotten.

I take a minute to set up for the first day of school tomorrow and grab my purse, but just as I'm about to flick the light off, a man wearing a suit and tie appears in the doorway along with a young boy.

"Knock knock, so sorry we're late. I had a meeting, and it went much longer than I had expected," the man says as he meets my gaze.

No, no, no. This cannot be happening.

"Wait, Sophie?" None other than Bradley from Saturday night's blind date stands before me.

"Bradley, hi. This is a surprise." I smile, trying to keep things professional. I look back at his son, who's a spitting image of his father. "You must be Peter?"

He glances down at his feet bashfully and avoids eye contact. "Yes, ma'am."

Aw, he seems really sweet and shy. I feel lucky to have such a sweet group of kids this year.

"Welcome to Heartland. It's a great school and I'm sure you'll feel right at home here."

"Yes, I'm sure you'll be at the top of the class." Bradley interjects.

I purse my lips, annoyed that he didn't allow his son time to respond.

Turning my attention back to Peter, I reply, "I went here when I was a kid! I know it can be intimidating to start at a new school, but you just let me know if you need anything, okay?"

He glances up at me through his thick black lashes. This kid is seriously a miniature Bradley. "Yes, ma'am."

As I'm giving them a quick tour of the classroom, Drew and Penny appear in the doorway, Drew still in his black scrubs, looking devastatingly handsome. My breath hitches at the sight of him.

Penny runs and hugs me. "Sophie!"

"Hey sweetheart! Don't forget it's Ms. Miller here at school." I say with a wink. She tries to wink back but ends up blinking both of her eyes dramatically, making me laugh.

"I just wanted to make sure you're still okay with Penny riding home from school with you?" Drew asks as his eyes go back and forth between me and Mr. Vanderven.

"Yes, of course! See you both tomorrow."

Drew is standing straight with his shoulders back. The way he's standing reminds me of a guard dog. He's still looking at Bradley Vanderven, his eyes slightly narrowed.

He looks back at me. "Are you heading home soon?"

I glance between Bradley and Drew, who are apparently having some kind of visual standoff. Bradley has his chin raised as if he's daring Drew to do something. I have no idea what's going on between them.

I clear my throat, pulling their attention back to me. "Yes, actually. I need to lock up my classroom, then I'm heading home." I turn to Peter. "It was very nice to meet you. I'll see you in the morning, Peter. Nice seeing you again, Mr. Vanderven."

Bradley puts his hand on my arm gently.

"Please, call me Bradley," he says with a quick glance back at Drew. "And yes, it was nice seeing you *again,* too. I really enjoyed our date the other night," he says with a smug look on his face.

He seems awfully confident, considering I said no to a second date.

Drew stays in the doorway holding Penny's hand. He looks tense. "I'll wait for you to lock up and walk you to your car. It's dark outside already."

I smile at him. "Thank you, I appreciate that."

Bradley and Peter continue to stand there awkwardly.

"See you tomorrow. Thanks for coming out tonight," I say, hoping my dismissal is clear.

Bradley hesitates, but finally smiles curtly and leaves with his son.

Chapter 16

Drew

Something about the way Bradley freaking Vanderven was looking at Sophie has my blood boiling. He was devouring her with his eyes! Like she was the funnel cake at a carnival his parents wouldn't let him have. And she went on a date with him? I'm not typically a jealous person, but knowing Bradley Vanderven got to take Sophie on a date makes me want to punch something. Did he hold her hand? Did he *kiss* her?

There was no way I was going to leave her alone in her classroom with him. What kind of creep dates his kid's teacher? I guess the same kind of creep who would want to date his kid's babysitter. Ugh.

I drag my hand down my face as I walk Sophie to her car. The sun has set, but I can still hear the cicadas chirping. It's so peaceful outside, this would be perfect if we were alone and I could reach out and hold her hand. Not that she'd let me. But this is *my* daydream, and in it we're alone and holding hands.

Thankfully, Penny is walking between us, forcing me to keep my distance. It's safer this way. As much as I want her, she can't be mine. Not only would Ted and David take turns tearing me limb from limb, but I don't want to be a creep like that Vanderven guy, making advances on his child's caretaker.

"Penny, did you like your new class?" Sophie asks in her honeyed voice, a voice that never ceases to make my stomach flip. In a good way.

"Yeah! Mr. Kenshaw was super nice! He decorated his classroom with dinosaurs!"

"That sounds totally RAWRsome." Sophie says and they both burst into laughter.

I grin, finding myself amused by her quirky sense of humor. "You crack yourself up, don't you?"

I meet Sophie's gaze, and she smiles back. "My brothers always made fun of me for laughing at my own jokes."

"What was it like growing up with three brothers?" I ask, bewildered by the thought of having so many siblings around.

She looks up at the starry sky before answering.

"Hmm, it was chaos. They teased me relentlessly but were also fiercely protective. And they were always wrestling and tormenting each other. Which made Mom crazy." She laughs and I can't help but laugh along with her.

"Having a house full of kids sounds chaotic … but also fun." I smirk.

Penny tugs on my hand.

"Can I have three brothers, Daddy?" She asks, her eyes wide with excitement at the thought.

"Ha, I'd kind of need a wife to give you any brothers, Pen."

She wrinkles her nose while she thinks. "I know! Miss Sophie needs a husband! So just marry her!" She looks between the two of us with a confident smile, like she just solved all of our problems for us.

We've reached Sophie's car and stand there staring at each other, unsure what to say to diffuse the situation.

Sophie takes Penny's hand with a smile. "Trust me, you do not want three smelly brothers."

Penny purses her lips before responding, "True, three sisters would be better."

Sophie huffs out an awkward chuckle, then looks up at me. Her eyes meet mine and hold my gaze long enough for me to feel the familiar feeling of electric shock that I get so often when I'm around Sophie.

Penny is still looking between the two of us, waiting for a response. "Sophie doesn't want to marry an old man like me, Pen." I wink at Penny and she giggles.

Sophie laughs and it sounds strained, not her usual harmonic laughter. "Well, I'll see you tomorrow after school, Penny." She unlocks her car and opens the door.

"Bye Miss Sophie!"

I smile. "See you tomorrow, Soph. I'll be home around six. Thanks again for keeping an eye on Penny after school."

"Of course. Bye, Drew." She stares into my eyes for a few seconds before getting into her car and driving off.

Penny runs into my bedroom at six o'clock in the morning already dressed in her school uniform, shoes on her feet, and backpack on her back.

She jumps on my bed and squeals. "Daddy! Hurry! It's the first day of school!"

I run a towel through my wet hair and chuckle. "Hey! No jumping on the bed!"

She hops off the bed with a thud and runs out of the room. I get dressed in my grey dress pants and a white button-down shirt. It's an office day, so no scrubs today. I secure a black leather belt through my belt loops as I walk down the hallway and into the kitchen.

"Penny, how about some eggs for breakfast?"

"I already ate!" She exclaims, just as I notice the cereal and milk mess on the countertop.

I look at her with one eyebrow raised, and she walks into the kitchen and grabs a cleaning towel from the drawer and wipes up her mess.

"Thank you." I tousle her hair. "I'm proud of you for making your own breakfast, but we always need to clean up our mess."

"Yes, sir." She says before running down the hallway to toss the towel into the dirty hamper, then bounding back into the kitchen.

"You excited for today, little miss?"

"So excited! Aunt Em is coming, right?"

"Yep! She's meeting us there," I tell her.

She scampers off down the hallway once more, returning with two hair ties and a brush. "Daddy, will you braid my hair in pigtails like Miss Sophie does?"

I roll my lips together to keep from laughing. I'm absolutely terrible at braiding. You'd think if I can perform surgeries, I could braid hair. But that's not the case. I grab the brush and hair ties from her and she hoists herself up onto the barstool next to me. My large hands make the hair ties look tiny, but I separate the hair as best I can and do a quick three-strand braid on each side. They look messy, but not terrible. I secure each one and admire my work.

"Okay, there you go."

Penny jumps down and runs to the bathroom to inspect the braids. "Daddy!" She yells from the bathroom. "These don't look anything like the braids Miss Sophie does!"

I walk to the bathroom and my shoulders slump when I see her disappointed expression. "I'm sorry, hon. But Miss Sophie is busy this morning, and that's the best I could do. I'll keep practicing, okay?"

"Alright, I know you can get better. With practice." She says with one hand on her hip.

An hour later, we're at Heartland Academy. Penny and I walk into the school hand in hand and spy Emily at the front desk.

"Aunt Em!" Penny exclaims as she runs to embrace her.

"Hey you! I've missed you," Emily says as she buries her face into Penny's neck. When she pulls back, she looks over Penny's hair. "Did your dad braid your hair?" She asks with a tight smile.

Penny wrinkles her nose. "Yeah, Miss Sophie was busy." She looks back at me and grins. "But he'll get better with practice."

Emily smiles, but her eyes look sad. She had a hard time on Penny's first day of kindergarten, but I was hoping she'd be okay this year.

"You okay?" I ask as the three of us walk down the hallway toward the first grade classroom.

"I'll be fine," she says without meeting my gaze, her voice sounding strained.

"Em—" I start, but she interrupts me.

"Don't. I'm fine."

I bite my tongue and the three of us walk in silence. The school is alive with people: students finding their way to their classrooms, parents saying goodbye, some taking pictures with their new teachers.

We walk into Penny's new classroom and Emily gives Penny a hug and takes a picture of her at her desk. Penny grins at the phone. She loves getting her picture taken. I introduce Emily to Penny's new teacher, Mr. Kenshaw, and then we say our last goodbyes to Penny. She adores school. Last year she was a total teacher's pet. She's not the least bit sad to watch me and Emily walk out of the room.

I glance over at Emily as we walk and she has tears streaming down her face. I don't want to make things worse, so instead of talking, I just wrap my arm around her shoulders as we walk. Sophie stands in the doorway of her third-grade classroom and eyes Emily with sympathy, or perhaps concern.

Maybe both. She gives me a sympathetic smile then ducks back into her classroom.

I continue to walk with Emily until we reach her car.

I open my mouth to speak, but she cuts me off. "I don't want to talk about it, Drew." She takes a deep breath. "I'm still watching Penny Friday while you go out, right?"

I shove my hands in my pockets and nod. "Yep, see you Friday." I frown, wishing I could say more, but knowing she doesn't want me to.

She hesitates for a second, then opens her door and slides into her car. "See you then."

For five days, I have come home to Sophie and the girls. Every evening I walk into my living room to the delightful sound of the girls playing and Sophie at the table working on grading papers or sometimes in the kitchen getting dinner started.

The sight of Sophie in my kitchen is enough to make my heart burst. I also love watching Penny and Samantha play together. Penny has taken it upon herself to play the big sister role, and she's so great with little Sam.

The fact that Sophie is off-limits feels heavier on my heart each day. It feels so good to have her here in my house, and with each day that passes, I wish she was in my arms, too. Greeting me with a kiss each day when I walk through the door. I wonder if Sophie feels this too. Whatever *this* is.

Maybe it's all in my head, but I feel like she looks at me differently now. She seems to hold my gaze longer and I've even noticed her watching me out of the corner of her eye.

It's becoming more and more difficult to keep my distance.

The close proximity is wreaking havoc on my nerves and my heart. I've been dreaming of Sophie every night. I never remember my dreams, but this one is clear as day. Sophie is twirling in a pink sundress in my backyard. It's dark outside and the yard is lit only by the Jefferson bulb lights. Her ringing laughter fills the air, then she walks over to me and kisses me softly.

Every morning I wake up in agony that it wasn't real. That I have to long for her but can't have her.

I'm losing my mind.

I'm sitting on the couch with Penny while we wait for Emily to arrive. Tonight, I'm meeting up with my two closest friends for some much needed guy time. I think my life has been filled with way too much estrogen lately. Hopefully James and Conner will be able to talk some sense into me.

An hour later, I'm walking into our favorite brewery in town. It's filled with pool tables and has an excellent IPA selection.

I spot the boys already playing pool, beer in hand, and stride over to meet them. We greet each other with a half hug and a clap on the back, the way all men do.

Conner's green eyes take me in, and his eyebrows draw together. "What the hell, man. You look like someone kicked your puppy."

I grab his beer and take a big swig of it. "I *feel* like somebody kicked my puppy."

"Hey! That one was mine." He flags down the server and orders two more drinks.

James chuckles and eyes me curiously before collecting all the pool balls to start a new game. "So, what's new with you? We haven't seen you in like a month."

I take another drink. "You just saw me yesterday."

"You know I meant outside of work." James frowns, then crosses his arms.

"Yeah, seriously, what's going on with you?" Conner mirrors James's expression.

I shake my head from side to side, then look at my feet. "I think I'm falling for my babysitter."

Conner chokes on a sip of his beer and James pounds him on the back.

James's eyebrows shoot up in surprise. "But ... Dr. Windell's daughter is your babysitter, right?"

"Yes, Sophie." I sigh.

Conner, who has now composed himself, replies, "Well, that's awkward."

"Thank you, Captain Obvious," I deadpan.

James's mouth is set in a straight line like he's deep in thought. "I mean, you're both single. So, it wouldn't be that big of a deal, would it?"

Conner flags the waitress down again and she shimmies over and gives him a flirtatious smile. He runs his fingers through his thick brown hair and smiles back at her.

"Hey, we're going to need some nachos." He glances back at me and his face goes serious, like he just remembered my dilemma. "Actually, make that two orders of nachos."

"You got it," she says with a giggle, then scurries off.

Conner always seems to attract the ladies with his chiseled jaw, brown hair, and emerald eyes. He looks like he came straight from Ireland.

"You're an idiot, Conner. How are we supposed to play pool while we eat nachos?" James rolls his eyes and sets his pool stick down. "Let's grab a table while we eat and help Drew with his love life."

James is the more serious one out of the three of us. He seems grumpy upon first meeting him, but once you get to know him, you realize he's the most loyal friend you could ask for.

"My life is just fine, thank you. But nachos sound good." We walk over to a high-top table and take our seats.

Conner looks at me with a serious expression. "Okay, so you're in love with Dr. Windell's daughter."

"I didn't say I was in love, I just can't stop thinking about her."

"So? You're both consenting adults. What's the issue?" James asks before taking another swig of his IPA.

"The Windell's have welcomed me into their family. Her dad and I work together, she babysits for me, I'm her landlord, *and* apparently she went on a date last weekend."

Conner grimaces. "Sounds complicated."

"Was it just one date?" James asks. "Maybe it's not serious."

"Yeah, maybe you're right. She hasn't gone on more than one date that I know of. But it's not like I can make a move, anyway." I take a big gulp of my drink.

The waitress brings the nachos to our table and gives James a coy smile.

"Thanks, babe," he tells her with a wink. Once she leaves, he looks back at me. "You're being way overly dramatic, man. Just ask her out, throw caution to the wind and all that." He shrugs.

James looks deep in thought. "However, if it didn't work out between the two of you, things would be super awkward since she's renting your basement apartment and you're good friends with her father."

I slump back into my chair. "I know. But I don't know how to stop thinking about her, or how to stop looking for her everywhere I go, just hoping to catch a glimpse of her."

They both stare at me blankly.

"You're so far gone, man." Conner says as he stuffs a cheese-covered chip in his mouth and James nods in agreement.

"Don't I know it."

"What happened with that nurse you were going out with?" James asks.

I take a deep breath. "She ended things before they really began. She told me I should be with Sophie because we're obviously attracted to each other."

They both grimace.

"Awkward," Conner says and then blows out a deep breath.

"If she noticed, then I assume Sophie reciprocates your feelings?" James asks with a smirk.

I shake my head. "I don't know, sometimes I think she does, but then I wonder if it's all in my head."

James taps his chin with his index finger. "Her husband was killed in action a few years ago, right? Maybe she has feelings for you, but she's just guarded because she's still grieving the loss of her husband."

Conner looks at him with his mouth agape. "You sure are philosophical for someone who sticks people with needles all day."

James scowls at him. "I'm a well-educated anesthesiologist, not a heroin dealer."

I chuckle at their antics. Conner loves goading James.

"That's a good point though. Maybe she's not ready for a romantic relationship. But then why'd she go on a date with that other guy?" Closing my eyes, I massage my eyes with my thumb and forefinger. "It's been ages since I felt this way about someone. Actually, I'm not sure I ever have."

James runs his hand through his dark hair, pinning me with his brown eyes as he taps his fingers against his beer bottle. "Hmm, you're just going to have to talk to her, man."

"I agree with James. If you're serious about this girl, talk to her. She might be crazy about you too."

James eyes Conner skeptically before clinking his beer bottle with Conner's. "Mark this day on your calendar; Conner and I actually agree on something."

Conner blows James a kiss and winks at him, making James roll his eyes. I'll never understand how that goofball made it through medical school.

I ponder their words for a minute. I am already serious about my feelings for Sophie, but I'm positive that, if she even has feelings for me at all, they're not nearly as progressed as mine are for her. It's crazy that I've gone my entire life without having strong romantic feelings for anyone, and then after one month of Sophie living in my basement, I'd do just about anything to make her mine. Screw Bradley Vanderven.

"Thanks for talking this out with me. I feel like this has been consuming my brain for weeks now." I grab a chip from the nacho platter and pop it in my mouth.

As I'm reaching for another chip, the hair on the nape of my neck stands on end and I feel a tingle of awareness throughout my body.

Conner and James's eyes go wide and Conner angles his beer bottle to point at something behind me. I turn in my chair and see Sophie walking towards me, her face lit up with a friendly smile. My eyes take her in from the tip of her toes to the top of her head. She's wearing wedge sandals with a little denim skirt, and a white top that flows gracefully as she walks. Her hair is up in a ballerina bun, with just a few wisps of hair pulled down around her face.

She looks like an angel. A really hot angel.

"Hey Drew," she grins as she stops at our table. I quickly glance at the boys who are slack-jawed by her presence. "I'm here with some teacher friends. We're celebrating surviving the first week of school." She laughs before smiling politely at Conner and James.

I chuckle nervously. "Congrats on surviving the first week, Soph. These are my friends from work, James and Conner."

They each raise a beer bottle as they say hello with smirks on their faces.

"Well, I saw you over here and just wanted to say hi. I'll let you guys get back to your nachos."

"Thanks for coming over, enjoy your evening." I smile and feel my cheeks heat as the guys stare at us.

Sophie gives a little wave to us before making her way back to her group. I didn't realize I was watching her until James clears his throat.

"*That's* Dr. Windell's daughter?" James asks with his eyes wide.

"No wonder you're obsessed with her. I think *I* need a babysitter." Conner raises his eyebrows suggestively.

I playfully punch him in the shoulder. "Shut up, you don't even have a kid."

Chapter 17
Sophie

Of course Drew is here. I thought it would be nice to have a night out and get my mind off of him, but there he sits looking so freaking handsome I can't stop glancing over my shoulder at him. I came out tonight with three of the other ladies who teach at Heartland Academy. But a huge part of me wishes I was on the other side of the restaurant, sitting next to Drew instead.

Every exchange we've had this week has felt charged with electricity. Watching him walk through the door every evening, the girls running to him for hugs—yes, even little Samantha. He scoops her up for a hug everyday along with Penny like it's the most natural thing in the world. Samantha adores him. Ever since he rocked her to sleep after Penny's birthday party, she's been obsessed with the man.

And I can't even blame her. Is it weird that I'm jealous my three-year-old gets a hug from Drew every day and I don't? Probably.

I've also really wanted to ask him how Emily is doing, but that feels private. I just can't get the picture of her tear-stained face out of my head. What was wrong? Why was she so upset about Penny's first day of school? It seems like such an emotional reaction to have for a niece, but who am I to judge someone's emotional state?

Maybe since Penny never had a relationship with her mom (that I know of), Emily and she grew really close. Perhaps Emily even feels like she's her mother.

Either way, my heart hurt for her. I can't even imagine how emotional I'll be when Samantha has her first day of school someday.

I glance at Drew's broad shoulders across the brewery once more. His friends meet my gaze and eye me curiously. I wonder if he's talked to them about me? They most likely know my father, too. If they work with Drew, they must work with my dad.

"Does this place have wine? Beer is disgusting. And I really need a drink after dealing with these moody fourth graders all week," Mallory jokes. She looks sweet and angelic with her blonde hair and honey-brown eyes, but she's tough and demands respect from her students.

Josie nods in agreement, making her brown curls bobble around her face. "Ugh, right? The fifth graders aren't any better. The first week is a big adjustment for everyone though; next week will be less dramatic."

Sadie chuckles. "I don't know what you two are talking about. My pre-kindergarteners are sweet little angels." She takes a sip of her Coke. Her blue eyes meet mine over the glass. "So, Sophie ... who's Mr. Muscles?"

My shoulders tense, but I try to keep my facial expression neutral. "What are you talking about?"

Josie and Mallory lean in with interest.

"That guy you keep staring at, the one you went to talk to earlier. Don't play dumb." Sadie winks.

I can feel my cheeks flush. "Oh, that's Drew. I babysit his daughter. She's in first grade at Heartland, actually." I say in a nonchalant tone, but by the twinkle in their eyes, I know I'm not fooling them.

Sadie's eyes widen. "Oh! You live in his basement, right?"

"You *live* with him?" Mallory whisper-yells.

"No, no. He converted his basement into an apartment. I rent the apartment from him."

Josie glances over at Drew and his friends. "Who are his handsome friends? You should introduce us." She waggles her eyebrows.

I smirk. "Sorry, I don't know his friends."

"Darn." She pauses. "Don't look now, but Mr. Muscles is looking at you, and oh my gosh, his face is even better than his shoulders."

The girls burst into giggles. "Could you guys at least *try* to play it cool?" I bury my face in my hands.

"He's definitely into you. Why don't you ask him out?" Mallory asks.

The waitress brings our appetizer and places it on the table. We thank her and dig into the wings.

"Don't think these wings will get you out of answering my question." Mallory winks at me.

I shrug my shoulders. "Besides the fact I'm not sure if I'm even ready to date again? He's really good friends with my dad and he's technically my boss. That could get awkward."

"Well, I understand the not being ready to date thing, but so what if he's friends with your dad? Isn't that a good thing?" Mallory asks.

Josie takes a sip of her wine and nods. "Yeah, my dad always hates all the guys I date."

Sadie taps her glass against Josie's. "Same, girl."

"No, you don't understand. They work together, and Dad took a liking to Drew and basically adopted him into our family. Drew lost his parents years ago, so they come to all of our family holidays. Plus, he's gone out with this really great girl a few times. I'm not sure if he's still seeing her."

"Well, if you haven't seen her around lately, I think you have your answer." Mallory says, pinning me with a knowing glance. "And the family thing could be awkward ... but what if it ended up being great?"

I smile and glance back again at Drew. He's looking this way and our eyes meet across the restaurant.

He smiles at me and I feel like I'm melting from the inside out. Maybe my heart is beginning to thaw after all.

The next day, Samantha and I are chilling in our apartment. Samantha is playing while I sit on the floor and prep things for this next week of class. I've gotten all of my papers graded, and I laminated some number cards for a math game I'm doing with my class this week.

Sam runs across the room from where she was playing with her dollhouse and sits in my lap. "Mommy, can I have a snack?"

I glance at the clock on the stove and see it's almost noon. "Oh yeah, I guess it's lunchtime! You want mac and cheese?"

"Yeah!" She beams.

I hear my phone ping and walk over to the table to pick it up. My heart flutters when I see a text from Drew.

Drew: I grilled for lunch if you gals are interested in eating something that didn't come out of the microwave.

I laugh and type out a response.

Sophie: How do you know I haven't been baking up a feast all morning?

Drew: Well, seeing as your apartment doesn't have an oven, that doesn't seem likely.

Sophie: Is it a bad sign that I didn't even realize there wasn't an oven down here?

Drew: Yeah, that's pretty bad. Come up and eat with us.
Sophie: Alright, if you insist.

I grin at my phone. He's never texted to invite us over casually like this. It's usually only a question about Penny or him telling me he got called in. He's probably just being nice since he knows I don't cook much ... and apparently don't have an oven.

"Hey Sammy girl, you want to go up and eat with Drew and Penny?"

Instead of answering, she jumps up and down, then runs toward the door that leads to the stairway.

"I'll take that as a yes." I chuckle as I unlock the deadbolt and take Sam's hand as we walk up the stairs.

Once we're at the top of the steps, Samantha takes off in a run toward the kitchen, where she finds Drew. She hugs his leg, and he hoists her up for a hug. He's wearing his white apron and seasoning something with one hand while he holds Sam with his other arm. Samantha is giggling and Drew has a big smile on his face. Dan and Shay's newest album plays from the Bluetooth speakers and an overwhelming sense of happiness fills my heart. I think I'd be perfectly content to spend every day with the three people in this room.

"Sophie!" Penny exclaims as she runs toward me from the kitchen. "I didn't know you guys were coming over today!"

Drew sets Samantha back on the floor and replies, "I thought they could come eat lunch with us."

Penny smiles up at him, then grabs onto Samantha's hand. "Come on, let's go play!"

They run down the hallway together toward Penny's bedroom.

Drew chuckles. "I love how well they get along."

"Me too." I smile. "So, what's for lunch?"

"I grilled some pork chops and zucchini."

I narrow my eyes. "Sounds very healthy."

He slides a container across the countertop in my direction.

"Don't worry, we baked cookies too." He winks and my stomach does a little flip.

I try to remain unaffected and keep my facial expression neutral, but I can feel the corners of my lips tugging upward. There's just something endearing about Drew speaking my love language. Which is, of course, sugar.

"Thank goodness. You know I can't survive without sweets."

He laughs, and it fills the room in the most magnificent way.

"Do you need any help?"

He shoots me a quick smile, but continues prepping the food. "Naw, it's almost ready."

I sit on the bar stool across the counter from him and watch him work.

"Thanks for inviting us, we have nothing going on this weekend." I place my elbows on the counter and rest my face in my hands. "Do you have any big plans over the weekend? I can always watch Penny if you have another date." I really want to know if he's still dating Mariah, but I don't want to be too obvious.

"No plans, and no more dates."

Now I'm even more curious. "You're not going to see Mariah anymore?"

His eyes meet mine, and he holds my gaze for a few seconds before shrugging his shoulders. "We're better off as friends, so we decided not to get romantically involved."

His gaze is burning into me, almost like he's daring me to keep asking questions.

"Oh, why?" My voice cracks. "She seemed great," I add quickly.

"She is great, just not the one for me." He pauses and worries his bottom lip, as if he's not sure whether he should say more. "I think she felt like something was going on between you and me, actually."

I swallow hard. "Really?" I try to sound calm, but my voice is barely above a whisper.

He pins me with his hazel eyes again. "Really." He clears his throat. "How about you? Any more dates with Mr. Vanderven?"

I'd laugh but Drew looks dead serious. "Um, no. My parents set up that date, I didn't even know about it until right before he showed up. He made me drink cabernet."

He relaxes his shoulders, like he's relieved by my admission. He smiles at me, showing his beautiful white teeth. "You seem more like a moscato girl."

"You're correct." I bite my bottom lip to keep from smiling like a dork.

There's enough electricity flowing between the two of us at this moment to power the entire tri-state area. I open my mouth to respond, but the girls run into the dining room in a fit of giggles, pulling us out of our moment.

I can't help but feel a little disappointed that we weren't able to finish that conversation, but it's probably for the best, anyway.

Drew and I make plates for the girls and our conversation is all but forgotten. Out of the corner of my eye, I catch Drew stealing glances at me as he prepares a plate for Penny.

We all sit down at the table to enjoy the delicious meal Drew prepared. Thankfully, the girls are chatting and keeping us entertained, so we don't have to carry the conversation. My brain is still reeling from the way he was looking at me earlier. I think I'll probably have visions of those gorgeous hazel eyes with flecks of brown and green as I fall asleep tonight.

———

It's Monday and I'm having issues with Peter Vanderven *again*. He seemed so sweet and shy when I first met him, but after three weeks with him, I can tell his father's spoiled, entitled attitude has—unfortunately—rubbed off on him.

"Ms. Miller?" Elizabeth asks with her hand raised in the air.

"Yes, Elizabeth?" I respond with a smile. Elizabeth is a really sweet girl. "Do you need help on your quiz?"

"I don't actually, but Peter might." He sits at the desk next to hers and she shoots him a glare. "Since he keeps copying my answers."

Peter's jaw drops and he raises his hands to his chest like he's offended at her words. Ugh, not this again. Peter doesn't seem to want to do any of his own work. I stand from where I was sitting at my desk and walk over to look at Elizabeth and Peter's work. After looking closely at both of them, it's obvious Peter has copied everything she wrote word for word. At least he's bad at cheating, so it's easy to tell. I'm going to have to call his father and arrange a meeting. Bradley creeped me out the last time I saw him, so I was hoping it wouldn't come to this.

"Peter, please move to the front of the class." I gesture toward the empty desk right next to mine.

"But I didn't do anything!" He demands. "She's lying!"

"Peter, we will talk about this after class. Please quietly obey my request so the other students can finish their quiz."

He stands up and stomps over to the desk next to mine. He leers at me, his mouth twisted in anger. "Just wait until my father hears about this."

"Oh, don't worry, your father will definitely be hearing about this," I whisper, so only Peter can hear.

He smirks. "Don't get too comfortable here, Ms. Miller. Once my father is through with you, you'll no longer have a job."

I stop myself from rolling my eyes at him. "Please continue with your quiz, Peter."

"Fine." He sneers.

I sit at my desk and massage my temples with my thumb and forefinger. It's going to be a very long day.

The following afternoon, I'm in my classroom waiting for Mr. Vanderven. I emailed him last night requesting a meeting to discuss Peter, and thankfully 2:30 worked for him since the kids are at music class during that time. Looking at the large clock in my classroom, I see it's already 2:32. I'm hoping he gets here soon because I only have fifteen minutes before the kids will be back.

Just then, Peter's father sweeps into the room with his arrogant stride. He's wearing another expensive tailored suit. It's black with a light blue shirt underneath and a gold and blue striped tie. His dark hair is gelled perfectly in place. He's so well-coiffed and wrinkle-free, I can't help but wonder if the man stands all day to keep his suit flawless.

"Mr. Vanderven, thanks for coming." I reach my hand out to him for a handshake.

He steps forward and takes my hand, but once again, instead of shaking it, he brings it to his lips and kisses it. My face heats, but not with embarrassment. With anger. What makes this guy think he gets the privilege of kissing my hand? His audacity is outrageous.

I yank my hand out of his and sit in the chair behind my desk to put plenty of space between us. He stays standing, leaning on one foot and crossing his arms. He has a cocky smirk on his face. He must think I was blushing earlier when really I was just enraged.

Ugh, I can't stand this guy.

"So, did you call me here to talk about how brilliant Peter is?" He winks. "Or did you just want to see me again?"

I take a deep breath and calm myself so I don't speak out of anger. "I'd appreciate if we could keep this professional, Mr.

Vanderv—"

"Bradley." He interjects.

I set my mouth in a straight line so he knows how unamused I am. "Mr. Vanderven, I asked you to come here today to discuss Peter's behavior."

He scoffs. "His behavior?"

"Yes, I'm having difficulty with him. He's not completing his homework each day, and he's copying answers off of the other students. Cheating is not permissible here, sir."

His expression becomes indignant, and he takes a step toward my desk and slams his hands down onto it.

"Whatever little pipsqueak accused my boy of cheating is obviously incorrect. And I'm appalled you would believe such lies, Ms. Miller." He sneers.

"I have moved Peter's desk ten times, and every student he sits by has complained about him copying their answers. I don't believe all ten children are lying."

He smirks at me with a sardonic look in his eyes. "Do you realize how large of a donation I made to this school when I enrolled my son? Trust me, you do *not* want to get on my bad side."

"It doesn't matter to me how much money you have, *sir*. I treat every child in my classroom equally. And I hope you can respect me enough to talk to Peter about his behavior at home. I've avoided sending him to detention thus far, but going forward I'll have to get the headmaster involved."

"I would choose your actions and words carefully, young lady."

I stand so he's not hovering over me any longer.

With a neutral expression, I respond, "Like I said, please speak with your son about our zero tolerance policy for cheating. That is all I had to say, so you can be on your way. Thank you for coming in."

Before I can take another breath, he's on my side of the desk, towering over me in what I assume is an attempt to intimidate me.

"I do not get dismissed, I do the dismissing. And we're not done here," he hisses.

I open my mouth to respond when a deep voice comes from the doorway to my classroom.

"She said you can go. Respect her wishes and leave."

We glance over to see Drew standing in the doorway, wearing his scrubs and a deep scowl. His fists are clenched at his sides, like he's holding himself back from beating the crap out of Peter's father.

"I'm sorry, we have no need for a phlebotomist at the moment, and this conversation is none of your business." Bradley smirks as he gestures toward Drew's scrubs.

Drew takes two long strides into the classroom so he's standing right in front of Bradley. Peter's father is tall, but Drew stands several inches over him. Not to mention the extra twenty pounds of muscle he has.

Bradley appears to waver under Drew's glare. He takes a few steps toward the door before glancing back at me.

"Ms. Miller, the headmaster will hear from me this evening, so don't bother speaking with her on my behalf." He grins salaciously before turning on his heel and exiting the room.

I let out a breath that I've apparently been holding in and bring my hand to my chest. Drew wraps his arms around me in a comforting hug.

"Are you okay?" he whispers against the top of my head.

I sigh as I hug him back. "Yes, thank you."

The feel of his body against mine is warm and comforting. Once his arms were around me, I instantly felt calm. There's something about Drew that soothes me and makes me feel safe. I'm immensely enjoying this hug. But way too soon, he pulls away.

Drew studies my face for a second. "That guy is a dick."

I laugh. "I'd agree with you, but it's frowned upon for me to call my student's parents dicks. What are you doing here, anyway?"

"My last two patients for the day cancelled, and I wanted to pick Penny up from school. I tried texting you, but you didn't respond, so I decided to stop by your classroom and let you know Penny wouldn't need a ride today." He smiles.

"That's too bad your phlebotomy patients had to cancel." I bite the insides of my cheeks to keep from laughing.

Drew smirks. "Very funny."

"But seriously, thanks for saving me. That guy gives me the heebie jeebies." I shiver.

"Glad to be of service." He does a little bow. "Well, I'm going to go get Penny."

And with a smile, he leaves the classroom, and I stand there looking at the doorway with a big, stupid grin on my face.

Chapter 18
Drew

Hugging Sophie was a huge, life-altering mistake. I've been stewing over that hug for the last four days. *Four* days ... over a hug.

The problem is, now I know I can't possibly go my entire life without hugging her at least once a day. I think I will literally die if I can't freely embrace her.

Okay, as a doctor, I can admit I won't die, literally. But my *soul* will die a slow and painful death.

I've decided to tell her about my feelings and ask her on a date, a proper date. Not coming upstairs to have lunch with me and Penny, but a romantic night out, just the two of us. I'd whisk her off to Paris for the weekend if I could, but I know I'll need to move slowly so I don't spook her. She's still processing the loss of her late husband, and I'll give her as much time as she needs.

I love her daughter, she loves my daughter, I get along with her family. What's the worst that could happen?

Okay, there's a lot that could happen. But all I know is that in my heart, this feels right. And sometimes you just have to listen to your heart.

Ugh, listen to your heart? I sound like a Hallmark movie.

It's Friday night and Penny is already in bed asleep, which means Samantha should also be asleep. This is my chance. I type out a text to Sophie.

Drew: Hey, you up?

The three dots pop up like she's responding, but then they stop. I wait five full minutes, wondering what I should do. I decide to text her again.

Drew: I was hoping we could talk.

No dots, no response, no nothing. This isn't like Sophie at all, and now I'm worried something is wrong. I pace back and forth in my bedroom for several minutes before I conclude that it wouldn't hurt to check on her.

I walk down the hallway and down the steps. When I come to the door at the bottom, I knock gently, as to not wake Sam up.

It takes a minute, but finally Sophie opens the door. She gives me her best smile as she looks up at me, but I can tell from her red-rimmed eyes she's been crying. My eyebrows crease with worry before I can stop them. She straightens her shoulders, as if to fool me into believing she's okay.

"Hey, Drew." I can tell she's trying to be her usual happy self, but her voice is thick with emotion.

"What's wrong?"

She walks down the small hallway into her living room, and I follow her.

She turns to me and crosses her arms. "Nothing, Drew, I'm fine. You just caught me at a bad time."

I take the small apartment in for signs of anything out of the ordinary. Everything seems fine, except there's a pile of tissues on the sofa next to a guitar. I notice the guitar is covered in marker.

"Do you play the guitar?"

Her chin quivers. "No, I- I-" Before she can finish answering my question, she bursts into tears.

I've never seen Sophie cry, and it's absolutely heartbreaking. Tears don't bother me or make me uncomfortable, but seeing Sophie upset makes me feel miserable. I wish I could take this hurt from her.

I pull her into my arms, which I've been dying to do again, but not under these circumstances. "Shh, Soph. It's okay."

I rub my hand up and down her back until she calms down. "Can you tell me what's going on?"

She sniffs, but keeps her arms around my waist while she answers. "Sam played. I gave him that guitar for Christmas the year we were married. He adored it, played it constantly." She pauses as she wipes her face with her sleeve. "Besides our wedding rings and photos, this guitar is the only belonging I've kept of his. And Samantha colored all over it with permanent markers." She chokes back another sob.

"I'm so sorry."

She shakes her head. "I know it's stupid, it's just a guitar, and I can't even play it."

I pull back just enough so that I can see her face. "It's not stupid. It was important to your husband, so it's important to you."

"I just wanted to save some of his favorite things to keep his memory alive, you know? I even thought maybe someday Samantha might take guitar lessons and use it."

I put my hand under her chin and raise her face so I can look into her eyes. "The little things become important when it's all you have left. After losing my parents I kept random items of theirs too."

"Really?" She asks. "What did you keep?"

I smile. "I kept my Dad's Seattle Seahawks jersey, my mom's favorite Yo-Yo Ma C.D. and the rolling pin she always used when she baked."

One corner of Sophie's mouth turns up in a smile. "A rolling pin? Is it the one we used?"

"No, it's in a box in my closet ... along with the C.D. But I downloaded the album on my phone and Emily and I used to listen to it constantly." I take a deep breath, memories of my mother baking while listening to her favorite music filling my mind. "I wanted to keep memories alive for Emily *and* for myself. I get it."

She loosens her arms from around me and takes a step back. She looks at me with an empathetic expression.

"Thanks for understanding. Maybe Google can tell me how to get marker out. Hopefully I don't end up ruining the guitar."

"Actually, Penny colored on the wood floors with marker once, and Emily's fingernail polish remover got it out. We did have to re-stain that area though."

"No way, I have some nail polish remover. I'll try that." She smiles softly. "You're always rescuing me, Drew."

I smile back, looking into her ocean eyes. I could get lost in this ocean so easily.

She blinks as if suddenly remembering something. "Hey, sorry I didn't respond to your text. What did you want to talk about?"

"Oh, uh, nothing." I shrug. "Don't worry about it."

This is the worst possible time to bring up our relationship, not that we even have one. I'm not sure where Sophie's at in the process of grieving for her husband, but tonight she's been through enough emotionally. She obviously still misses her husband a great deal, and she probably always will have moments of sadness. I know I still have those difficult moments when the loss of my parents feels heavy. I would never expect her to stop loving her late husband. All I can hope for is that she might be willing to love me too, that she might be willing to let me make her happy. That we can experience a completely new love in each other.

But that's a conversation for another day. I'll keep waiting, as long as I need to.

Sophie's worth it.

On Monday afternoon, I receive a text from Sophie. I haven't seen her since the guitar incident, so my face lights up when I see her name on my phone screen.

Sophie: Hey Drew, sorry to bother you at work. I have some kind of stomach bug, and Samantha and I are headed home from school. I won't be able to bring Penny home today. I'm so sorry.

I frown. A huge part of me wishes I could rush home to take care of her.

Drew: That sucks you're not feeling well. Don't worry about Penny. I'll reschedule some patients and pick her up. Can I get you anything on the way home?

Sophie: I'll be okay! Thanks though. :)

Drew: Let me know if you change your mind. I am a doctor, you know.

Sophie: Oh really? I thought you worked in the phlebotomy dept.?

Drew: *gif of Robert Downey Jr. rolling his eyes*

Sophie: *gif of Ryan Reynolds smirking*

I laugh to myself. Only Sophie could have a stomach bug and still be able to make me smile.

Walking up to reception, I ask the ladies at the front desk to reschedule my last two appointments so I can pick Penny up from school.

An hour later, I just finished up with a patient for a post-op check when my phone vibrates in my pocket. I pull it out to see an incoming call from Heartland Academy.

"Hello, this is Drew Reed."

"Hello, Dr. Reed. This is Caroline from Heartland Academy. I'm calling to see if you can come get Penny from school early. She just threw up and the poor thing is feeling awful. There must be a bug going around the school. We've had to send ten kids home today, and a few teachers."

"Of course, my last patient just left so I'll be there in fifteen minutes."

"Thank you, see you soon."

After disconnecting the call, I write some patient notes on my computer as quickly as possible, then take my white coat off and hang it on the back of my office door.

Dr. Pham is in the office next door to mine. I knock on her open door and she looks up from her computer. "Hey, I'm heading out to pick up my daughter. The school called saying she's sick."

"Poor thing, hope she feels better soon." She gives me a sympathetic smile.

"Thanks. I already had the front desk reschedule the rest of my patients for the day. Could you ask them to reschedule tomorrow's patients too?"

"Of course, take care of that sweet girl."

"Will do," I say with a little wave as I walk away and head out to the parking lot.

Please don't throw up in my Bronco, please don't throw up in my Bronco. I internally repeat to myself on the way home from picking Penny up. Her face looks green as she holds her stomach.

"Alright, Pen. We're home." I park in the garage and rush to get her out of the vehicle before she explodes.

Picking her up, I carry her inside the house. She holds onto my neck with a grumble. "Daddy, I want to lie down. My tummy hurts."

"I know, sweetheart. We're almost there."

I walk to her bedroom with swift steps and lay her in her bed. Then I dart to the hallway to retrieve some towels. I put one under her and one on the floor, then grab her little trashcan and place it next to her bed. She grabs for her comforter and snuggles in.

"Thanks, Daddy," she mumbles and tries to smile, but it looks more like a grimace.

"I'm going to change out of my work clothes, then I'll be back to check on you," I whisper as I smooth her hair back away from her face.

Taking a deep breath, I walk to my room and get changed out of my dress pants and white button-up shirt. I throw on my favorite pair of comfy grey sweatpants and a black v-neck t-shirt then rush back to Penny's room to check on her. She has her eyes closed and looks content. I sit on the side of her bed and rub her back. Sick children are just about the saddest sight you'll ever see.

I pull my phone out of my pocket and shoot a text to Sophie.

Drew: Hey, Penny is sick too, so I got her from school early. We're home now. Do you need anything?

I wait for her to reply for five minutes before my phone finally pings.

Sophie: I just feel like I should warn you I have no clue what havoc Samantha is wreaking on this apartment while I'm overcome with this plague. But I promise to pay for whatever damages she's made.

Drew: Don't worry about the apartment. Can I help with Sam? She can watch TV upstairs.

Sophie: Would you really do that? My parents are out of town and I don't want to expose Odette to sickness, otherwise I'd ask them to help.

Drew: It's seriously no big deal. I'll come get her.

Sophie: I owe you big time.

Standing up from Penny's bed, I walk to the basement steps. Once I'm at the bottom, I knock a few times before opening the basement door. It's eerily quiet, which means Samantha is definitely getting into trouble. Three-year-olds and quiet are never a good mix.

I peek into her room and find her there with a marker in each hand. One black and one orange. She's drawn stripes all over her skin and smiles up at me.

"I'm a tiger! Rawr!" She giggles.

I shake my head but can't hold back the chuckle that escapes from my mouth. "You're in big trouble is what you are."

She scampers over to my side and hugs my legs. I pick her up and tousle her blonde curls. "Let's check on your mommy real quick before we head upstairs, okay?"

"Okay!" She responds, oblivious to the fact that her mother feels like crap.

Walking down the hallway with the naughty little tiger in my arms, I find Sophie curled up on the small sofa in the fetal position. There's a bucket by her side and her purse has been discarded in the center of the room. Like she was so desperate to lie down when she arrived home, she couldn't even make it to the table to set her things down. My heart wrenches at the thought.

"Hey, can I get you anything?"

She opens one eye and peeks up at us. I can tell when she spots Sam's stripes because her eyes fly wide open. "Oh my gosh, Samantha. You'd be in big trouble if I didn't feel like death warmed over."

Samantha giggles and then growls as she puts one hand up like a claw.

"Thankfully, it's washable marker this time." I smile. "Can I get you anything before we head upstairs?"

"You're a saint, Drew." The sound of my name on her lips sends a shiver down my spine. "Thank you for keeping an eye on Sam. Would you hand me that water bottle that's on the table?"

"Of course." If only she knew I'd bring her a mountain on a silver platter if she asked me to. I retrieve the water bottle and hand it to her. "Text me if you think of anything else."

"Thank you." She whispers, then closes her eyes.

Chapter 19
Sophie

The sight of Drew in that fitted black t-shirt and butt-hugging grey sweatpants should be enough to give me miraculous healing, but sadly it did not. Although my vivid memory of it is definitely taking my mind off of puking. But even with those blessed grey sweatpants etched into my brain, I still have to run to the bathroom every ten minutes.

Over the last three hours, Drew has come downstairs to check on me four times. If I wasn't convinced this man is husband material before, I am now.

Like, how has he stayed single for thirty-six years?! It's mind-boggling.

It's incredibly sweet of Drew to watch Sam for me, but he's also taking care of his own sick daughter. My stomach churns, but this time with guilt and not sickness. I've never allowed anyone to help with Sam except my family. But when I got home from school, I texted all of my brothers. Madden is in D.C., Brooks is entertaining clients from out of town, and David never responded. He's one of those super responsible people who turns his phone off when he's working.

Of course I would get sick when my parents are out of town on their anniversary trip. What are the chances?

Despite my sore abdominal muscles from getting sick so many times, and my limp and weary limbs, I'm feeling slightly better. Drew is already exposed to the germs, so I might as well head upstairs and check on Samantha.

Throwing on a sweatshirt and securing my hair into a messy bun, I trudge up the basement stairs. It's dinnertime, so I pad toward the kitchen. But on my way into the kitchen, I spy the back of Drew's head in the living room. He's sitting on the large sectional, his back to me. A princess movie is playing on the TV and he's eating something.

I tiptoe over to the sofa to get a better view. Sam is snuggled into his side on the couch and Penny is sprawled out on the other end of the sectional, wrapped in blankets, with a bucket by her side. Samantha and Drew are eating grilled cheese sandwiches and they're all watching the movie together.

Each interaction I witness between Drew and the girls chips away at the ice that has frozen my heart since losing my husband. I imagined my heart would stay in that hardened state forever, never to thaw again. But right here, seeing him look at my daughter with adoration while simultaneously caring for his own sick daughter? My heart is melting fast.

I clear my throat before walking into the living room, not wanting to scare them with my sudden appearance.

"Sophie," Drew says with a smile. "How are you feeling?"

"Hi, Mommy!" Sam grins and takes another bite of her grilled cheese.

"Hey, sweetheart." I take a seat next to her. "I'm feeling a little better, still woozy, but I think I got the throwing up part out of my system."

"Good. You look a little better." He glances at me over Sam's head. "Penny has kept some saltine crackers down, so hopefully no one else gets sick."

"Thanks again for helping. I don't know what I would've done without you." I hold his gaze for a few seconds, feeling the electric charge between us.

"I like being here for you, Soph." He opens his mouth to speak again, but he wrinkles his nose and his hand shoots to his stomach.

"Are you okay?"

Before he can answer, he jumps off the sofa and runs down the hallway to his bedroom. He slams the door, but we can all hear the sounds of sickness. Penny and I look at each other, both frowning at the sound.

After an hour, Drew still hasn't made it back to the living room. I hoist myself off the sofa and head to the kitchen and fill a water bottle with ice water. Just as I'm about to walk down the hallway to his room, Drew emerges from the dark hallway, looking miserable.

"Hey, I was just coming to check on you." I walk to him and hand him the water bottle.

He takes a swig of the cool water. "Thank you. I feel like trash."

One side of my mouth pulls up in a smile. I can't help it. He's the most adorable sick man I've ever seen. This big, brawny man, taken down by a stomach bug. His dark hair is messy, sticking up all over his head, and his eyes look tired and dark, his black t-shirt is rumpled.

"You wanna watch TV with us? I bet the girls will even let you pick the movie."

He smirks. "My arms could fall off and those two still wouldn't let me pick the movie."

I chuckle. "Yeah, you're probably right."

Penny is asleep on one side of the sectional, and Sam is sitting on the other end. A jolt of nervousness runs through my body, Drew and I never sit next to each other on the couch, and especially not this close. Not wanting to make things awkward, I take a seat near Sam, trying to leave plenty of space for

Drew. He sits down next to me, our arms brushing together, but he doesn't distance himself.

There's a soft blanket draped over the couch, so I grab it and hand it to Drew, since he's not feeling well. He smiles and takes the blanket, then proceeds to cover us both with it.

I roll my lips together, trying to hide my smile. He's sick, he's unwell. I'm sure in any other circumstance he wouldn't be behaving this way. He probably doesn't mean anything by it.

Biting my bottom lip, I risk a glance at him. He's looking at me, his eyes burning into mine. Our eyes hold, neither of us talking.

I blink slowly and take a deep breath before grabbing the remote. "So, what movie should we watch next?" I ask, my voice sounding raspy.

His jaw twitches, and he swallows. "Right. A movie. How about *Up*?" He looks over at Sam for approval.

"Yeah! *Up!*"

He starts the movie, and before I know it, all of us have drifted off to sleep.

We're 1,000 feet up in the Blue Ridge Mountains of North Carolina. My husband stands in front of me, his brown hair blowing in the mountain breeze. He looks back at me with a wide smile on his face, his deep-brown eyes twinkling with delight.

"Baby, come look."

We hiked for hours to make it to John's Rock. We've heard there's a magnificent view of Cedar Rock Falls from up here.

Discarding my backpack on a large rock, I take careful steps to meet Sam on the cliff. He pulls me into his side, and I close my eyes as his scent envelops me. He smells the way he always does: woodsy and masculine. But after our hike, that scent is mixed with pine sap, sweat, and the mountain breeze. I want to savor it, to remember it forever.

Finally, I open my eyes and gasp when I take in the view. The sky is big and blue, not a cloud in sight. It's the perfect backdrop to the mountain landscape, filled with the most gorgeous fall foliage I've ever seen. A swirl of reds, oranges, yellows, and greens flows over the mountains, making it look like the most impossibly beautiful painting you've ever seen. Only this is real life.

"Oh Sam, this is the most beautiful sight I've ever seen."

He doesn't answer, so I glance over at him. His chocolate eyes are wide and glossy with unshed tears. "The mountains are stunning, sure. But you're the most beautiful sight I will ever see. Past, present, and future. Nothing compares to you, Soph."

The breeze blows and a few strands of hair flutter into my eyes. Sam reaches out and sweeps them out of my eyes with his hand. This tough, military man. But when it comes to me, he couldn't be more gentle.

I step closer to him and link my arms around his waist. "Oh Sam, you're so good to me. What am I going to do without you for nine months?" *A tear escapes down my cheek.*

He frowns. "I'm dreading being away from you for so long. You are my home. I'm afraid I'll feel lost out there without you. But at the same time, I'm looking forward to doing my job. My duty."

Laying my head on his chest, I listen to the steady rhythm of his heart, taking it in. Knowing next month he won't be here, he'll be in the Middle East, surrounded by danger.

"I'm so proud of you. But I'll miss you more than I can ever tell you."

He kisses the top of my head. "I'll miss you too. My heart aches just thinking about it." *He lays his head on top of mine as we stand there in each other's arms, taking in the magnificent view surrounding us. "Promise me something."*

I move my head to look up at him. "Of course. Anything."

His jaw tenses and his expression turns serious. "If anything happens to me, promise me you'll move on."

"Sam—" I begin, but he interrupts me.

"You're young, Sophie. You have a beautiful heart full of love. I don't want you to be alone if something happens to me. I want to know you'll take care of yourself, that you'll move forward with your life and be truly happy. A long life filled with love, happiness, and children. Promise me."

I'm about to argue, but I can tell he means what he's saying. His eyes search mine earnestly, waiting for my answer.

"I promise," I whisper. Tears flowing steadily now. "But nothing is going to happen to you, Sam. You're going to be okay." I force a smile.

"Thank you. I love you so much."

"I love you too, Sam."

I startle awake to see my brother, David, standing in front of me in Drew's living room. I'm reeling from my dream. It was so vivid, like I was watching a film. It felt so real.

I blink a few times, trying to wake myself from my stupor. Looking down, I see Drew also fell asleep, and he's slumped over with his head in my lap. Samantha is curled up on the other side of me, dreaming peacefully. A surge of emotion flows through my veins at the memory of my husband, and then waking to Drew snuggled up on my lap… but instead of my usual guilt, I only feel peace. Maybe that dream was a sign? Or maybe it was Sam sending me a reminder that it's okay to move forward and be happy again. To fill another person's life with love and allow them to do the same for me. I have the irresistible urge to run my fingers through Drew's thick hair, but remember David is staring at us and resist.

"David," I whisper. "What are you doing here?"

He looks stunned by the sight of us all snuggled up on the sectional. Not angry like I'd expect, but more curious about how we ended up like this.

"I'm so sorry, I didn't mean to wake you."

I remove myself from Drew's heavy sleeping form and scoot out from the couch. He doesn't even stir. The man sleeps like a rock.

With my hand, I gesture for David to follow me downstairs so we don't wake the others.

Once we're at the bottom of the stairs, David looks me over. "I got your text late and stopped by your apartment to make sure you were okay. You weren't here, and the door to the stairway was open." He pauses and shuffles his weight awkwardly from one foot to the other. "I didn't mean to be nosey. I just got worried when neither you or Drew responded to my texts and went upstairs to see if everyone was alright. You were all asleep, and I was going to turn around and leave, but I just—" His voice falters.

"You just what?" I urge him to continue.

He looks down at his feet, then back up at me. "You looked so peaceful, Soph. Happy. It's been so long since I've seen you look so happy." He smiles. "You guys looked like a family, falling asleep after a movie night. It was ... beautiful."

He clears his throat and straightens his shoulders, almost like he's proving his own manliness to himself after having an emotional moment.

I smile at his sweet words. "I feel happy. More like myself lately. But that wasn't what it looked like ... I was so sick, and Drew offered to help with Samantha since Mom and Dad are gone. Penny also got sick, so the three of them were watching movies. I went to check on Samantha, and then Drew got sick. So I stayed to help, and we were all so tired, we must've just conked out."

"I wasn't accusing you of anything." He puts his hands in his pockets. Only David would still be wearing dress pants and a button-down shirt at 10:45 p.m. "I know I overreacted when you first moved in here, but if Drew is the one putting that look of peaceful contentment on your face, then I'm all for it."

My face turns bright red, making David chuckle. "Sorry, your love life isn't my business. Are you all good here, though? Can I get you guys anything?"

"I think we're all good now, but thank you for stopping to check on us."

"Alright, well, goodnight then."

After seeing David out, and locking up the house, I tiptoe back up to the couch and squeeze myself back into my comfortable spot between Samantha, Drew, and now Penny, who has scooted over to cuddle up against her daddy.

Chapter 20

Drew

Squinting my eyes to dull the brightness gleaming through the windows, I try to move into a more comfortable position. Why is my pillow so hard? Why is my body so weak? And why is my bedroom so bloody bright?

Then I feel someone stirring beside me, and my eyes fly wide open. I'm in the living room, I must've fallen asleep watching *Up*. Looking around me, I see Penny is using my butt as a pillow, and Samantha is running around the living room, still covered in tiger stripes, and has a marker in hand. Oh boy.

She runs up to me giggling and says, "Mustache!"

I look back at her in confusion. The crick in my neck is making it impossible to think straight.

"Um, good morning …" Sophie's undeniable voice comes from above me.

Glancing up I see her lovely face and realize I'm laying on her lap. Okay, the crick in my neck was totally worth it to wake up to Sophie.

I use my arm to prop myself up into a seated position. "Good morning." I rub the back of my neck. "Sorry for commandeering your lap."

Her cheeks blush slightly, although it's hard to tell since her skin is so pale from being sick yesterday. "That's alright." She rolls her lips to keep from laughing.

"What's so funny?"

She smirks. "Well, I think Sam found Penny's marker stash while we were asleep."

Penny stirs next to me and sits up. She yawns and stretches her arms with her butt in the air like a cat. She smacks her lips a few times, then looks up at me.

"You look like a huge dork, Dad."

Samantha runs back into the living room. "Mustache!" She exclaims before running away giggling again.

"She drew a mustache on me, didn't she?" I ask and then glance from side to side to see both Penny and Sophie nodding and trying not to laugh.

"I think we're going to have to confiscate every marker on the premises at this point," Sophie says, then wrinkles her nose. Which is one of the many things she does that I find absolutely charming.

I stand up and extend my hand to help her up. She grasps it and I pull her to her feet.

"That's probably a good plan."

She smiles up at me, making me feel woozy. And not just because I'm dehydrated and my stomach is completely depleted. I hold her gaze, and the only thing stopping me from pulling her into me and kissing her is that my breath must smell atrocious. And our daughters are here. And I apparently have a fake mustache drawn on my face.

Sophie pats my arm, then glides past me. "I'm going to shower and give Sam a bath."

"No!" Samantha whines. "I wike my stwipes."

Sophie gives a heavy sigh before picking Samantha up and heading toward the basement steps. I watch her walk away, loving the sight of her in my house in pajamas and a messy bun. She looks back at me and smiles before going downstairs.

Penny comes to my side and takes my hand. "Daddy, you need to shower, too. You smell horrible."

The next morning, I drop Penny off at school and cross my fingers she doesn't pick up more sick germs anytime soon.

Pulling into the drop-off line, I spot Sophie greeting the children as they hop out of their vehicles and head to their classes. She's wearing a black pencil skirt today with black pointed-toe flats and a silky white blouse tucked in. She looks scrumptious. If any of my teachers had looked like Sophie, I definitely would've enjoyed school more. Pulling down my sun vizor and opening the mirror, I make sure I look okay. My black scrubs are clean and pressed and my face is freshly shaven. No crumbs in sight. Whew.

When it's our turn, I roll down my window. I have no doubt I'm grinning at her like an idiot, but I'm past the point of caring.

"Good morning, Ms. Miller. You look like you're feeling 100 percent healthy now."

"Good morning, Drew—er, Dr. Reed." She smirks. "I am. So are you, and I can see you were able to remove your marker mustache."

I shake my head with a laugh. "It took some scrubbing, but I got it off."

She chuckles. "Good morning, Penny! Have a great day."

"Thanks, Sophie! I mean—Ms. Miller! Bye Daddy!" Penny grins, then scampers off inside the school.

"Bye, Pen!" I shout, then direct my attention back to Sophie. "I'll see you tonight?"

She bites her bottom lip, looking a little shy. "Yeah, see you tonight."

She holds my gaze for a few seconds before we're interrupted by the car behind us.

HONK HONK HONK. "Move it! Some of us need to get to work!"

I look in my rearview mirror and spot a shiny black Mercedes, with none other than Bradley Vanderven behind the wheel. His eyes are narrowed as he sends invisible lasers at my Bronco.

I roll my eyes, drawing a giggle from Sophie. I wave to her and then pull out of the line of vehicles.

Taking my exit for the highway toward the hospital, I call Emily on speaker phone. She won't be at work yet and I have fifteen minutes on the road to chat.

"Hey, bro! Haven't heard from you in a few days."

"Hey! Sorry, Penny and I had some sort of plague." I sigh.

"You guys were sick?!" She sounds panicked. "Why didn't you call me?"

"Calm down. We're all fine now. It was just a stomach bug." I shrug my shoulders even though she can't see me.

She pauses, and I can almost picture her on the other side of the phone fuming. "You know I like to be kept informed on Penny. You could've just texted me and let me know what was going on."

"Emily, you moved out and started a new job to get some distance from us, to move forward with your life. Me texting you every time Penny has any scrape or sickness isn't going to help with that."

She gasps audibly. "She has scrapes too?!"

"No! I was just being facetious. Good grief."

Emily sighs. "Okay, sorry for freaking out. I'm just used to being there and knowing what's going on."

"I know." I tell her, trying to sound sympathetic. "So, I actually called to talk to you about this weekend."

"Yeah? Can I come see Penny?" She sounds excited at the thought.

"You know you can see her anytime. I was wondering if you could watch her Friday night?" My hands tighten on the steering wheel, nervous about what I'm going to say next. "I was hoping you might watch Samantha too."

"Drew …"

"Emily."

"What are you doing?" I can hear her release a deep breath.

"I haven't talked to Sophie about it yet, but I'm going to ask her to dinner on Friday. I was hoping having a sitter lined up would make the offer all the more enticing."

"Are you sure about this?" she asks. I imagine her tapping her foot and crossing her arms with a judgemental look on her face.

"Em, I've never been more sure about anything in my entire life."

She sighs again. "Of course I'll watch Samantha. If that's okay with Sophie."

"Thank you, I owe you." I'm smiling so big my face hurts.

"Just make me your best woman at the wedding and we'll call it even." I can practically hear her smirk through the phone.

I laugh light-heartedly, admittedly not minding the idea. But I'm getting way ahead of myself. "You're the best. Wish me luck! I just pulled up to the hospital, so I'll see you Friday?"

"Sounds good, see you then."

We hang up and I park in my designated parking spot in the parking garage. And I stride into the hospital with an extra pep in my step.

Chapter 21
Sophie

I'm sitting at Drew's table upstairs, finishing up some grading, when he comes in through the garage door. He's still in his scrubs and despite his tired eyes—performing surgery all day has got to be exhausting—he still makes my heart skip a beat. Before I can stop myself, my face morphs into a big smile. Like a small child looking at a puppy.

"Hey, Soph." He smiles back. "Sorry I'm late; my last surgery ran longer than I expected."

Something has shifted between us in the last forty-eight hours. I'm not sure if it was caring for each other when we were sick, or if it just gradually shifted over the last two months. There are so many sparks flying between us lately, we could use them to power our own defibrillator. I roll my eyes at myself. Spending this much time with Drew has me thinking in medical euphemisms.

Anyway, it feels like we're on the precipice of a huge transformation between landlord and lessee to something much different.

"No problem, spaghetti is on the stovetop waiting for you." Gathering up my papers off the table, I put them in a folder. "I need to get Samantha to bed, so I'll leave you to it."

I pull my bottom lip into my mouth, stalling because all I really want to do is sit with him while he eats and ask him all about his day.

He runs one hand through his hair and takes a deep breath. "After we get the girls to bed, can we talk?" He clears his throat, seeming abnormally nervous.

I freeze. Maybe I completely misread him. He sounds so serious, not at all the casual and confident man I've come to know so well.

With a feeling of dread in the pit of my stomach, I nod. "Yeah, sure." I fake a smile.

An hour later, I'm sitting on the sofa in my apartment downstairs, wringing my hands together while I think about each interaction Drew and I have had over the past two months. Wracking my brain to see if I've mistaken the connection between us, and coming up with a list of things he might want to talk about. None of them good.

So far my list looks like this:

1. He might tell me to stop holding eye contact for so long.

2. He might've found a sitter who can actually cook.

3. Perhaps Emily is coming back, and he needs me to move out.

4. Maybe he will point out how inappropriate it was that I was drooling all over him when he wore those fitted, grey sweatpants. (Although, in my defense, I was sick and delirious).

Just as I've nearly worried myself into a full-blown panic attack, a knock comes from the basement door. I rush through the main area and down the small hallway to let Drew inside.

He smiles when I open the door, making me feel slightly more calm. He must have taken a shower because his hair is wet and he smells like heaven. Also, I think he takes pleasure in torturing me because he's wearing another pair of sweatpants along with a white hoodie.

I gesture for him to come in and he follows me into the living room. Taking a seat on the sofa, I take a deep breath. Drew sits next to me and his eyes shift around the room. If he's avoiding eye contact, this can't be good.

I gulp down the lump in my throat and wait for him to speak.

"Soph—" He stops and then runs both hands down his face. He looks frustrated, tortured even. "Damn it. I've never been so nervous."

"Drew, you're scaring me. Just spit it out. Did you find a new sitter or something?"

He looks into my eyes for the first time since entering my apartment, and then he laughs. An exuberant, booming laugh.

"A new sitter? Sophie, the problem I'm having isn't that I'm not happy with your babysitting services." He laughs again. "I'm nervous because I want you to be *more* than just the babysitter, and I'm not sure how you feel about that."

I release the breath I've been holding in, and now it's my turn to laugh. "Oh my gosh, Drew. You had me so worried something was wrong."

He grins at me, and then his face turns serious. "Getting to know you these past few months and watching you with Penny has been a special kind of torture ... because I often find myself wanting you all to myself." He smiles again. "I know you're grieving the loss of your husband, but if you think there's room in your heart for me, I'd really like to take you on a date."

My eyes fill with tears as another layer of ice melts away from my heart and I feel it leap to life with rapid beats. Good thing Drew's a doctor. He might need to check my heart rate after this conversation.

He looks at me with concern as a tear releases from each of my eye sockets. He releases my hands. "A- a- and if you're not ready, or if you don't feel the same, I completely understand. I know I'm older than you, and I'm friends with your dad, and we have the girls to consider—"

He's talking a thousand miles a minute, and a giggle bubbles up through my lungs and releases from my mouth before I can stop it.

"Drew, stop." I place my hand on top of his. "I would love to go on a date with you."

He releases a deep breath, then his face lights up. Knowing I'm the reason for that smile on his face makes my heart nearly beat out of my chest.

"I was hoping I could take you to dinner on Friday?" He ducks his head down then looks back up at me through his thick lashes. "I hope this wasn't too presumptuous, but I asked Emily to babysit for us."

I chuckle. "So you were pretty sure I'd want to go to dinner then, huh?"

"I was cautiously optimistic." He winks.

"That actually works out. Otherwise, I'd have to ask my parents, and they'd inevitably want to know what plans I had." I bite my bottom lip. "Not that I'm ashamed to go to dinner with you... it's just that I'm unsure how they'll respond."

He nods. "Yeah, I had the same thought. David is going to kick my butt when he finds out."

I recall David's words the other day when he found us on the couch upstairs, asleep. "I'm not so sure about that, actually."

Drew raises one eyebrow in question. "So, Friday night then? We can leave after I get home from work and shower, around 6:30?"

"Perfect."

We grin at each other as we stand from the sofa. I follow him as he heads to the stairwell door, and we bid each other goodnight.

Even after closing the door and telling Drew goodnight, my heart is still racing. I'm half nervous and half excited. Nervous that my relationship with Drew is about to drastically change, but excited at the possibility of a future with him.

Chapter 22

Drew

The next two days drag by. I'm counting down the hours until I have Sophie to myself and we can have an uninterrupted conversation. I'm so ready to explore the romantic side of our relationship and see where this can go.

I blink to bring my focus back to the patient in front of me. He won't stop talking about his dog, Barry. Who names a dog Barry?

We've already discussed the process of his knee replacement surgery next week, but the older patients seem to be extra chatty. Usually, I don't mind taking the extra time to listen to their stories, but all I want to do is get home, shower, and take Sophie out.

His story pauses, so I clap my hands together and interject before he begins another story about his dog. "Alright, Mr. Paulson, I'll see you Wednesday bright and early for your surgery."

He stands and smiles. "Right, right. I'm sure a strapping young man like yourself has exciting plans tonight. I need to get home to Barry, anyway."

I chuckle and open the door for him. "Enjoy your weekend."

"You too, Dr. Reed." He shakes my hand and walks out the door and down the hallway to the reception area.

I breathe a sigh of relief before turning to walk toward my office, but instead, I smack straight into Ted Windell.

"Whoa there, son!" He puts his hands on my shoulders. "You're in some kind of hurry, huh?"

Huffing out an awkward laugh, I drag my hand through my hair. "Yeah sorry, I have plans tonight and am running late."

"Hot date, huh?" He winks.

The color drains from my face. Trying not to give myself away, I attempt my most genuine smile.

"Uh, yeah. You know it. Ha." Wow, Drew. Real smooth.

He grins and takes a step away before turning back to me again. "Oh, hey! You're coming to our Labor Day BBQ next Sunday, right?"

I had completely forgotten about that. Labor Day is always on a Monday, but being in the medical field, we often celebrate holidays on our days off instead.

"Yeah, of course." I smile. "See you next weekend."

Ted claps me on the shoulder, then turns and walks away. Waiting a few seconds to make sure he's out of sight, I bound toward my office and shuck off my white coat. After draping it over my office chair along with my stethoscope, I log out of my computer.

I take a quick peek out of my office door to make sure the hallway is empty before walk-running down the hallway and through the exit like a kid at a pool in a no-run zone.

Finally, I make it to my Bronco and head home ... to Sophie.

Thirty minutes later, I'm showered and dressed and ready. I've never gotten ready so fast. I opted for some dark wash jeans and a black button-up shirt. Since it's still fairly warm outside, I rolled my shirt sleeves up to my elbows. I complete the ensemble with a cognac belt and leather oxfords. Just as I'm about to leave my bedroom, I remember the cologne Sophie liked.

In the past, I've always kept first dates casual. But there's nothing casual about tonight. I wanted to do more than just take her to the taco truck. I planned a fun evening for us and I really think Sophie will love it. It's definitely not your typical first date, but I think it's just what we need tonight. I've never gone on a date with a woman I've had strong feelings for before, but my heart is already involved here, so I put a lot of thought into our date. Sophie deserves the best.

Grabbing the bottle of cologne from the bathroom, I give myself one spritz and then walk out to the living room. Emily is on the couch with the girls, looking like she wants to tease me, but holding back since Sophie is standing between us.

Sophie grins up at me with a blush on her cheeks. Her fitted pink dress matches her cheeks perfectly. The dress is understated but still gorgeous, just like the woman wearing it. The dress has a deep-v neckline and the length of it hits just a few inches above her knees, showing off her long legs. Her shiny blonde hair is down and smooth, and she has something on her lips that makes them look extra glossy and tempting.

I have to stop myself from licking my lips.

"You look beautiful, as always," I whisper so only Sophie can hear.

Her cheeks turn even pinker. "Thank you. You clean up pretty good yourself." She winks.

She winked at me. Holy mother of Moses, I want to drop to my knees and worship the ground she walks on. Sophie Miller winking is quite possibly my new favorite thing in the world. I love that she goes after what she wants. She's not shy and reserved like some of the women I've dated.

"You ready to go?" My voice sounds hoarse.

She nods, then walks over to give Samantha a kiss. "Be a good girl, okay?"

Samantha smiles. "Bye, Mommy!"

Sophie turns to Emily. "Thank you so much for watching her."

"Of course. It's not a problem." Emily pulls Samantha into her lap and tickles her sides, making her giggle.

Penny looks between Sophie and I with a look of confusion in her big brown eyes. "Daddy, where are you and Miss Sophie going?"

"I'm taking her to dinner. She's done such a great job babysitting. I thought she deserved a treat." I shoot Sophie a quick wink. Apparently winking is our thing now.

Penny looks satisfied with that answer. "Good idea! Have fun."

"Goodnight, ladies." I put my hand on the small of Sophie's back and direct her toward the garage door.

After driving across town, we pull up into a large parking lot surrounded by evergreen trees. Sophie looks bemused as I get out of the Bronco and walk around to open her door for her. Now that we're out of the vehicle, we can hear music and laughter nearby.

I smirk at her and take her hand in mine. "Don't worry, there's something fun just on the other side of those trees." I point to the row of evergreen trees a few yards from us.

As I lead her through the small path between the trees I hear her breath catch when she sees the carnival on the other side of the trees. She looks up at me with a breathtaking grin.

The area is lit up with lanterns and decorated in a country theme. Hay bales line a wooden dance floor, and plaid fabric covers the tables at the various booths. They have half a dozen small carnival rides in one area, and there are booths that have different carnival games set up on the opposite side. There are food vendors scattered throughout, some making funnel cakes and cotton candy, others offering nachos, corn dogs, pretty much every kind of carnival food you can imagine.

Her jaw drops as she takes it all in and I chuckle. "I wish you could see your face right now."

"This is possibly the best first date I've ever been on," she says as she loops her arm through mine.

I glanced down at her, my expression serious. "Me too."

We walk arm in arm into the carnival, which is a fundraiser for a highschool in town. I randomly saw a flier for it a few days ago and it screamed *Sophie*.

"I knew they'd have plenty of junk food here for you." I tease.

We head to get some cotton candy and corn dogs before walking around to play all the games. My stomach will not be happy with me in the morning. But it's worth it to see Sophie so excited.

As we walk around the carnival, we take turns asking each other questions, some silly, some serious.

"Okay, my turn," I tell her. "If you were stranded on a desert island. What three items would you want with you?"

Sophie releases one of her larger than life laughs, a laugh that all the Windells seem to share. I chuckle as I watch her. She laughs with her entire body.

"Hmmm." She taps her index finger on her chin while she thinks. "A French press, coffee grounds, and a big bag of sugar."

I shake my head in dismay but smile at her so she knows I'm being sarcastic. "You're out of control with the sugar."

She smacks my arm playfully with her free hand. "Okay, my turn to ask a question. This one is more serious."

"Shoot."

"I've never heard any talk about Penny's mother. Does she have any contact with Penny? Or … with you?"

My skin prickles, a cold sweat breaking out along my back. I was hoping she'd heard the one-night-stand tale from her father and I wouldn't have to say much else.

"Oh, well. Did Ted, I mean, your father, mention anything about it?"

She twirls a strand of her hair. "He said you had a one-night stand and got a woman pregnant. But I'd like to hear about it from you."

"Right. Um, the woman became pregnant rather—unexpectedly—obviously. She didn't want the baby, and signed full custody over to me."

"And she hasn't been in contact since?" Sophie asks incredulously.

I swallow the lump in my throat. I hate lying to her. "No, she hasn't."

"Wow," Sophie responds, seeming surprised. "I can't imagine not wanting contact with my child. I'm sorry."

"It's okay. It's for the best." I clear my throat. "So, my turn to ask a question?"

Chapter 23
Sophie

Drew was so fidgety when I asked him about Penny's mother. I'm not sure why talking about her would've unnerved him so much.

I have a feeling there's more to this story than meets the eye. But I also don't want to push and ruin our date. And this is only our first date after all. Perhaps he'll be more comfortable telling me about her mother once we've gotten to know each other better.

His shoulders relax instantly once the subject is changed. His relief is palpable. Even his facial expression goes from tense to smiling again. I will definitely get to the bottom of this eventually.

He thinks for a moment, then asks, "Why did you rent my apartment when you could have easily purchased a house with your trust fund, or your husband's life insurance? What you do with your money is your business, I've just always wondered."

I give him a tight smile, slightly aggravated that I'm willing to share everything about myself with him, but he's obviously holding back for some reason.

"Well, Sam didn't have much of a relationship with his parents once he finished school. They lived in an old trailer park and never cared to put much effort into raising him or to provide for him. Which meant he didn't have a college fund or anything like that."

Drew's eyes widen in surprise and I continue, "That's why he joined the Army right out of highschool. He wanted to serve and also to earn his G.I. Bill for college. He was the hardest working person I had ever met." I smile at the memory. "He was determined to take care of me and our future children. He wanted to be an example of having a strong work ethic and providing for those you love. And because he wanted our children to learn those values, we agreed not to use the trust fund."

Drew concentrates on his hands folded in front of him while he listens. "I respect his determination." He pauses. "So, then, what are you going to do with the money?"

I shake my index finger at him. "No, no. It's my turn to ask a question."

He chuckles. "Oh right, go ahead."

Clearing my throat, I muster up the gumption to ask the important question that's been on my mind. "Do you … want more children?"

He sits up straighter, seemingly taken aback by my question, but one side of his mouth pulls up into a boyish smile.

"Absolutely. It was just me and Em growing up, and we weren't close until we lost our parents. I've always wanted a large family. I just never met anyone. Or more accurately, didn't have time to meet anyone."

I bite the insides of my cheeks to keep from smiling, but it's impossible.

He looks amused by my expression. "Do *you* want more children?"

"Yes," I blurt.

Drew laughs. "Should I be concerned by how quickly you answered that? Do you want like twenty kids?"

I nearly choke, trying to contain a laugh. "Oh gosh, no. But a few more would be great."

His lips pull up into a smile, and his eyes swelter as he looks into mine. Drew's gaze gets hotter as the seconds tick by. How can I be *this* affected by something as simple as eye contact?

We continue walking around the carnival, stealing glances at each other and playing carnival games, until a small band assembles in front of the dance floor. It's just a vocalist, a drummer, and an acoustic guitarist. They're pretty good for how young they are, as they begin playing covers of popular country songs.

Linking his fingers through mine, Drew leads me toward the dance floor. "Dance with me."

"Okay." I scrunch up my nose. "But I haven't danced in ages."

He rolls his eyes playfully. "Please. I know your mother probably made you take a million dance classes. I'm sure you'll be fine."

I smirk and shoot him a side glance, letting him know he's correct. Then he whisks me onto the dance floor. He puts one hand on my waist and takes my hand with the other.

My arm curls around his neck, his skin is hot against mine. It feels good to be close to him. His warmth radiates through his clothes as we twirl in step to the fast-paced music. The air has cooled now that the sun has gone down, making me want to curl up into his warm body like a cat with a cozy blanket.

The twinkle lights surrounding the dance floor gleam as we laugh and swirl, enjoying each other's company. I'm relieved there's only joy in my heart. No guilt, no second-guessing. Being in Drew's arms gives me an overwhelming sense of safety and contentment. Déjà vu sends goosebumps over my flesh like this very moment, here in Drew's arms, was exactly where I was meant to be at this very moment in time. Almost as if Sam sent Drew to me and is giving me his blessing to move on.

My eyes lock with Drew's. His expression is gentle. I have the unnerving sense that he's thinking the same thing I am. We twirl together on the dance floor, eyes locked on each other.

The jubilant music fades to a stop and so do we. The band begins again, but the lights around us dim and the song is slow. The air between us is charged with whatever this feeling is passing between us. Without hesitation, Drew pulls me closer to him, looping both hands around my waist. My hands link around his neck. We step in pace to the music, our bodies pressed together in the most delicious way. I can feel the rise and fall of his broad chest as he breathes and his hands pull me a little tighter, like he never wants to let go.

As we sway from side to side, enjoying the feel of holding each other tight, all the other couples become invisible to us. It's just Drew and I, dancing in our own dreamland.

As each brutal second passes, His face comes closer to mine. Our noses are almost touching now, and I know he's letting me decide if I want to come the rest of the way. If I'm ready to close the distance between our lips and bring us to a new sensation we've never felt between us before.

Oh Drew, if only you knew how ready I was for this.

My feet lift me the rest of the way, making our lips brush ever so softly. Only a whisper of a touch. He stills, his eyes are closed like he's relishing in the way our lips are barely touching. I pull back just enough to see his eyes. His lids slowly open and meet my gaze. He has the most beautiful eyes I've ever seen, sometimes brown, sometimes green. But always with flecks of gold woven throughout. His expression looks amused, like he's waiting to see what I'll do next.

"Kiss me, Drew," I whisper, unable to wait another second.

His eyes go dark and he closes the distance, making our lips more than just brush this time. He kisses me with firm strokes, like his life depends on this kiss. My lips are water and he's a man who's been stranded in the desert for way too long. Our lips dance and sway like they're moving in time to the slow music, but our feet are stopped.

His mouth tastes sweet like cotton candy as it presses into mine over and over again. His kisses are achingly sweet.

Drew stops abruptly, and that's when I realize the music has stopped. I open my eyes and glance around. The teenage couples on the dance floor are watching us with stars in their eyes, but the adults are scowling. I can only assume those are the parents. And they're probably wondering who invited this entirely inappropriate couple to the high-school's fundraiser.

Drew takes in my embarrassed expression and bursts into one of his loud, sincere laughs. The sound fills me with warmth all over again, but I start laughing as well. He takes my hand and pulls me off the dance floor and we laugh on our way back to the Bronco.

Drew opens my door, still grinning. "Whew, that was a close one. I thought those parents were going to call the bouncer to kick us out."

I slide into the Bronco, my face heating at the reminder of our very public kiss. "Yeah, pretty sure all those kids are getting an abstinence talk tonight." I grimace.

He bursts out laughing. "I never know what you're going to say." He shakes his head. "That's one of my favorite things about you."

With one hand braced on the door of the Bronco and the other on the roof, he leans in to give me one more swift but achingly soft kiss. I'm still closing my eyes and savoring it when he pulls back and closes my door for me.

Chapter 24

Drew

The morning after my date with Sophie, I wake up with a grin on my face. I casually put my arms behind my head while I lay on my back in bed and look up at the ceiling.

My time with her was incredible. And that kiss. What a kiss it was. I want to kiss her again and again. The memory of her sweet, pouty lips moving perfectly in sync with mine makes my stomach do a little swoosh.

Sure, I've kissed women before. And it was nice. Who doesn't enjoy kissing? But never have I experienced a kiss filled with heat and passion like the one I had with Sophie last night.

Good grief. I'm acting like a swooning teenager. I grin to myself again.

I stretch, urging my muscles to come back to life after sleeping so peacefully and dreaming of the woman in my basement all night.

Wow, it sounds sketchy when I refer to her as the woman in my basement.

Dragging myself out of bed, I shoot Sophie a text. I think there are rules about waiting a certain amount of time to contact someone after a date, but I don't even care.

Drew: Good morning, beautiful.

She texts right back.

Sophie: Good morning, Drew. I really enjoyed our date.

Drew: Me too. Best first date in history.

Sophie: It was pretty amazing. ;-)

With a wistful sigh, I head to the bathroom. I glance at myself in the mirror and notice I'm smiling and didn't even realize I was smiling. I shake my head at my dopiness before walking out of my bedroom and down the hallway with an extra pep in my step.

Emily is in the kitchen leaning against the countertop, a steaming mug of herbal tea in her hands. She arches an eyebrow at me before taking a sip.

"What's that look for?" I ask before walking into the kitchen, grabbing the coffee pot, and filling it with water.

"I'm assuming your date went well by the stupid grin on your face."

I narrow my eyes at her. "It went very well, as a matter of fact."

Glancing around the main area of the house, I notice Penny isn't awake yet. Perfect, because I need to have a serious conversation with my sister. I twist my lips as I ponder my words.

"Oh no. I know that look." Emily says before setting her mug down.

Releasing a heavy sigh, I rest my back against the countertop opposite of my sister. "We need to talk."

She wrinkles her nose. "Nothing good ever comes after someone states 'we need to talk.'" She makes air quotes with her fingers.

"I have to tell her, Em."

Her eyes widen in shock. "Drew, no." She takes a step toward me and lowers her voice. "You've been on *one* date."

"I can't lie."

My heart constricts inside my chest. My one and only regret last night was not being able to open up about Penny's birth to Sophie.

Emily shakes her head, her eyes filling with tears. "You promised. You promised no one would ever have to know."

My eyebrows furrow. I hate that I'm upsetting her. "That was over seven years ago, Em. You had to know someday I'd have a serious relationship or get married. Obviously, I'd tell that person everything."

"Drew, please." Her eyes shift back and forth, the look of desperation on her face palpable.

"I can't begin a relationship with a huge lie like this. I am serious about Sophie. Dead serious."

"I need more time."

I throw my head back and run my fingers anxiously through my hair. Bringing my head back down, I look at Emily.

"She asked last night, asked about Penny's mom. And I had to deflect." I shake my head as I remember the look on her face when I clammed up. "And yet she shared everything with me. Answered every question with pure honesty." Tears are streaming down Emily's face now, her cheeks are red, and her expression looks angry. "We can trust her, Emily. She'd never tell a soul."

"It's not your story to tell. It's mine, and I'm not ready," she says matter-of-factly, her eyes glazing over, which tells me she's done with this conversation.

Anger bubbles up inside of me and threatens to boil over.

I take a deep breath, trying to calm myself before responding. "I know it's your story, but Penny is my daughter. This affects me too!"

Emily doesn't respond. She just looks down at her feet, tears dripping onto the kitchen floor.

"I'll wait two weeks so you can get used to the idea. No longer." I pause and step toward my sister, but she backs away from me. "I've never wanted this to come between us. Don't let this come between us."

"I have to go," she says, still looking at her feet. "Tell Penny goodbye for me."

"Em, wait." She quickly paces back to the guest room to pack her overnight bag. She always spends the night after babysitting, so I've kept the guest room ready for her whenever she wants to use it.

I follow closely behind her. "Don't leave like this, let's talk this out."

"I have nothing more to say," she says, her voice flat.

She pulls her backpack onto her shoulder, then turns to walk out of the guestroom.

I grab her gently by the arm. "Don't drive when you're upset. Please," I beg.

Emily tugs free from my grasp and rushes from the room. She stops in the hallway just long enough to look back at me, her eyes displaying the hurt behind them.

Then she leaves.

Chapter 25
Sophie

It's the morning after my date with Drew and I'm walking into my Wonderful Widows meeting with a smile on my face. I keep trying to stop smiling and play it cool, but the smile seems to be permanently plastered on my face.

I have read Drew's text about a million times. *Good morning, beautiful.* My heart flutters every time I read it. I can practically hear him saying it in his deep, manly voice.

Taking a seat in the circle, I glance around the room and notice everyone has stopped their conversations and is staring at me quizzically.

"What?" I ask, looking around at the group of women.

Gerda smirks. "That's an awfully big smile on your face, young lady."

Bernice pulls her sunglasses out of her handbag and puts them on her face. "There, that's better." She sighs dramatically. "Now I won't be blinded by Sophie's beaming smile."

Ashley giggles. "Care to inform us what——or who——put that smile on your face?"

I feel my chest and face heat. "Well, a lot has happened in the two weeks since I've seen you all."

Lisa claps her hands together. "Okay, spill the tea, girl."

I roll my lips together to contain a girlish giggle, but it escapes, anyway. "I've gone on two dates in the past few weeks."

"With the hot surgeon??" Lisa asks.

I blush again. "Yes, well, my second date was with him. And our date was amazing. And ..." I pause, deciding how many details I should give them.

"And what??" Ashley asks impatiently, literally sitting on the edge of her seat.

"We kissed."

The room erupts in claps, and squeals like we're all a bunch of middle schoolers.

Bernice waves her hands and shushes the ladies. "Quiet down. We need more details here. Was it like a peck?"

Slowly, I shake my head from side to side. "No. It was more like he'd been waiting to kiss me for a thousand years and finally found the right moment."

A collective swoon fills the small room.

Gerda smiles. "Sounds like a pretty amazing date. How are you feeling, emotionally?"

I ponder her question for a few seconds before answering. "Fantastic, actually. I don't feel guilty at all. I feel lighter, happier than I have in a long time." I swallow a lump in my throat. "But it was only one date. Who knows what will happen."

"I hope it continues to go well. It's wonderful to see you so happy!" Bernice says with a sweet smile. "But didn't you say you had two dates?"

"Ugh, yes. The first one nearly convinced me I shouldn't even bother dating. My parents sprung a blind date on me, and I humored them by going," I say. "I figured it might be good for me to just rip the band aid off and go on a date. The guy was super stuffy though." I roll my eyes and the girls laugh.

"Anyway, enough about me. Ashley, how are your wedding plans coming?"

Ashley grins. "Great!" She grabs a stack of envelopes from her backpack. "I brought an invitation for you all." She stands from her chair and passes them out. "Sorry it's so last minute, but our engagement was pretty short."

I open the envelope and slide out a white invitation with gold foiled letters. Her wedding is in one week. I wonder if Drew would go with me? I think he's on-call next weekend though. And maybe he's one of those guys who hates going to weddings.

Bernice slides her arm around her sister. "We wouldn't miss it for the world!"

"I'll be there unless Drew gets called into work and I need to watch Penny," I say. "Your invitations are lovely! I'm so happy for you."

"Thank you! And please bring Drew as your date if you'd like! You're all welcome to bring a plus one." Ashley is beaming with excitement as she speaks. The joy on her face is contagious. If I wasn't already in a really good mood, Ashley's smile would be enough to put me in one.

"Can my four-year-old be my date?" Evie asks.

"Of course! I'd love to meet your adorable son, Evie," Ashley answers, then pats Evie's shoulder.

Lisa smirks. "How about cats?"

"Animals are welcome too." Ashley winks at Lisa.

We all chuckle.

Chapter 26

Drew

Between my sister's silent treatment and the fact that Sophie has been busy all weekend, I'm feeling down. Is it pathetic that I miss her after only two days? Probably.

I heave a heavy sigh as I load the last of the dishes into the dishwasher and turn it on.

Penny runs into the kitchen and looks up at me, her hands on her hips. "Okay, you've been sad all day." I frown, not realizing I'd been so bad at hiding my downcast mood. "I say we go to Whole Foods. Whole Foods always makes you happy."

A chuckle escapes from my throat. I kneel so Penny and I are at eye level. "Sorry I've been moody. Get your shoes on and we'll head out."

She smiles and places both of her small hands on my cheeks, then kisses the tip of my nose. Before she can see the wetness forming in my eyes, she scampers off in search of shoes.

This little girl has brought so much joy into my life. Some days I feel like she's taken care of me just as much as I've taken care of her.

Thirty minutes later, we're browsing the deliciously healthy aisles at Whole Foods. I am a sucker for a fancy grocery store, probably because I like when things are done well. And Whole Foods' marketing and store setup is genius. Even the smell in here makes you feel healthier.

Or perhaps I just enjoy overpriced salsa.

Penny and I load the cart with our usual healthy, organic items. We have lots of fruits and veggies, hummus, protein powder, bacon, and then there's candy and caramel macchiato creamer thrown on top. I'm on call next weekend, and I didn't want Sophie to have to bring her own creamer upstairs if I get called in.

Although I find it adorable to see her with her creamer in hand when I get called in on Saturday or Sunday mornings.

We round the corner into the next aisle and I hear Penny gasp before she gleefully runs down the aisle toward none other than Ted and Diane Windell.

"Penny! How are you?" Diane asks as she uses her hand to smooth the top of Penny's messy hair.

"Great! Daddy loves this place." She holds her arms out at her sides, gesturing to the entirety of Whole Foods.

I smile as I wheel my shopping cart down to meet them.

Ted laughs. "So does Mrs. Windell. But then again, she loves anything that's expensive," he says with a roll of his eyes.

Diane playfully swats at his arm. "Oh, you stop that! You know how frugal I am!"

Diane turns her attention to Penny and Ted looks at me with one eyebrow raised, almost as if to say, "she's definitely not frugal."

"So what are you two up to on this lovely Sunday evening?" Diane asks, looking between me and Penny.

"Just getting some shopping done for the week," I reply.

"I didn't peg you for a man who likes caramel macchiato creamer … or Sophie's favorite candy," she says as she pins me with a direct stare.

"Ha. I'm not, really." I laugh nervously. "I'm on call next weekend. I figured I'd pick up a few things for Soph in case she needs to watch Penny for me."

She gives me a tight smile. "Right." Her facial expressions tells me she's unconvinced.

A few seconds pass and she's still staring me down. I change the subject, "So ... what are you two up to?"

"We're on a date. Isn't it obvious?" Ted says flatly.

"So grouchy." Diane shakes her head. "We're grabbing some charcuterie supplies then going on a picnic."

"Yes, because apparently eating outdoors is romantic." Ted smiles endearingly at his wife.

"Exactly." She smiles back before linking her arm through his.

It's nice to see them getting along and being affectionate. Until a few years ago, I was pretty sure they hated each other by the way they acted toward one another.

I smile fondly at them. "Well, we won't keep you. Enjoy your date."

"Alright, see you this weekend for the Labor Day BBQ!" Ted yells as he and Diane walk away.

"See you then!" I yell back.

Monday evening I head home from work, my stomach flips at the realization I finally get to see Sophie again. Just being near her lightens my mood. Coming home to her every evening after work never gets old.

I pull into the garage, and my heart is pounding in anticipation. Three days and I'm acting like I've been stranded in the Sahara Desert without water.

Opening the garage door, I enter the kitchen and see her standing at the kitchen counter, slicing potatoes. She has the air fryer preheating, good girl. She thinks she's a terrible cook, but she learns quickly.

I tiptoe through the kitchen to peek into the living room. The girls aren't in here. They must be playing in Penny's bedroom. Turning back around, I clear my throat so I don't scare Sophie. She *is* holding a knife, after all.

She looks over her shoulder, and a smile overtakes her entire face. I put my index finger over my lips, gesturing for her to be quiet.

"What are you doing?" she whispers.

I take two long strides towards her and spin her to face me. She gives me a coy smile and I remove the knife from her hands, making her giggle. Then I lean in and kiss her softly. My hands go around her waist, pulling her closer.

She melts into me with a happy sigh. Her arms go around my neck as she kisses me back for a few seconds before breaking off the kiss. She backs away, but has a smirk on her face.

"Drew!" She whispers. "The girls could have walked in!"

I groan. "I know, I know. But I've been thinking about doing that for three days and couldn't wait any longer."

She pats my chest and shakes her head. "You're incorrigible."

Realizing her hand is still on my chest, I grin at her. She looks from my eyes to her hand resting on my pec. Her cheeks turn bright red and she whips her hand away.

I waggle my eyebrows. "You like my muscles, huh?"

Her jaw drops. "Someone is awfully vain." She lifts her chin up haughtily.

Moving in, I place my hands back on her waist and tickle her sides. She squirms and giggles. Sophie is ticklish. I didn't realize that before now. I'm intrigued. I want to find out every little thing about this woman.

The girls rush into the kitchen and storm into us. "Tickle fight!" they yell just before using their tiny hands to tickle me and Sophie.

Their small hands don't phase me at all, but I pretend they do and chortle with laughter.

I straighten up and chase after them both with my fingers wiggling in front of me. "Tickle monster!"

They squeal as they attempt to run away from me toward Penny's room. But I grab them both, one in each arm and stride back to the couch and throw them both down onto it and tickle them.

"Daddy!" Penny giggles so hard she can barely talk. "Stop!"

I stop and let them catch their breath. Samantha grins up at me. "Daddy is the tickle monster," she says in her sweet little voice, then stands up and hugs me.

My eyes fly wide open. "You mean, Drew? Mr. Drew is the tickle monster." I ask playfully, sweeping her blonde curls out of her eyes.

"No ... Daddy." She hugs me tighter.

I turn my head to glance back at Sophie. Her face is blank as she listens from the kitchen. I have no idea what to do. I stand there slack jawed and as still as a statue.

"What's for dinner? I'm hungry!" Penny asks, saving me from responding.

I clear my throat. "Sophie is getting dinner ready, sweetheart."

"Okay, we're going to play in the backyard." Penny takes Samantha's hand and leads her to the French doors. She opens one and they run hand in hand toward the play structure in the backyard.

I hesitate before walking over to Sophie. Her hands are shaking slightly as she fusses over the potatoes, obviously rattled by Samantha calling me daddy.

Smoothing my hand down her arm, I try to soothe her. All I want to do is take away all of this woman's worries, all of her hurt. I want to carry all the difficult things for Sophie and let her experience only joy and happiness.

"Hey, talk to me."

She stands still and grips the counter top, lowering her head between her arms.

Taking a deep breath, she glances back up at me. "Sorry, I just wasn't expecting that. For her to call you that. It took me by surprise."

"I know. It surprised me too. I didn't know what to say. I didn't want to upset her."

"I think we should keep our relationship just between the two of us, Drew. It's so new, we need to be careful in front of them. And my family. I just don't want to deal with the drama yet, you know?" Her voice is laced with worry.

Leaning back against the counter top, I respond, "Whatever you want Soph. You set the pace. I want you to feel comfortable and I definitely don't want to add stress to your life."

I know my feelings are progressing faster than hers, and that's okay. She hasn't dated at all since losing her husband—that I know of. I'll move this along at a snail's pace as long as I get to be with her.

With an aching gentleness, she places her hand on my shoulder. Her soft touch soothing my entire body, easing my fears.

"You're not adding stress to my life, Drew," she says, looking at me with her big blue eyes so tenderly it makes my heart leap. "You've done nothing but bring me joy. I just want to enjoy this for a little while. And I have no idea how my parents will react."

I nod, bringing my hand up to cover hers. "I get it." I smile. "When can we go out again?"

"Actually, I need a date for a wedding this Saturday." She grins. "I know you're on call, but if you don't get called in, it would mean a lot if you came with me."

"Of course. I'd love to go." I stand and go to the cabinet and pull out some plates for dinner. "Whose wedding is it?"

She pulls the silverware drawer out and grabs some forks. "A friend from my Wonderful Widows group, her name is Angela." We walk over to the table and set the places for dinner. "I may have told them about you ... They're excited to meet you."

"Oh, really? Did you tell them about my muscles?" I hold both arms up and flex them through my dress shirt.

She wrinkles her nose and crosses her arms. "You're ridiculous." But she can't hide her smile.

I laugh. "Now I really hope I don't get called in. I want to meet these ladies."

The air fryer beeps from the kitchen.

"Alright, dinner's ready," Sophie says before opening the back door and calling the girls in.

A feeling of warmth passes over me as I picture us being a family, coming home to Sophie and the girls each night. Setting the table, eating dinner together.

I've never wanted anything so badly.

Chapter 27
Sophie

Friday, my students are at lunch and I'm relishing my quiet classroom. On Fridays, my friends Mallory and Josie come and eat lunch with me. It's the only day none of us have lunch duty and we take full advantage of it.

Mallory walks through my door with our Chipotle order in hand. Her blonde hair trails down her back in a long braid.

"You're like the blonde Katniss Everdeen, taking care of us by bringing the food," I say with a grin.

Josie trails behind her carrying the drinks, her wild curly hair looking especially untamed on this windy Kansas day. "Yeah, except she hunts with her debit card instead of a bow."

Mallory rolls her eyes. "Please, if I was Katniss, I would've 100 percent chosen Gale over Peeta."

My jaw drops, and Josie looks offended.

"No way, she was meant to be with Peeta!" Josie says with conviction, bringing her hand to her chest.

Margaret, who works at the front desk of the school, peeks her head into my classroom. She has a huge smile on her face when she sees me. "Oh good! You're here." She waltzes in holding a gigantic floral arrangement.

There's a plethora of what appears to be every different yellow colored flower imaginable. It's a bright and cheery bouquet. It instantly fills my classroom with a delicious scent.

"This was delivered for you." Margaret grins at me as she sets the arrangement on my desk, then turns to leave the room.

As soon as the door closes, Josie and Mallory nearly pounce on me. "Oh my gosh! Who are they from?!" Mallory is basically yelling in my ear.

I wince. "I haven't had a chance to even look at the card!" I try to act like I have no idea who they could be from.

Josie places a hand on her hip. She's giving me a look that tells me she sees right through my facade.

"Let's read the card then." She raises her chin like she's challenging me.

I swallow slowly, my heart beating faster by the second. I'm hoping he didn't sign his name and I don't have to tell them about Drew and me just yet. We've had the most perfect week. Every night, we put the girls to bed and wait for them to fall asleep. Then I come back upstairs—baby monitor in hand—and we sit on his sofa and talk for hours. We've talked about every subject possible. He's told me about his parents and what it was like for him and Emily after losing them. I told him about Sam and all the hiking we did in North Carolina. We've talked about the future, and what it could look like. We've dreamed together, gotten to know each other. And in just a week. It feels unreal how much closer I feel to him after just one week.

And in between those conversations, there was a fair amount of kissing ... but we tried to keep it at a minimum. I just can't help it. Kissing Drew transports me into some kind of magic dream land where anything is possible. Where there's no sadness. Only happiness. The stress of real life melts away a little with every kiss, and I can't seem to get enough.

Slowly, I pull the small card from the bouquet and open it up. Mallory and Josie look at me wide-eyed.

Hey Beautiful,

The color yellow always makes me think of you. Everything about you exudes joy and happiness, despite all that you've been through.

Thank you for one of the best weeks I've ever had.
Yours,
Mr. Muscles

"Hmm." I shrug and tuck the card into my pocket. "They're from my dad. That was sweet of him."

"Yeah, right! Let me see that card!" Josie dives and grabs the card from the large pocket on the side of my pink cardigan.

Mallory runs to her side as they read the card together. "That's really strange that your dad signs cards from, 'Mr. Muscles.'"

I nod. "Yes, he's a very strange man."

"Sophie Miller! You're holding out on us and we know it!" Mallory all but squeals. "Pleeeeaaaase tell us."

"Who is Mr. Muscles? I have to know," Josie asks, grabbing me by the shoulders and giving me a gentle shake.

Mallory's jaw drops and her eyes go wide like she just had an epiphany. "It's your landlord! Isn't it? The smoking hot one."

I can feel my cheeks heat, and even my ears feel warm.

"It is, you can tell by her blush." Josie grins.

Mallory rubs the side of my arm, her eyes fill with empathy. "We shouldn't have been so nosy if you weren't ready to say anything. I'm sorry. We just got excited for you."

Josie hugs me. "Yeah, sorry, Soph. We're just living vicariously through you."

Exhaling a ragged breath, I hug Josie back.

"It's okay. We were just hoping to keep it between us for a bit longer. I'm not quite ready to tell my family since they all know Drew. They'll be all up in our business in an instant."

Mallory smiles, her expression gentle. "That's understandable. We won't tell a soul."

Josie slides her thumb and forefinger along her mouth like she's zipping it shut.

"So, since we've already been nosy ... why was it the greatest week of his life?" Mallory asks with a wink.

A dreamy sigh escapes from my mouth before I can stop it. "We've just stayed up late every night talking after the girls go to bed."

"Talking ... or *talking*." Josie waggles her eyebrows.

"Just talking." I roll my eyes with a laugh. "I feel like we've gotten to know each other so well in just a week. It's such a unique situation. We were barely even friends at first, just seeing each other in the mundane everyday life. And somewhere amidst the mundane, things began seeming not mundane at all. Every glance, every brush of the hands, every time he helped Samantha with something. I began to fall for him."

Mallory and Josie take a seat in the small chairs made for children right in front of my desk, their elbows resting on their knees, and their hands holding their faces. Their eyes are glossy and they look like they could fall out of their chairs at any second as they swoon.

"Oh, Sophie." Josie sighs. "That sounds so romantic."

"It really does. I need a Drew." Mallory smiles up at the ceiling, like she's picturing her own knight in shining armor. "Not your Drew, obviously. But my own."

"I knew what you meant." I smirk.

We continue to chat and eat our lunches quickly before the kids come back. Just as the girls are leaving, Headmaster Williams knocks on the door frame. She says hello to Josie and Mallory, and I give them a little wave as they leave.

Headmaster Williams is a stately woman, probably in her mid-fifties. She's an intimidating height, easily five inches taller than me, and that's without her heels on. She has friendly, brown eyes, but when she's getting down to business, they turn steely. And you do not want to be under her steely gaze.

Thankfully, her gaze is kind at the moment, and her shoulders relaxed. She's always wearing a tailored blazer with a button-up shirt underneath with trousers or a pencil skirt. All of her blazers are emblazoned with our school logo on the lapel. When she walks in the room, everyone sits up a little straighter, even those who know her well. When someone said women can do anything a man can do, and they can do it in heels? This was the woman they were talking about.

"Headmaster Williams." I smile and gesture for her to come into my classroom. Not that she needs an invitation. "To what do I owe the pleasure?"

She smiles back politely as she strides into the room with her long legs. "Thank you, Ms. Miller. Oh!" She spies my flowers on my desk and grins. "Those are gorgeous!"

I blush. "Thank you."

She doesn't ask questions about the bouquet of bright yellow blooms. Thankfully, she's too busy to be nosy. I'm going to have to chat with Drew, aka Mr. Muscles, about sending extravagant gifts to me at work. I'm already cringing at the comments I'll inevitably have to field from my students.

She smiles again before getting straight into business. "I just wanted to stop by and follow up on your student, Peter Vanderven. How are things with his behavior? And have you had any more issues with his father?"

"Actually, Peter has been doing much better. His attitude towards completing his work isn't stellar, but as far as I can tell, he's no longer copying his classmate's work."

She secures her hands behind her back and stands up straight as she nods. She has the posture of a soldier. I straighten my spine, absently trying to emulate her perfect posture.

"And I haven't had any more interactions with his father since that day we previously spoke about."

"Good, good," she says in a clipped tone. "I had a meeting with him soon after that and told him we will not tolerate bullying from him *or* his son. I'm happy to hear he took our conversation seriously."

My students burst through the door as they begin haphazardly dashing to their desks. As soon as they notice Headmaster Williams standing next to me near my desk, their eyes go wide and they slow their strides and continue single file to their desks. More quietly than I even knew they were capable of.

When they're all seated, they greet our guest. "Good afternoon, Headmaster Williams."

"Good afternoon, children." She nods her head, seeming pleased with their respectful greeting. She turns her gaze back to me. "Ms. Miller, I'll leave you to your students. And enjoy your weekend." She takes one last look at the flowers, then winks.

My eyebrows shoot up before I school my features. "Um, thank you. You as well."

She glides out of my class without another word.

And for the rest of the day, my students take guesses as to who sent me the giant flower arrangement.

Chapter 28

Drew

Saturday evening is finally here, which means I get to go on another date with Sophie. I've been antsy all day that I might be called into work, but I haven't. Usually when I'm called in I get a call well before five p.m., so I should be good to go. But just in case, I pack a pair of scrubs to leave in the Bronco.

On Saturdays, Ted and Diane usually watch Samantha for Sophie. She asked them to keep her overnight so she can attend her friend's wedding this evening and they agreed. She just left out the part that I'm her date to said wedding.

I texted Emily a few days ago asking if she'd watch Penny for me tonight, and she responded with nothing but a "yes." That was the only word she's spoken—er, texted—since she abruptly walked out of my house last weekend. I'm hoping this means she's coming around to the idea of me coming clean to Sophie. Because this secret has eaten away at me for seven years. And the longer I wait to tell Sophie, the harder it will be.

Sophie said the wedding is a casual outdoor event, taking place in the botanical gardens here in Wichita. I glance at myself in the mirror, taking in my tailored black trousers, matching vest, and white button up dress shirt underneath, completed with my oxford dress shoes and a green plaid tie.

Hopefully, this isn't over-the-top. This is probably the fanciest outfit I own, aside from the tux I have for formal occasions.

But Sophie makes me want to go all out. To give her my very best.

After a quick spray of the cologne Sophie adores, I stride out to the living room at the same time Emily comes in the front door.

We stand there in silence for a few seconds. She's looking everywhere but at me.

I swallow the lump in my throat. "Em, thanks for coming. I —"

She cuts me off. "No, Drew. Don't." Shaking her head, she continues. "I'm not ready to talk about it, okay?"

"Okay." My voice comes out raspy, my throat feels thick with emotion. "Thanks for watching Penny."

"You know I'll always be here for you and Pen. No matter what," she says as she finally meets my gaze. She looks tired, with dark shadows under her eyes. It looks like she hasn't been sleeping.

Penny skips down the hallway, and her entire face lights up when she sees her aunt.

"Aunt Em!" She runs over and Emily kneels down to embrace her.

I smile as I watch their interaction, noticing for the millionth time how much they look alike.

"I'm going to head out." I smile, and Penny pulls away from Emily just long enough to hug me around the legs. "Love you, sweetheart. Be good for Em."

"I will!"

One side of Emily's mouth pulls up in a smile. "You look pretty snazzy."

Penny nods "Yeah, Daddy! You look like a prince."

I shrug like it's not a big deal. "People have to dress up for weddings."

I told Penny I was going to a friend's wedding, but not that I was going as Sophie's plus one. We've managed to keep our relationship platonic in front of the girls, giving our relationship the time it needs to grow before bringing the girls in on it. I don't see any reason why Sophie and I would ever part ways. But if we did, we wouldn't want it to affect the girls. Penny would be devastated if Sophie was no longer in our lives. Almost as devastated as I would be.

With a wave, I go out the garage door and back my Bronco out of the driveway. Once I turn the corner and know I'm out of sight of my living room windows, I park and walk over toward the entrance to Sophie's apartment.

My entire body feels rattled with nervous energy. Like I haven't seen Sophie in weeks when in reality we watched a movie on my sofa after the girls fell asleep last night.

I knock on her door then smooth my hands down my vest, making sure I look alright. She opens the door with a bright smile and my breath leaves my lungs. My eyes widen, my jaw drops. I'm speechless. Like that cartoon wolf that goes "AOOOGAH!"

She stands there and I drink her in. Starting at her toes, then slowly dragging my eyes back up to her face. She's wearing strappy nude stilettos and a silky cocktail dress in a color that reminds me of rust. If rust were really freaking sexy.

There's a small pendant necklace around her neck with a pale white stone resting right between her collarbones. Her hair is piled up one top of her head and has been curled into loose waves. She left a few wispy strands of blonde hair dancing around her face and dusting the skin by her neck. Her lips are shiny, plump, and inviting and her eye makeup is dark and smoky.

"Wow," is all I can say once I finally remember how to speak.

She giggles. "You like it?"

She glances down at her outfit and then does a little spin. She's adorable *and* sexy. Adorably sexy. Apparently that's a thing.

"Sophie, you're gorgeous."

She takes a step closer to me. "You look pretty handsome yourself, Mr. Muscles," she says, leaning in for a kiss.

Closing the distance, I press my lips to hers. She tries to step back after giving me a quick peck, but I sweep my arm around her waist and pull her into me.

"Drew!" She throws her head back and laughs. Which makes me want to kiss her neck. "We're going to be late," she says, playfully swatting at my chest.

I groan. "Okay, fine." I remove my arm from her waist and thread our fingers together instead.

We walk to the Bronco hand in hand, smiling at each other like fools.

When we walk into the botanical gardens, there's acoustic guitar music playing in the background and twinkle lights draped in the trees and bushes. There are only about fifty guests here, if I had to guess. It's twilight, and the setting is incredibly romantic.

Sophie's face lights up when she spots two older ladies standing near the chairs that have been set up for the wedding guests.

Taking my hand, she pulls me toward them. They both grin when they spot us, but not in a sweet grandma-like way; more like two Cheshire Cats who are up to no good.

"Oh my goodness, is this the hot surgeon?" one of them asks Sophie and then shoots me an ornery wink.

Sophie's cheeks pinken. "You two behave yourselves!" She glances at me and tightens her grip on my hand. "This is Drew."

I reach my free hand out to shake their hands, but one pulls me into a big hug and the other follows suit.

"We're huggers!" The slightly taller one says before turning to Sophie and quietly stating, "Wow, you're right. Good muscles on this one."

I think it was meant to be a whisper, but was definitely loud enough for me to hear. I pretend to be oblivious to the comment, but Sophie's face continues getting redder by the second. Sophie raises her eyebrows at the women, as if silently pleading them to play it cool.

She clears her throat. "Drew, this is Bernice and Gerda. They're sisters and they started Wonderful Widows together."

"Pleasure meeting you both." I nod my head at them and then slip my arm around Sophie's waist. The silky fabric of her dress is calling to my fingertips like catnip to a cat. My hands can't seem to stop reaching out for her.

Bernice and Gerda's eyes trail down to my hand on Sophie's waist and they give each other a look. Like they're speaking to each other telepathically. I wish I knew what they were communicating to one another.

"Ashley saved a row for us. Lisa and Evie are already seated." Bernice points to a row where two women sit chatting amiably.

The music changes and a man steps under the floral canopy at the front of the ceremony area. Everyone seems to take that as a signal that the ceremony is about to start and finds a seat. We follow the sisters to the seats they saved for us, and they introduce me to Evie and her son and also a woman named Lisa.

The ladies hug Sophie and they all look genuinely thrilled to see each other. There's a closeness between the five of them that makes it seem like they've known each other all their lives.

I can see the joy exuding from Sophie by being with them, and it's then that I realize this group of widows is probably the entire reason Sophie's heart has healed enough to allow me inside. They've really helped her move forward and process her grief.

The feeling of gratefulness to these ladies brings a sudden bout of fresh tears to my eyes. I blink several times and gulp down the lump in my throat, trying to keep the tears down.

Sophie takes her seat next to me and puts her hand on my knee. I cover her slender hand with mine and she smiles up at me. "Aw, Drew. Are you crying?"

I sniff. "Probably just allergies."

We both know it's a lie. I kiss her temple and bring my free hand around her shoulders, slowly rubbing circles with my thumb on her bare skin. Her gorgeous skin feels even softer and silkier than her dress.

"It's okay," she whispers, laying her head against my shoulder for a moment. "Weddings make me cry, too."

Smiling against her temple, I pull her into me, just a little tighter.

After the bride and groom's parents are seated, the guitarist strums Adele's, "Make You Feel My Love."

Sophie leans in to whisper, "Sam used to play this song, it was one of his favorites."

I swivel my head to look at her and realize the memory makes her happy. Not sad. I smile at her, remembering back when I could finally think of my parents with happiness and not in mourning. My heart felt so much lighter when their memories brought me joy instead of grief.

The officiant at the front gestures for the audience to rise, and we turn to see a bride at the opposite end of the aisle. The groom has taken his place at the front and he's a wreck. The man has tears streaming down his face as he looks at his bride. She has a little girl on one side, and a little boy on the other.

The three of them walk down the aisle together. The bride is all smiles as she holds the gaze of her tearful groom.

Sophie sniffles next to me and whispers, "Those are her children walking her down the aisle. So sweet."

She pulls a tissue from her clutch and dabs at her eyes. I don't think there's a dry eye in the entire botanical garden at this point. Even a few of the tears I've been holding back break free. Sophie hands me one of her tissues.

This is just such a vivid picture of what me and Sophie's wedding would be like. Joining together as a family. It's absolutely beautiful and breathtaking.

If I was ever uncertain where I wanted my relationship with Sophie to go, this would've solidified it. But I was never uncertain.

The ceremony continues and I can't seem to pry my eyes away from the couple standing before us. They're probably around my age, and the ceremony is simple. The bride is wearing a dress that's fairly casual, and she doesn't even have a bouquet. The groom is wearing dark jeans and a button-up shirt tucked in. There's nothing fancy or over-the-top, just two people whose love is palpable. And the beauty of these four becoming a family.

The officiate announces it's time for the groom to kiss his bride, and the groom dips her back and kisses her. The kids jump up and down, cheering along with the rest of the crowd. The guitarist starts playing again, an upbeat song that I don't recognize. The couple walks down the aisle together, the kids trailing right behind them.

All four of them look incredibly happy.

Chapter 29
Sophie

Ashley and Mike's wedding ceremony was wonderful. Not because it was fancy or expensive— it was actually quite simple—but because it was so sweet to see their love for each other and how much Ashley's children adore Mike.

Drew walks by my side as we make our way over to the small reception area. We walk hand in hand, enjoying the lovely September evening and the comfortable silence that passes between us.

Watching Mike and Ashley—and her children—made me hopeful that Drew and I might get married someday. I never thought I'd be in a place emotionally to even desire getting married again. My grief after losing Sam was so crushing, I didn't think I'd ever feel like myself again. But slowly, over time, I've grown through it. I might be a different woman now than the barely twenty-one-year-old girl Sam married so many years ago. But this new, mature woman I've grown into is worthy of love. And I have so much love to give.

I want to give that love to Drew—and Penny—and any other children we could have. For the first time, I can picture a new life, a new family, a new love. For me *and* Samantha. Watching Drew interact with her always makes my heart swell. It's different from watching my dad and brothers with her.

There's a new hope blooming in my heart that she could grow up with a daddy.

A cool breeze brings out goosebumps along my arms. Drew glances over and we make eye contact. A shiver runs through me.

"Soph, you must be freezing in that dress. I don't even have a jacket to offer you." His brow furrows. He looks adorable when he's unnecessarily concerned. But it's also kind of nice to be fussed over.

"I'll be fine. I probably should've grabbed a sweater." I snuggle into his side as we continue walking.

We enter the outdoor reception area and it's just as pretty as the ceremony. There are white chairs in circles for the guests and a small wedding cake at a round table surrounded by gifts from the guests. The botanical gardens are beautiful, so they really didn't need to add a bunch of decorations to distract from that. I love the simplicity of it all.

We wait in line with the other guests to congratulate the couple. Bernice and Gerda are in front of us, and Lisa and Evie, as well as her adorable little boy, are in line behind us.

Drew pulls his phone out of his pocket and glances through the messages.

"Nothing from the hospital." He sighs with relief. It's sweet he wanted to come with me tonight so badly. He shows me his phone screen. "But Emily sent me this."

His shoulders shake as he laughs. I take his phone and look at the photo. It's a picture of Penny and Emily covered in black spots.

"What in the world?" I squint my eyes to read the text under the photo.

Emily: Penny said she and Samantha like to use washable markers and make themselves into different animals... She was bummed Samantha isn't here to play with and practically made me choose an animal. So, we're dalmatians.

I can't contain the giggle that comes out of me, which makes Drew laugh even harder.

"Tell her I'm really sorry Samantha is such a terrible influence."

He shakes his head and tucks his phone back into his pocket. "I really hope that the washable marker comes off easily."

"It does. Don't worry. I'd know ... I've washed various animal prints off of Sam probably a dozen times by now." I roll my eyes, but I'm still laughing.

The line has continued moving while we were reading Emily's text and now we've made it to the newlyweds. Ashley is wearing a gauzy dress that falls just a few inches above her knees. The fabric blows in the breeze, creating an angelic effect. The top has spaghetti straps, showing off her slim shoulders and neck. Her hair is down in loose curls. She looks effortlessly stunning.

"Ashley! You look beautiful. Congratulations." I pull her into a hug.

We release each other and she loops her arm through her husband's. "Sophie, this is Mike. Mike, this is Sophie."

Mike shakes my hand with a grin. He looks just as happy as Ashley. They make a handsome couple.

"So nice to meet you." I grab Drew's hand and bring him closer to us. "This is Drew. Drew, this is Mike and Ashley."

Ashley shakes Drew's hand and looks from me to him and then back again, like she's assessing us as a couple. "We've heard so much about you at Wonderful Widow's, it's great to meet you."

"Great to meet you both as well. Your wedding was lovely," he says with a smile.

"Oh, you're so sweet. Thank you," Ashley replies.

Drew takes my hand and we start to walk away. Ashley taps my shoulder as I'm leaving. I turn just in time to see her silently mouth, "Wow, he's handsome!"

I nod in agreement, and she winks at me.

Drew is walking me to my apartment door after an evening of laughing with friends, eating wedding cake, and dancing beneath the twinkle lights. I feel like I'm in a dream. And I don't want to wake up. My chest feels tight at the thought of saying goodnight to Drew and going our separate ways tonight. I always feel a little bummed out when we say goodnight to each other, but tonight it feels heavier.

Watching Mike and Ashley together filled me with longing that, someday, maybe that could be me and Drew. Drew lingers at my door, looking down at our joined hands. His hesitation to say goodbye makes me wonder if he's feeling the same heaviness I am.

Neither of us makes a move to open the door or to say anything. We just enjoy the warmth of our hands linked together. Drew leans against the door frame with a sigh.

"I don't really want to say goodnight. Every time I say goodnight to you it gets harder." One side of his mouth pulls up into a smile, but his eyes look a little sad.

"I feel the same way."

He tucks a strand of hair behind my ear, but instead of pulling his hand away, he slowly brushes his finger down my ear and the side of my neck. I lean into his caress.

He pulls his hand away, and his head falls back against the door frame. "This is agonizing."

I giggle at how dramatic he's being.

"I should probably let you know that I'm serious about you, Soph. I plan to marry you someday. I'll wait until you're ready, but it's going to happen. And you're going to sleep in my bed every night." His eyes darken as he says it.

He's completely serious. There's not even a hint of humor in his expression.

I whisper, "Sounds good to me... I'm not going to argue with you." It comes out in a rasp.

He slides one hand around my waist and pulls me close. His other hand goes to my jaw, his thumb sliding along the edge.

"I'm going to kiss you goodnight, and then I'm going to be a gentleman and walk away."

He kisses me and my hands go to his chest and clutch his shirt, trying to pull him closer. He angles his head to the side to lean into my lips, then pulls back.

"Goodnight, Sophie."

I gulp, still reeling from his kiss and his intense gaze. "Goodnight."

I wake up early; the sun is barely up. The first thing I do is check my phone. Madden texted last night that Odette was in labor. Their first was born pretty quickly; they barely made it to the hospital, so I'm anticipating my new nephew is already here. Sure enough, there's a text from my brother.

Madden: Bradford Theodore Windell is here! 21 inches long and 8 lbs, 1oz. He's healthy and Odette is doing great. She's a rockstar as usual. :-)

I grin as I read his message and type out a reply.

Sophie: Yay! I can't wait to meet my new nephew! Send pics when you can.

I jump out of bed and throw on some bike shorts and a baggy t-shirt. Mom and Dad kept Samantha last night and I'm sure they ended up with my nephew Oliver as well. Odette's parents are in their late-seventies, so they don't normally ask them to watch Oliver overnight.

Grabbing my phone, purse, and keys, I head out the door. After sliding into my car, I check my phone one last time and see Madden sent a photo of little Bradford. He has chubby cheeks and is wrapped in a blue blanket. He has a wisp of blonde hair peeking out from under his little beanie.

I respond quickly before I start the car.

Sophie: Another blondie! You're going to have to have half a dozen babies to get one with red hair.

Madden: Ha. Not even funny. I'm willing to try ONCE more. That's it.

Sophie: *gif of Justin Timberlake doing the shifty eyes*

I glance up and see the sun rising, a brilliant cascade of pinks and yellows. For the first time in a long time, I feel nothing but joy and hope.

Life is good.

Chapter 30

Drew

"Daddy! Wake up!" Penny's voice yells, way too loudly, as she jumps up and down on my bed.

Emily didn't stay the night last night like she usually does. She's distancing herself from me, and it breaks my heart. I never wanted anything to come between me and my sister, but I don't know how to fix this.

Penny jumps off the bed and runs to the window in my room, throwing the curtains open. I throw one arm over my eyes, protecting them from the blaring sunshine.

Grabbing my phone from the nightstand with my free hand, I bring it to my face and see it's already almost 9 a.m. I have several missed messages from Sophie, making me shoot up in bed to a sitting position. Penny notices I'm up and snuggles under the covers right next to me.

I pull up the texts from Sophie and read through them.

Sophie: Thanks for being my wedding date. It was amazing. :-)

Sophie: Odette had her baby late last night, so I'm heading to my parents' to get Samantha. I'll probably stay for the day since they're watching Oliver. But let me know if you get called in and I'll be back in a flash!

The last text is a photo of her newest nephew, Bradford. He's a very cute baby.

Penny makes an "aw" sound next to me. "Oh my goodness, whose baby is that? She's so cute!"

I chuckle. "He's a boy. His name is Bradford, and he's Madden and Odette's new baby."

"I hope I can hold him next time I see them!" Her eyes look excited at the thought.

"We'll have to ask them." I slip my arm around her and pull her into a hug.

With my other hand, I shoot Sophie a reply.

Drew: He's a cutie! Enjoy time with your family. I'll text you if I get called in. And being your wedding date was amazing, so no need to thank me for that. ;-)

The following evening, Penny and I drive over to the Windell's house. They were insistent upon continuing to host a Labor Day BBQ, despite watching their grandson while Madden and Odette are at the hospital.

We ring the Windell's doorbell and Sophie answers the door. Her bright smile is contagious and I can't help but grin right back at her. Her hair is in a high ponytail and she's wearing skinny jeans and some kind of wrap-top that ties at her waist. I definitely don't imagine what it would be like to pull the strings on the tie and watch it unravel. Nope. Perfect gentleman over here.

"Hey you two! I'm so glad you're here." We step inside and she gives us each a hug.

She keeps it short, probably not wanting to seem overly affectionate in case someone in her family walks in. Penny runs off in search of Samantha, leaving Sophie and I in the entryway.

"We brought deviled eggs. Where should I put them?" I ask, holding up the plastic container.

She smirks. "Had to bring some protein, huh?"

I roll my lips together, trying to stay serious. "Well, I've been told certain ladies like my muscles. So I've gotta get enough protein in."

"Is that right? Well, you wouldn't want to disappoint said ladies," she says before reaching for the container.

Her hands brush mine when she takes the container from me, and I wink at her. She giggles and then turns toward the kitchen, presumably to put the deviled eggs with the other food.

I swagger through the house, feeling a little manlier after flirting with Sophie over deviled eggs. What is my life? Two months ago I was totally cool—man-card still intact. Now I'm all amped up over brushing fingers while passing a Tupperware container. Who knew finger brushing could be so exhilarating?

Before heading out to the back patio, I peek into the Windell's former office, now turned into a playroom for their grandchildren. Penny, Sam, and Oliver are busy coloring at the small table in the center of the room. I duck out before they spot me and walk out the back door.

"Drew! My man!" Brooks holds his hand out for a high five as I step onto the patio.

We give each other a high five, then pull each other into a brief one-armed hug while pounding each other on the back. The worldwide greeting between all men.

As I release myself from Brooks' man-hug, I spot David behind him. He gives me a genuine smile. He's looking at me differently than usual. I can't put my finger on the look he has in his eyes, but I want to say it's affection?

Despite the kindness in his eyes, he thrusts his hand forward for a handshake. He's the only Windell that's not a big hugger.

Giving him a firm handshake, I greet him, "Hey, David."

"Drew." He nods his head instead of saying more.

Ted and Diane turn their attention from the large outdoor kitchen to me. "Drew! So glad you made it! Now we're just waiting for our friend, Bradley. He's new in town so we invited him and his son to join us."

"Ugh." Brooks groans before taking a sip of bourbon.

Somewhere in the last sixty seconds, Brooks has managed to get himself a bourbon on the rocks.

"Starting early, huh?" My eyes flick to his glass.

He shrugs. "It's a holiday." He leans toward me and covers his mouth as he whispers, "and also I'm gonna need several of these to be near Dad's new friend. I had the displeasure of playing a round of golf with him and Dad. The guy is a complete tool."

Before I can ask more about that, a tall man with dark hair walks onto the back patio. He has a young boy with him who looks like a miniature of the man beside him. Sophie is following them, her lips set into a terse line.

At first I'm confused by her expression, but then I recognize the man before me. He's the jerk Sophie went on a date with several weeks ago. The one who called me a phlebotomist. My entire body tenses and I clench my jaw. My body goes into protector mode, my head arching to the side to crack my neck of its own volition. My fists clench at my side. I'm all wound up, ready to fight. I breathe in a deep breath through my nose and close my eyes for a second.

Alright, Drew. This is a Labor Day BBQ, not a fight club. Bradley Vanderven is Ted's friend, not a volatile criminal. Calm down, buddy.

"Mom, Dad, you didn't tell me Mr. Vanderven and Peter were coming today." She tries to smile as she says it, but her expression is strained.

Ted smiles at her. "Of course, they're new in town. And the more the merrier! Right?"

"Yes, the more the merrier," she says, smiling between her dad and Bradley. But her eyes are wider than usual, like she's saying HELP ME through her eyeballs. "Peter is in my class at Heartland."

"No way! I didn't realize you were his teacher. What a small world," Ted responds as he fiddles with the grill.

Bradley laughs sardonically. "Yes, Sophie has been keeping Peter in line at school, hasn't she?" He glances at Peter, then his eyes flick to Sophie.

"Peter has been doing great the last few weeks," she says, then looks away.

She seems uncomfortable, but Peter looks thrilled with her praise.

Diane, who's been busy fussing over the food, walks over to join our conversation. "Bradley, has anyone introduced you to Drew yet?" She pats my arm. "You two are around the same age. I bet you would get along great. And Drew is a single dad also!"

"Seems we have a lot in common," Bradley says with a smile, but it looks more like he's baring his teeth. Like an evil cartoon character.

I thrust my hand out in front of him, not wanting to make this any more uncomfortable than it already is. "Great to meet you, Bradley."

He shakes my hand, his grip much tighter than necessary. "Nice meeting you as well, Drew." His nostrils flare as he says my name.

"Drew is a work associate of mine. We've basically adopted him into our family," Ted says with a lighthearted chuckle.

"Ah," Bradley nods, "So that would make you a—"

I cut him off short. "An orthopedic surgeon. Kind of like a phlebotomist, but with a scalpel."

His nostrils flare again, and I wink at him.

Ted laughs, but it sounds stilted. Pretty sure he's picking up the tension between me and Bradley.

"Anyway," Ted clears his throat and gestures toward the grill. "The food is ready! You all can select your steaks from the grill, and the rest of the food is in the kitchen."

"I'll get the kids," Sophie announces before ducking back inside.

Brooks sidles up next to me again. This time, he has a second glass of bourbon and hands it to me. "I'm sensing you want a drink now."

I fill my cheeks with air and slowly blow it out through my mouth before taking a sip. "Thank you."

He raises his glass to me, then spins on his heel and stalks off toward the grill.

A half hour later, we're all seated outside on the patio, with plates full of food. The Windell's have a large, farmhouse-style outdoor table. It's perfect for seating large groups of people like this. Bradley and I sat at opposite ends, obviously not wanting to be near each other.

Sophie didn't sit right next to me, which is probably good. Not sure I could keep my hands to myself if she was that close. But she's sitting across from me. David is next to her and Brooks is next to me. Penny, Samantha and Oliver are seated in the middle of the group. Ted and Diane are next to them, helping their grandkids cut up their meat into small bite-sized pieces.

"So, David. How's the neighbor situation? You guys best friends yet?" Brooks asks before taking a bite of his steak.

David rolls his eyes. "Not even close. The other evening, I opened my windows because there was a nice cool breeze. So there I was, minding my own business in my living room, reading *The Journal of Accountancy*, when I heard a meow."

Sophie giggles. "A meow?"

"Yep. So I glanced over and saw her cat had crawled through my window and was sitting on my dining room table. It scared the shit out of me."

"Language!" Diane scolds from the opposite end of the table.

David grimaces. "Sorry, Mom." Then continues, "But it's not a normal cat. That thing is huge. It looks more like a baby tiger, or a bobcat."

Brooks and Sophie are about to fall out of their seats laughing.

"You're so dramatic, David." Sophie spits out between fits of laughter.

"I'm serious! It's huge!" He holds his hands out about two feet apart. "It's like this big!"

"There's no way." Brooks chuckles. "So what did you do?"

"I opened my front door and tried to shoo him out. But he just sat there with this look on his face like *I* was the one in his space."

Sophie, who has just taken a sip of water, nearly spews it out of her mouth. Brooks and I are trying, unsuccessfully, not to laugh at his story. He seems genuinely upset about his neighbor's cat invading his house.

"So I go over to my neighbor's house, fuming. I rang her doorbell, probably more times than I needed to. And she flings the door open, looking annoyed with *me*. So I tell her to come get her dam—I mean—dang cat."

At this point, the entire table is listening to David's story. Even Bradley Vanderven looks amused, and I've never seen him genuinely smile.

"So she walks over to my house, waltzes inside like she owns the place, grabs her giant cat—who is seriously like half her size. Then walks back to her house. And right before she closed her front door, she *grinned* at me."

The entire table erupts in laughter.

"It's not funny," David mutters.

Brooks raises one eyebrow at him. "You know, there's a fine line between love and hate."

"What's that supposed to mean?" David snaps back.

"I think you and your neighbor secretly have the hots for each other," Brooks says nonchalantly, popping another bite of steak into his mouth.

"That's absurd." David's jaw tightens.

"Next time, just kiss her and see what happens." Brooks shrugs, as if it's no big deal.

"A man should only kiss a woman when he actually *likes* her." David snaps back.

Penny, who I didn't even realize was still listening to the conversation, pipes up, drawing everyone's attention. "My dad must really like Sophie then!" She beams.

Everyone's eyes nearly bug out of their eye sockets as they stare between me and Sophie. She nearly chokes on the bite of steak she has in her mouth.

I laugh nervously and rub the back of my neck, which suddenly feels very hot. "Penny ... what on earth are you talking about, sweetheart?"

Everyone's eyes turn to my daughter, waiting expectantly for her response.

"Every night, I get up from bed to go potty, and you and Sophie are usually on the couch kissing." She shrugs her shoulders innocently.

Sophie's hands come up to cover her face. Brooks looks between us with a very amused twinkle in his eyes. David is wearing a satisfied expression, which isn't what I would've expected. But Ted's face is turning redder by the second. I can practically see the steam coming out of his ears. And there's that terrifying vein in his forehead again ... Diane just sits there with her mouth slightly agape.

Bradley Vanderven leans over so he can make direct eye contact with me. "So, if Ted and Diane adopted you into their family, wouldn't that be like kissing your sister, Drew?" He smiles, obviously enjoying my discomfort way too much.

"Drew. Sophie. Kitchen. Now," Ted says as he rises from his seat and walks through the French doors into the house. Diane follows him.

I feel like a kid about to be grounded for eating cookies before dinner. It's been a long time since a parent has been angry with me, and it feels even worse than I can remember.

Sophie and I stand and follow them inside. I take her hand in mine and give it a squeeze. I'm hoping it will ease her mind and let her know we're in this together.

We walk into the kitchen and stand opposite of Ted and Diane in the center of the large open space.

"Does one of you care to explain what is going on here?" He looks at our entwined hands and crosses his arms.

"Calm down, Ted. Did you really not see this coming?" Diane shakes her head.

Sophie releases my hand and absently rubs the side of her arm. "Me and Drew started seeing each other officially a few weeks ago. We were going to tell you, but we've barely been on two dates. We weren't in a hurry to announce it to the world."

Ted is now looking at his feet. He shakes his head. "Drew, I trusted you."

Diane smacks his arm. "Would you stop!" Her fists rest on her hips as she looks at him. "Have you really not noticed the way they look at each other? Or how Drew always jumps in to help her with Samantha? Or how about how he was buying all of her favorite grocery items at Whole Foods?"

"Or how about how happy Sophie has been lately?" David's voice comes from behind us, making us jump.

Ted rubs his temples with his thumb and index fingers.

"They're obviously smitten with each other. They would've told us when they were ready," Diane adds, seeming perfectly at ease with the prospect.

"I can't believe I didn't notice." Ted looks between us. "Yeah, I guess you have seemed happier, Soph." One side of his mouth pulls up into a hesitant smile.

"I never meant to make you feel deceived, but I wanted to wait to say anything until Sophie was ready. Sophie's feelings are really my only concern here, and our girls, of course," I say as I rub my hand down her spine, trying to help her relax.

She smiles up at me.

"I can respect that." Ted takes a deep breath. "I guess it's all out now, though. You can't hide much from children." He smirks.

David walks forward to stand next to his father. "And, of course, if you hurt Sophie for any reason ..."

"Yeah, I know. You'll kick my ass."

"Language!" Diane yells.

I stand up straight under her glare. "Sorry, ma'am."

Chapter 31
Sophie

That conversation with my parents went much better than I was expecting. I guess we weren't as elusive as we'd thought. Not only has my mom picked up on things, but Penny has seen us on the couch almost every night. How embarrassing.

Although I definitely feel lighter now that it's all out in the open and we don't have to hide anything. And things with Drew are amazing, so why hide our relationship?

Dad was definitely more freaked out than anyone else, but David's input was helpful. I'm going to have to inform Drew later about David finding us asleep on his couch together back when we all got sick.

The family drama proved to be a little much for Bradley Vanderven. He and his son suddenly had somewhere else to be once we all returned to the patio after our kitchen conversation. And I'm definitely not complaining about their early exit. I feel like I can breathe now.

Once everyone has finished their dinner, we all help clean up the mess. The kids run back to the playroom to play, and the adults open a bottle of wine and sit on the patio. You never know what September in the Midwest will do, but this September has been extremely pleasant. None of us are in a hurry to go back indoors. It's actually really nice for Drew and

I's relationship to be out in the open now, especially since everyone seems fine with it. Aside from Dad's initial angry outburst, of course.

Drew sits next to me and keeps our hands intertwined. Every so often, the breeze blows a strand of hair in my face, and Drew brushes it aside.

Amidst all the hubbub, I had completely forgotten that Madden and Odette were stopping by to get Oliver on their way home from the hospital. They walk through the patio doors. Madden is carrying little Bradford in his car seat. The car seat swallows him up and makes him look so tiny.

They both look exhausted, but happy. Obviously excited to show off their new baby. Odette's hair is in braided pigtails and she's wearing her glasses, which mostly hide the dark circles under her eyes. She looks comfortable in a t-shirt and yoga pants. Even Madden is in casual wear, which looks weird since he's normally very put together. But today he's wearing sports shorts and a t-shirt that says, "Today I don't feel like doing anything. Except my wife, I'd do her."

"Madden, what on earth are you wearing?" Mom asks with a disgusted look on her face.

"Mom, I'm so tired. You're lucky I'm even fully dressed at all. I grabbed the first t-shirt in my drawer without even looking at what was on it." He finishes his sentence just before a big yawn takes over his face.

She rolls her eyes. "I'll let it slide this once. Now, let me hold that baby!"

She makes grabbing motions with her hands toward the car seat. Madden and Odette wanted to have privacy at the hospital, like they did when Oliver was born. My parents took Olly to meet his baby brother yesterday, but besides them, none of us have seen him yet.

We all surround my mom as she unbuckles Bradford from his car seat. He has thick blonde hair curling around his nape and forehead and he curls up like a little hedgehog as Mom pulls him out of his car seat.

Everyone in the room makes a collective "aww" sound.

I clutch my heart and move forward to pet his soft baby-hair. "Oh my gosh, he's just so precious."

My mom snuggles him close and Dad sidles up next to her to kiss his new grandson on his chubby cheek. Oliver runs out onto the patio with the girls trailing behind him.

"My baby brudder is here!" He exclaims, putting his hands out to stop the girls from coming any closer. "Don't get your germs on him." He states with his lisp, drawing a laugh from all of us.

"Okay, Mom, you got to hold him, now it's my turn!" I reach for my new nephew and Mom begrudgingly relinquishes her grip on him. I snuggle him into my chest and smell his head. "Oh, he smells so good."

"New baby smell is the best," Odette says as she comes up next to me.

She lays her head on my shoulder to look at her son, but her eyes close the minute she lays her head down. Madden comes up beside her and grasps her shoulders, bringing the weight of her onto himself instead of me.

Drew is on my other side, staring at Bradford with a tender gaze. "I really miss the baby stage," he whispers, his lips brushing against my ear. He kisses me on the cheek without thinking, and Madden's eyes bulge out.

"Um, did I miss something while my wife was giving birth to a tiny human?"

"Oh yeah, Drew and Sophie apparently make out all the time on Drew's couch," Brooks says with a shrug of his shoulders.

Now Odette's eyes fly open. "I'm sorry, what?"

"We do not make out all the time!" Drew whisper-yells. "Only after the girls go to sleep … or, at least, we thought they were asleep. And we're dating, not just making out."

Odette looks up at Madden with a smirk. "You owe me $100."

Madden heaves a heavy sigh. "My wallet is in the car."

My jaw drops. "Wait, you made a bet about this?"

"You two haven't been able to keep your eyes off of each other for two months." Odette smiles, then leans back into Madden and closes her eyes again.

Brooks steps in and gestures for me to hand over the baby. "Alright, it's Uncle Brooks' turn."

I place Bradford gently into his arms. He coos and baby-talks to him. Brooks will make a great dad. Someday. Once he grows up a little.

After a few minutes, Brooks walks over to David. "Okay, Uncle David's turn!" David stiffens and holds his arms out straight like Brooks is handing him a platter of hor d'oeuvres.

"Not like that, you dope! Curve your arms more, pretend he's your neighbor's cat." Brooks scoffs, like he's some kind of baby expert.

"I would *never* touch that monstrosity of an animal," David spits. But he cradles his arm to support Bradford's neck and cuddles him into his chest.

After we've all passed the baby around and gotten in some newborn snuggles, Odette releases a loud yawn. "Alright, I have unmentionable places that are sore and tired and I need to go home and sleep for about thirty hours."

I giggle at her comment. When Odette is well-rested, she would never make a comment about unmentionable places. That just goes to show how delirious she is.

"Alright, sweetheart. Let's get you home," Madden says before placing a kiss on top of her head.

She points at me and Drew, her eyes half-closed. "You two invite us to the wedding, okay?"

Drew takes her comment in stride. "Don't worry, you'll all be invited."

He winks at me. He doesn't seem even remotely phased to be talking so openly about marrying me. He's just standing there grinning like he loves the idea. My stomach does a flip-flop and my heart flutters in my chest. It feels like there are about a million butterflies doing some kind of gymnastics routine inside my body.

I really like the idea of marrying Drew.

The next day, life goes back to normal. School is back in session after a long weekend and Drew is back at work.

At the end of the school day, I'm on pickup duty at the front of the school, making sure each kid gets into the correct car in the pickup line. All the cars are nice, shiny, and new. The parents are all well-coiffed, usually coming from work to pick up their kids. Some have nannies that pick up instead. But every child who attends Heartland Academy is from at least a semi-wealthy family.

Heartland strives for excellence, so the coursework and homework can be grueling. But by the time the students graduate, they're well prepared for college. Watching all the fancy cars pull up and then pull away leaves an ache in my heart. This is such an amazing school, but middle and lower-class families would never be able to send their kids here. We have a few scholarships, which is how my sister-in-law, Odette, attended high school. But I wish we had more available.

Another shiny black SUV pulls up and I open the door so a first grade student can hop inside. "Bye, Ms. Miller!"

"See you tomorrow, Caroline." I smile and close the door and wait for the next vehicle in the line of cars.

As a military family, Sam and I never would have been able to afford to send Samantha here. But there are so many advantages, not only the after-school courses like STEM lab and art classes, but a speech therapist as well.

I wonder if there's more we could do. Perhaps running fundraisers to give us the ability to give more scholarships. Since most of the families associated with Heartland have plenty of money to donate, I wonder why we're not doing more to help the community. It's something I've pondered since starting my job here. When I attended this school as a child, I never even thought about it. But after meeting Sam, he opened my eyes to the way things are for other families and the financial struggles that can leave you with very few options.

Bradley Vanderven's black Mercedes pulls up next. He rolls down the window and gives me a salacious grin.

Peter comes up beside me. "See you tomorrow, Ms. Miller." He gives me a shy smile.

His behavior in class has greatly improved now that he takes me seriously and knows I'm not going to shy away from talking to the headmaster or his father.

"See you tomorrow, Peter." I open the car door for him and he scoots inside.

Bradley slides his designer sunglasses down his aristocratic nose. "Surprised to see you here today, figured you were grounded." He winks.

I inwardly hold back a groan and an eye roll. "Nope, everything is just fine. Thanks for your concern."

I wave before closing the door in his smug face, forgetting he had rolled the window down. It didn't have the dramatic effect I was hoping for. He chuckles, and it sounds cold and fake, unlike Drew's.

I actually feel bad for Peter. His dad is such a twerp.

The girls and I arrive home an hour later. I hustle them both inside and turn a show on for Samantha so I can help Penny get her homework done.

Penny beelines to her room the moment she gets inside. She's always ready to change out of her school uniform and into comfy clothes. While she's changing, I open up her sparkly pink backpack. She has so many key chains attached to it, it jingles when I pick it up. The zipper is way more difficult to slide open with all the flare she's added.

Sliding out her homework folder, I open it up to see what she needs to do this evening. There's a note on top from her teacher, so I read it, assuming it's a note about her homework for tonight.

Dr. Reed,

The office informed me today that they never received Penny's shot records from you prior to school starting. If you could send a copy with her to school tomorrow, I'd appreciate it! The office changed to a new computer system, and some paperwork was lost in the process. My apologies for the inconvenience!

Mr. Kenshaw

I sigh. This happened to a few of my students as well. As a private school, shot records aren't mandatory, but the office prefers to have them on file if the parents don't have an issue with it.

Drew texted an hour ago letting me know he has a surgery that might run long, so he'll be home later than usual. I could probably locate Penny's shot records somewhere around here and make a copy so he doesn't have to worry about it.

Penny runs into the kitchen where I'm standing. She's wearing striped rainbow leggings paired with a bright pink princess shirt. It's sparkly, of course.

"Hey, sweetie, do you know where your daddy might keep important paperwork?"

"Oh yeah! He has a desk in his room and a filing cabinet." She grabs my hand and drags me in that direction.

I've peeked inside Drew's room before. Curiosity got the better of me one day when the girls were occupied. I was too busy admiring the way his room smelled and how comfortable his big, king-sized bed looked to notice the desk in the corner next to his dresser. There are five bedrooms upstairs and only three are full, so I have no clue why he doesn't turn one of them into an office.

"Dad keeps everything here. The key to the filing cabinet is in his nightstand," Penny explains before running back down the hallway, probably to find Sam.

A key? His nightstand? Okay, this feels like an invasion of his space. I grab my phone out of my pocket and shoot him a text.

Sophie: Hey Mr. Muscles ;-) the school lost Penny's shot records and wants you to send a copy with her to school tomorrow. I was going to do it for you, but Penny says the key is in your nightstand and I didn't want to overstep. LMK if that's okay and I'll take care of it for you!

I head back into the living room and pry Penny away from the TV. I grab her homework folder again and we sit down and get to work on it.

An hour later, we're finished with homework, and I start dinner. I check my phone. Nothing from Drew. He's probably still in surgery.

I keep dinner simple as usual. We're having spaghetti and steamed broccoli. Drew likes to make sure there's a vegetable with every meal. I definitely eat much healthier since I started watching Penny.

It's almost seven p.m. by the time we eat and I get the kitchen cleaned up. Checking my phone one more time, I see there's still no response from Drew. I slide my phone back into my pocket and pad back down the hall to Drew's room.

I'm being ridiculous. It's just a filing cabinet. If Penny knows where the key is, he must not be that private about it. I walk over to his nightstand and hesitate for a second before sliding it open. The drawer is mostly empty. There's only a tube of chapstick, a few granola bars, and a small key.

I smile, making a note to ask him about the granola bars later. I take the key out, close the drawer, and make my way to the filing cabinet. The key slides right in and the wooden filing cabinet opens easily. I thumb through the well-organized folders and find one marked *Penny*.

Shaking my head, I internally berate myself for not doing this earlier. It's just one simple thing I can do for him since he's working late tonight. I pull the file out and flip through the papers inside. Her shot records are easy enough to find and there's even a printer on his desk. Turning it on, I flip through the shot records to see how many pages I'll need to copy.

My eyes flick back to the open folder and something strange catches my eye.

I think it's Penny's birth certificate, but Emily Reed is listed as her mother. I blink several times and look at it again. I'm holding it close to my face. Drew's name isn't even listed here. What on earth? Actually, the area that asks for the father's name and signature is blank.

I glance down and see more papers in the folder. My body goes still, the blood running through my veins feels like it has turned to ice. This can't be true.

The other papers in the folder are adoption papers. There has to be a perfectly reasonable explanation for all of this. There's just no way Drew would hide something this big from me. I mean, surely he wouldn't lie to me, right?

Something about this feels off. My gut is telling me something is wrong here. My head is spinning with questions.

Putting the papers carefully back in the folder, I take a deep breath. I take a seat in his office chair and check my phone one last time to see if he's texted back. He hasn't. Still in surgery.

We both agreed our relationship wouldn't affect the girls, and I will stand by that no matter what. I make a copy of the shot records and place the originals back into the folder. Unsure what else to do, I file Penny's folder back where it was and leave the key on top of the filing cabinet.

I inhale one last deep breath to calm myself and walk back out to the main area of the house. The girls are in Penny's room playing with her dollhouse, so I put the shot records in Penny's backpack and zip it up.

My phone pings with a text message, and I take it out to read it.

Drew: Hey gorgeous, don't worry about the shot records. I'll do it. On my way home now!

I swallow the lump that has been lodged in my throat ever since my eyes landed on Penny's birth certificate.

Walking down the hallway, I tell Penny to get her pajamas on and brush her teeth, then I run downstairs to grab some jammies for Samantha. The girls giggle and smile as I help them get dressed and ready for bed, and I try to put the birth certificate out of my head.

I'm reading the girls a bedtime story when Drew appears in Penny's doorway and grins as he looks at all of us cuddled up on her twin sized bed.

"How are my girls?" Drew asks in his warm, husky voice.

He looks so handsome in his black scrubs. I smile back at him, but it feels forced.

"Daddy! I need a bedtime kiss!" Penny jumps up from her bed and runs over to him, hugging him around the legs.

Drew must have noticed my expression because he's looking at me with concern. I get out of Penny's bed and Samantha stands up and holds her arms out for me to hold her. Picking her up, I start to walk out of the room.

"Soph, what's wrong?" he whispers as I walk past him.

It's difficult to look at him, his eyes are so warm and I'm usually comforted by that warmth. But I feel so confused.

"Nothing, I'm alright. Just tired. Samantha and I are going to head to bed, okay?"

His eyebrows furrow like he's unconvinced I'm okay. "Get some rest."

I slide past him into the hallway and carry Samantha downstairs.

Chapter 32

Drew

I have no idea what's going on with Sophie. I'm trying to focus on finishing Penny's bedtime story and enjoying a few minutes with her, but my thoughts keep drifting back to the look in Sophie's eyes.

I've seen her when she's sad, but this was different. Since I've known her, she's never looked at me like that before. If I didn't know any better, I'd say she looked hurt. I don't like it. All I want to do is run to her, pull her into my arms, and kiss the anguish off of her stunning face. But that can wait a few minutes while I put Penny to bed.

I finish the bedtime story, having no clue what I just read as I couldn't focus my thoughts. Tucking the blankets around her, I lean in and kiss her on her cute little forehead.

She grins up at me. "I love you, Daddy."

My heart instantly feels a little lighter. "I love you too, Pen."

I give her one more kiss, then turn her light off and softly close her bedroom door. I walk to my bedroom and open the door. I always keep it closed so Penny doesn't jump on my bed when I'm gone. I don't turn the bedroom light on, but walk straight to the bathroom, strip down, and throw my scrubs into the hamper. I take my time in the shower, letting my muscles relax after spending hours performing surgery.

After my shower I'm feeling a little more relaxed. I throw on some black sweatpants and a plain white t-shirt.

When I step out of the bathroom, my bedroom is still completely dark. Except for a small green light that's blinking in the corner. It draws my eye instantly. I frown as I walk across the room and flick my bedroom light on. The green light is coming from my printer. That's strange. I can't even remember the last time I used that old thing.

Then I see it. The key.

Sophie must've made a copy of Penny's shot records after not getting a response from me.

The blood rushes from my face. I feel cold all over, like I'm going to either pass out or throw up. Then I remember the look on Sophie's face as she walked past me this evening.

"Oh no. No, no, no."

I drag both hands through my wet hair. My phone is in the bathroom, so I turn and walk back over to grab it and check the time. It's been at least half an hour since Sophie went downstairs. Hopefully Samantha's asleep by now.

My stomach roils as I walk down the hallway and then down the basement steps. I don't even bother knocking on the door. My body is on autopilot, I can barely think.

Sophie is sitting on her couch, hands in her lap. She doesn't even look up at me as I enter the room. She has changed into light-pink pajama shorts and a black tank top.

I drop down onto the couch next to her and stretch my arms out to reach for her hands, but she pulls away from me.

"Soph—"

She holds a hand up to stop me. "I saw Penny's birth certificate... I'm so sorry. I didn't mean to intrude. I was trying to help."

"It's okay, I know you were being helpful."

"Can you explain her birth certificate to me? I don't understand."

"Well, I- I- I want to tell you everything, Soph. I just need more time. I need to talk to Emily first."

She finally meets my gaze, her eyes are glossy with unshed tears. "Have you been lying to me this entire time?" A tear slips down her cheek.

"Sophie, you have to understand. I promised my sister I wouldn't say anything. I was trying to give her time to get used to the idea of you and I being together."

"So is Emily Penny's mom? I just want you to tell me the truth." Her lips are set in a straight line and her eyebrows pinch together. "I've been completely honest with you from the start. About me and Sam, about grieving the loss of him… everything." Her voice cracks on her last word. "But you didn't trust me enough to be honest with me. And that really hurts."

This is an unfamiliar expression from Sophie. I can't tell if it's anger, disappointment, or maybe sadness. It might even be all three.

She stands from the couch and paces back and forth in the small living room. I rise from the couch and reach for her, but she pulls away again.

"Sophie, I'm so sorry. I'll tell you the whole story, I promise. I just have to talk to my sister first. I want to do right by you, but I also have to consider Emily's feelings."

"Drew, I was just starting to heal. To feel happy again. To feel like myself. I can't do this." She looks down at her feet, her head shaking back and forth.

I grab her shoulder and urge her to look at me. Her face tips up and my heart wrenches at the sight of tears steadily streaming down her face. I hate being the cause of those tears.

"I've never lied about anything else. Please believe me."

"How am I ever supposed to trust you again, Drew?" She crosses her arms. "I need time to process this."

"Soph. Please."

"We agreed not to let our relationship impact the girls, so I will continue watching Penny after school."

I don't know what else to say, and she wants me to leave. I don't want to go. I want to stay and talk this out, even if it takes all night. But she's upset and hurt and maybe some time to think will be helpful. Maybe she just needs some space and then she'll listen to what I have to say.

She has to. Because I love her and I can't possibly let her go.

It's taken me thirty-six years to find the love of my life, and now that I've found her, there's no way I'm going to give up.

The next day drags by. I barely slept last night, tossing and turning. And the one hour I was actually asleep, I dreamt of Sophie. But it wasn't a pleasant dream like the others. In the dream, she was on a cliff, dangling by one arm. I was on the ground, and the cliff was so steep I couldn't get to her. When her hand slipped and she began to fall, I woke up with a start.

I never got back to sleep. And I've had a throbbing headache all day. No amount of ibuprofen seems to help.

Sophie won't respond to any of my texts. I know a simple "I'm sorry" text isn't enough, but I have no idea how to fix this.

I walk through the door when I arrive home from work and Sophie is in the kitchen as usual. Dinner smells good. Sophie is wearing the apron I got her for our cooking lessons months ago. I'm aching to wrap my arms around her and kiss her neck, to find shelter from this hurt in my heart. To have her comfort me with an embrace and her warm smile.

Closing the door behind me, I walk into the kitchen from the garage. Sophie hears the click of the door and spins to face me.

We stand there, looking at each other but not knowing what to say.

She turns back around and unties her apron before hanging it on the hook by the refrigerator.

"Samantha, get your shoes," she calls as she walks down the hallway towards Penny's room. "We're heading home, okay?"

The girls meet her in the hallway. "Aren't you guys eating dinner with us?" Penny asks, her brow furrowed in confusion.

"Sorry, Pen. We need to get home. I have papers to grade."

I can't see her face, but her voice sounds as sweet as always. She pulls Penny into a hug and that seems to ease her worries. Penny smiles and hugs Sophie back.

"Alright, bye Sammy!" Penny turns to hug Samantha too.

"I wanna pway wip Penny," Samantha grumbles.

Sophie crouches down and picks her up before turning back towards me. "See you tomorrow, Drew."

She smiles at me, but her eyes are sad. She's not looking at me with the familiar affection I've come to crave from her.

I swallow, my throat feeling like sandpaper. "See you tomorrow. Goodnight Samantha."

My voice comes out hoarse. I can't even manage to smile. The muscles in my face can only seem to manage a frown at the moment.

She turns and carries Sam down the stairs. Penny walks into the kitchen and hugs me around the legs.

"Hey, Daddy. Don't pout, we'll see them tomorrow."

Penny and I spend the rest of the evening together until I put her to bed. I love my time with Penny and I cherish it, but I miss having Sophie and Samantha here. I miss feeling like a family.

I miss feeling whole.

And it's only been one day.

After Penny goes to bed, I shower, then pick up my phone to call my sister. I need to tell her Sophie knows about Penny, but I also just need to talk to someone about all of this.

I find her name in my contacts and tap the call button.

She answers after two rings, "Hey bro, what's up?"

"Hey," I croak before climbing into my bed.

"Are you okay? You sound sick." I can hear music and voices in the background.

I lay my head back against the headboard. "Sophie found Penny's birth certificate."

She's quiet on the other end. I can only hear the background noise.

"Let me find a quieter spot." I can hear her flip-flops smacking against the floor and then the click of a door. "Okay, sorry. So you told her?"

"No. She *found* the birth certificate." I rub my temples with my thumb and index fingers.

She breathes heavily. "What do you mean she found it?"

I clear my throat. "The school asked for Penny's shot records. She was just trying to be helpful. So she got them out of my filing cabinet. And all the other paperwork is in the same folder. The birth certificate, the adoption papers, everything."

She gasps, it's small but audible. "Oh no. What did she say?"

"She was confused and asked me to explain it, but I told her I needed more time and needed to talk to you before saying anything. Now she feels like she can't trust me, Em. She'll barely look at me, let alone speak to me."

"I'm so sorry, Drew. I feel like this is all my fault," she pauses. The phone makes a crinkly sound, like she's switching it to her other ear. "I've been seeing a therapist."

"What? Since when?" This is a surprise, but I also feel relieved. I've been trying to get her to see a therapist since she told me she was pregnant with Penny.

"I've only met with her twice. I set up an appointment when you talked to me about telling Sophie."

I'm quiet, waiting for her to continue.

"I realized it made sense for you to tell Sophie. You obviously really care about her, and I can tell she makes you happy. The more I thought about it, the more I realized I was wrong to expect you to keep it from her. My therapist said I was probably projecting my own trauma onto you. And I'm sorry. I was going to talk to you about it, but I haven't see you much lately, and the timing never felt right."

"I'm sorry I haven't been around to hang out with you as much," I tell her, realizing that my relationship with Sophie has affected the time I've had to spend with my sister.

"Don't apologize. You've spent years focusing on me and Penny, taking care of us. I want you to be happy. I want you to spend time with Sophie. She's really good for you."

"Thanks, Em. But I'm not sure I can fix this. I don't know what to do." I shake my head and release a heavy sigh.

"Is it okay if I talk to her? I'll tell her everything. I promise. She's just finding out about it for the first time, so she might need some space to wrap her head around it."

"Are you sure you want to talk to her about it? I can tell her everything, I was just worried you'd never speak to me again if I did."

"I'm sorry. I shouldn't have expected you to keep it a secret from her. It's my story to tell, so I'll be okay talking to her about it."

"Alright, if you're comfortable with that. Hopefully, once you explain the situation, she'll talk to me again. I think she's worried everything I've ever said to her was a lie."

She takes a deep breath. "I can see how she'd feel blindsided. I'm so sorry I messed this up. You wanted to tell her right away, and I stopped you."

"It's okay. We can't change things now. I just want to move forward." A loud yawn comes out of my mouth before I can stop it.

"You sound exhausted."

"I *am* exhausted, I'm going to head to bed."

"Of course, sleep well."

"Bye, Em."

Ending the call, I plug my phone in and then fall back onto my pillow.

Chapter 33
Sophie

It's Friday night. Finally, an end to the longest week ever. It's been exhausting to act normal when I'm falling apart inside. I have to stay positive for Samantha and my students, and it's not like I haven't been through difficult things before.

I tuck Samantha into her little bed and give her a snuggle and a kiss goodnight.

"'Night, Mama." She smiles and pats my cheek.

I smile back. She's always the light on my darkest days. "Goodnight, Sammy girl."

Softly, I close her door behind me and pad across the hallway to my bedroom. I just want to lie in bed and binge watch the rest of *Bridgerton* on my laptop. I press play on my screen, but my mind continues to wander.

Grief and heartbreak are achingly similar.

Drew has been giving me the space I asked him for, which I appreciate. He hasn't been pushy or impatient. He texted me yesterday, telling me he misses me and asking that I come talk to him when I'm ready. I wanted to tell him I miss him, too. I miss him so much. I miss what we had and the trust there was between us.

Every time I see him he looks heartbroken. All I want to do is put the happiness back into his beautiful hazel eyes. But I don't know if I can trust him with my heart again. And how can we have a relationship when he won't even explain the situation to me? I understand his loyalty to his sister, but what about our relationship? We have to be able to be honest with each other.

I have so many questions.

It really sucks to feel happy again, just to have it all ripped away.

A knock comes from the stairway door, jolting me from my thoughts. I ignore the knock. It's probably Drew. And I'm too exhausted to talk this out tonight. My phone pings from my night stand, I hesitate before glancing at the screen, expecting it to be Drew urging me to come open the door. But it's from Emily.

Emily: Hey, it's just me. Can we talk?

I exchanged numbers with Emily a few weeks ago when she watched Samantha and Penny so Drew and I could go on a date. We've never talked much, especially without Drew present. But I'm interested in what she has to say, so I get out of bed and walk to the door and open it.

Emily stands there with an apprehensive look on her face. She's in comfy clothes like she's ready for bed: black leggings and an oversized Seattle Seahawks sweatshirt. She crosses her arms and hugs herself, like she's nervous.

"Hey, come in," I whisper.

She walks inside, and I lead her into the living room. She takes a seat on the couch, but avoids eye contact. "Thanks for letting me in."

"Sure." I take a seat next to her.

She glances at me briefly, then looks back down at her lap where her hands are. "I wanted to explain the situation with Penny." She absently picks at her fingernails.

"First, Drew came to me after your first date. He told me he was serious about you. Really serious. And that he needed to tell you about Penny." She swallows. "I begged him not to. Actually, I left because I was upset. We barely spoke to each other for a week."

"Oh, I didn't know that." It makes me feel a little better than he at least *wanted* to be honest with me. But he still chose not to be.

"Back when I was getting my undergrad, a few of the courses I was taking on campus were in the evening. And by the time class got out, it was dark." She closes her eyes, her chest heaving as she takes deep breaths. "I was alone, walking to my car when a man came out of nowhere. It was too dark to see his face." Her hands are trembling as she recounts the details to me. "But he …. he assaulted me. I didn't report it or tell anyone. Not until a month later, when I found out I was pregnant."

She pauses. "This obviously isn't something I enjoy talking about. When I was pregnant with Penny, I was in a really dark place … emotionally."

Her voice falters and I cover her trembling hands with mine. Her whole body is shaking now.

"Emily, I'm so sorry you went through that."

"It was horrible. Drew was so angry—not at me, but at himself. He was angry he hadn't been there to protect me. It was hard for me to move forward, and Drew was carrying the weight of the world on his shoulders, as usual. He tried so hard to get me to see a therapist or talk to someone. But I just didn't want to relive the whole thing again."

I nod, trying to wrap my mind around what that must have been like for them.

"I knew I wasn't in a good mindset to raise a child, and I wasn't financially independent. So I asked Drew to adopt the baby and raise her. I knew he'd be an amazing dad." Her lips pull up into a sad smile. "And he is. I've never regretted my decision." She takes a deep breath. "I told him I never wanted Penny to know she was conceived that way. I didn't want her to carry that kind of trauma, and he agreed. We came up with that story about a one-night stand so he wouldn't have to tell anyone what happened."

I run my hand through my hair. "I feel awful that I was so hard on him. I had no idea."

"You had no way of knowing. Drew has been an amazing brother and such a wonderful father to Penny. You can't let him go, Sophie. There's not a better or more trustworthy man out there." She looks at me, her lips curving into a genuine smile.

"Thank you for trusting me with this. I can't imagine how difficult it must be to talk about. I think you did an amazing thing for Penny. Please know that I would *never* tell anyone."

She fidgets with her fingers again. "I know."

Before I can stop myself, my arms wrap around her shoulders. Her spine straightens, which makes me remember that she's not a big hugger. She relaxes slightly and wraps one arm around my back.

We pull out of the hug and stare at each other, I think we're both unsure where to go from here.

"So, is Drew home?" I ask.

She wrinkles her nose. "No. I practically forced him to go out. He's been a mess all week. I thought it would be good for him to go out with his buddies."

My eyes fill with tears. "Ugh, I feel awful. I'll talk to him tomorrow."

"Please do. He's called me every evening this week. And I love talking to my brother, but he's being a little needy." She smirks.

"I've missed him like crazy all week." I admit, slumping back onto the couch.

She stands to leave. "He's missed you too."

The next morning, I wake up early, eager to talk to Drew and sort this out. It's barely seven, and Sam isn't even awake yet.

I jump in the shower and think about what all I want to say to Drew today. I understand now why he didn't tell me about Penny. And I should've heard him out instead of just pushing him away and shrinking back to avoid anymore heartbreak.

The tricky thing about love is you have to be willing to put your heart out there to be broken. You never know what the future holds. But you can control your actions and live life the best you can. And the best life for me is a life with Drew.

There's no doubt our future will hold trials and difficulties, but I'd much rather go through those things with Drew by my side than face them alone.

After my shower, I begin my fanciest primping routine. I even dry my hair with a blow dryer and curl it into beachy waves. Samantha appears in my doorway after a while, her eyes are bleary like she's still trying to wake up. Her blonde curls are matted down on one side of her head while the other side is all fluffy.

"Good morning, sweet girl."

She rubs her eyes with the backs of her hands and then looks up at me. "Mommy looks pwetty."

I kneel on the floor in front of her, holding back a chuckle at how crazy her hair is. "Thank you, sweetie. We need to get you ready to go to Grandma and Grandpa's for the day."

That wakes her up instantly. She loves spending her Saturdays with my parents. She runs into her bedroom and starts grabbing clothes out of her dresser.

Together, we pick out her clothes and she helps me select which sundress I should wear. We agree on the yellow one. I'm pretty sure that's Drew's favorite anyway.

Two hours later, I've dropped Samantha off with my parents, and I'm parking in front of Drew's house so we can finally talk. I step out of my car and close the door. As I begin my ascent to his front door, I squeeze my fists together and then release them again. My palms are so sweaty because I'm nervous.

I've pushed him away all week, which only caused heartache for us both. All I want is to talk this out and for our relationship to go back to normal. I want him to wrap me in his big muscular arms and forget about the emotional angst of this past week.

I nearly trip over the last step that leads up to Drew's front porch, but I catch myself and smooth out my dress with my sweaty palms.

Lifting my hand to ring the doorbell, I take a deep breath. Before I can ring it, the door swings open. Emily stands before me, her lips forming an uneasy smile.

She looks me up and down, taking in my dress and my hair. She smiles, but the smile looks sympathetic and unhappy.

"Hey, Sophie, I saw you walking up the steps. I was just going to text you."

"You were?"

"Yeah, Drew isn't home."

My shoulders sag in disappointment. "Oh, when will he be back?"

"Well, he used to camp at least once a year with James and Conner, but they haven't been in ages. So apparently last night when they were out, they decided to camp tonight. They packed up and left about thirty minutes ago."

I groan. "I should have texted him. I was so preoccupied with thinking about what I wanted to say to him, I didn't even consider it."

"I'm sorry, I almost said something about you wanting to talk, but I didn't want to overstep." She steps out onto the porch and closes the door behind her. "They always camp out on James's property. Do you know where it is?"

I shake my head. "I don't. Does he live out in the country?"

Emily crosses her arms and leans against the side of the house. "Yeah, he has a plot of land about forty-five minutes outside of Wichita. That's where they camp, but the cell service out there is terrible."

With a sigh, I ask, "Do you happen to have the address? I could type it into Google Maps."

"I don't think Google Maps is going to work out there."

I slump back against the banister on the front porch. "Well, my parents have Samantha for the day. Surely it couldn't be that hard to find. I have to at least try."

Taking a deep breath, I continue, "I don't think I can wait another day to talk to him."

She nods. "I get that. I'll text you his address, but be careful. There's a twenty percent chance of storms today. The guys ignored my warning, but you know how unpredictable Kansas weather can be."

She pulls her phone out of the front pocket of her hoodie and types out a message.

My phone pings with James's address. "Thank you so much, Emily! I'll screenshot the directions now in case I don't get any service out there."

"That's a solid plan. Good luck, Sophie." She smiles.

"Thanks." I pull her into a big hug before she can stop me.

Chapter 34

Drew

It feels great to be out in nature. I forgot how clear my mind feels out here. No traffic, no street lights, no noise. Just peace and quiet.

"So, your sister's pretty cute, huh?"

Oh, and Conner and James. Only Conner would be brave enough to make a comment about my sister.

"Seriously, Conner?" I pick up a sleeping bag that's still rolled up and throw it at his head.

He blocks it with the back of his arm. "What?" He shrugs. "It's true."

James hammers the last tent peg in the ground and then glares at Conner. "Leave Drew alone. The whole point of this camping trip is so he can relax and get away from his woman problems."

I roll my eyes. "That is *not* why we're camping. We're camping because we love it and we haven't done it in forever."

"Right." Conner raises his eyebrows and gives James a knowing glance.

James stands to his feet and brushes the dirt from his hands onto his worn jeans. "Alright, the tent is up. Now we can make a campfire and relax with some beers."

Conner has the kindling and logs placed in the firepit that James built out here when he first bought the place. His country house and sixty acres of land are way too much for a single man, but James likes his space. And he likes being out here where it's quiet.

And I'm more than happy to take advantage of the peace whenever he invites us out to his place.

I throw the sleeping bags and our pillows into the tent along with the flashlights we packed. It's a four-person tent, so plenty of room for the three of us.

When I look back over my shoulder at James and Conner, I see they have the fire going. We packed plenty of beer, s'mores supplies, and hot dogs to feed us for the night.

It's barely noon now, but it's a perfect day for camping. There's just enough cloud cover to keep us shaded, a cool breeze that tells us fall is creeping in on us, and a large pond that reflects the sky. I'm sure we'll go fishing in the pond later.

The three of us sink back into the Adirondack chairs surrounding the fire pit, and I breathe out a long sigh. "This is the life."

Using the edge of my chair, I pop the cap off of my beer and take a drink from it.

"It really is." James agrees. His eyes are closed, and his ball cap is pulled down over his forehead.

We sit in silence, enjoying the sound of the crackling fire as we sip our beers.

And then I feel two drops of water land on my arm. I whip my head over to look at Conner, thinking he flicked water on me or something.

Conner is looking up at the sky. Even James is alert now, sitting forward in his chair.

"We should've listened to Emily." Conner grimaces.

"Would you quit talking about my sister?"

He rolls his eyes. "I'm serious! She warned us there was a chance of storms today."

"Only a twenty percent chance!" James says, throwing his hands up.

Conner shrugs. "You never know what Kansas weather is going to do, man."

The rain picks up from a few drops here and there to a steady sprinkling.

James stands from his seat. "Alright, let's turn on the radio in the truck and see what they're saying about the weather."

Conner and I follow James to his large pickup. I hop in the front seat and Conner gets in the back. James walks around and gets in the driver's seat, then turns the key in the ignition and flips to a local radio station.

We all listen intently as the meteorologist tells us the chance of storms today has escalated dramatically in the last hour. He also mentions that we're now in a severe thunderstorm warning, and a flash flood warning.

James drags his hand down his face with a groan. "You've gotta be kidding me."

"Apparently Drew's sister is beautiful *and* smart." Conner says, then has the audacity to wink at me when I turn to look at him.

"Shut up, Conner," James and I grumble in unison.

Conner throws his hands up in defense. "Okay, okay. Just trying to provide some comic relief while we're on the cusp of death."

James scoffs. "Between the three of us, we have a surgeon, an anesthesiologist, and a medical doctor." He gives Conner a sidelong glance. "Although sometimes I question how on earth you got a doctorate."

We give Conner a hard time, but he's actually an impeccable doctor. And his patients seem to appreciate his zany sense of humor.

"True. We can handle anything the storm throws at us." I agree with James.

"Unless it's a tornado," Conner mutters under his breath.

After a quick discussion, we all agree it's best to pack up the campsite as quickly as possible then head back to James's house for safety.

As soon as we step foot outside of the pickup, the rain pours down on us. I grab everything out of the tent and throw it in the back of the truck so James can remove the tent pegs. Conner walks over to load up all the food and our cooler. The rain puts the fire out for us, so I guess that's one less thing we have to worry about.

We take a good thirty minutes to take down our campsite and load everything back up. We're all soaking wet by the time we get back inside the warm cabin of the pickup. The rain is pouring down now. We can barely even see the pond that's probably about twenty yards away from us.

James grimly looks out at the rain. "Ugh. The dirt road I have to take to get back to the house floods like crazy in storms like this. It's the downside to living out here." He shifts the pickup into drive and we begin our descent.

The rain is a torrential downpour now and the windshield wipers can barely keep up. The wind is blowing hard. I can feel it shaking the pickup as James slowly creeps forward through the field.

Between the wind and the rain, the cabin of the truck seems loud. James turns the radio up even louder as we continue to listen for weather updates.

"Next time, I'm listening to Emily!" Conner yells from the back seat.

I ignore him.

James continues driving agonizingly slow through the large field, trying to make it to the country road before it gets too muddy out here. It takes us ten minutes just to make it back to the road. We still can't see anything more than five yards ahead of us, but at least we're back on the dirt road. Which is already flooding with water.

We're probably twenty minutes away from his house on a normal day, but who knows how long it'll take us to get back at this rate.

James drives carefully through the large puddles filling up the road and we all listen intently to the weather on the radio. We really should have listened to Emily. But this morning there was only a twenty percent chance of rain. It didn't seem like a big deal.

I wonder how Emily and Penny are doing. Penny isn't a huge fan of storms. I hope Sophie and Sam are okay too. I wish I was there with all the girls, taking care of them. Not that Sophie would even let me at this point.

"What's that?" Conner asks, squinting as he looks through the front windshield.

James brings the pickup to a stop and we all squint to see what's going on. There's a Subaru Outback stopped in the middle of a flooded spot in the road. The water is only about six inches deep. I'm unsure if the vehicle is stuck in the muddy water, or if the driver just got scared. As I'm squinting through the windshield, deciphering the situation, realization hits me.

"That looks just like Sophie's car," I stammer, opening the door and hurling myself out of the truck without another thought.

A blonde woman who looks like Sophie opens the driver's side door of the Outback and stands on the front seat and waves her hands in the air.

"My car is stuck!" She yells.

It *is* Sophie. My heart races. I know she's fine, and it's just a minor flood. But my body goes into beast mode as I splash through the water. My tennis shoes and jeans are covered in the murky water that comes up to my shins.

I wade over to the driver's side door and have to yell over the wind and rain so she can hear me. "What the hell are you doing out here?!"

Once I reach her, she ducks back into her vehicle, sitting in the driver's seat.

"I had to see you!" She says breathily.

Her hair is soaked and plastered to her face and shoulders. She's wearing her yellow sundress—which looks even brighter amidst the dark and stormy sky. Her dress is sopping wet and clinging to her body. I stare at her, waiting for her to continue.

Her chest is heaving as she breathes, "I love you, Drew."

I duck down and pull her into a hug, which leaves half of my body awkwardly hanging out of the vehicle, But I don't care, I *have* to touch her. She returns the embrace, wrapping her arms around my neck, then kisses me, hard. Like she's desperate and this could be her last chance to kiss me.

We're cold and wet and there's a storm brewing all around us, but I'm completely oblivious to anything but the warmth of her lips on mine. The sky might be grey and cold, but my body is all sunshine and rainbows.

I pull away and put my hands on both sides of her face. "I love you too, Sophie."

She smiles and her chin quivers. Her face is already so wet I can't tell if she's crying or not. A sharp crack of lightning in the sky brings us back to our surroundings.

"Would you two get in the pickup already!" Conner yells.

We look over and see his head peeking out of the passenger window. Effortlessly, I pick Sophie up and carry her in my arms as I wade back through the water. Conner has moved to the front seat so I open the backdoor and Sophie and I pile in.

Her teeth are chattering and her body shakes with a shiver. I grab my sleeping bag from the seat next to her, unravel it and wrap it around both of us. Sophie raises her chin, and her eyes meet mine. I smile at her before going in for another kiss. She kisses me back without restraint.

We hear someone clear their throat from the front seat and I glance up to see James in the rearview mirror.

"You guys realize we're still here, right?" He asks.

Conner punches him in the arm. "Leave them alone, they're in love, man."

Once we make it back to James's house, I give Sophie a pair of dry sweats and a t-shirt to change into. They're going to be gigantic on her, but she was freezing in her soaked sundress. I change into some sports shorts and a hoodie in one of the guest rooms, and then walk back into the upstairs living room.

Conner and James have made themselves scarce, probably retreating to the basement to play video games.

I sit on James's plush grey sofa and wait for Sophie. She comes out of the bathroom in the hallway with her wet hair pulled up into a messy bun and wearing my clothes. I swear I could drop down and propose to her in that instant. Something about seeing a woman wearing your clothes brings out the primal urge to wife her up.

Sophie smiles as she walks into the room. She doesn't even bother sitting next to me. Instead, she drops down right into my lap. And I'm definitely not complaining.

"I'm so sorry for not telling you about Penny." I nuzzle my face into the side of her neck.

She smells amazing, like flowers mixed with how I imagine a rainforest would smell.

"I'm sorry for not listening." She leans back so she can see my face. "Emily came over last night. She told me everything."

My eyes widen. I wasn't sure when Emily would be willing to talk to her, or if she would end up deciding not to open up about it. She hasn't even been willing to talk to me about what happened. Her therapist must really be helping.

"Really, she did?"

"You're such a wonderful man, Drew. I think it's amazing that you adopted Penny. And that Emily still gets to be in her life."

My eyes fill with tears, but I blink them away. "It means so much to me to hear you say that."

"I mean it. You lost your parents and then stepped in to raise your sister, and then Penny. All without complaint. I see how much you love them, and how well you've taken care of them." She smooths her hand down the side of my face. "I'm so lucky to be loved by you."

I lean in so our foreheads rest against each other. "I love you so much."

"I love you too. So, no more secrets, right?"

I kiss her again. "No more secrets."

Chapter 35
Sophie

There's a beautiful disaster that is the post-Christmas-morning massacre surrounding us. It's Christmas day and Samantha and I are celebrating with Drew, Penny, and Emily. Christmas music hums through the bluetooth speakers in Drew's kitchen, courtesy of Michael Bublè, and wrapping paper in a myriad of colors and patterns covers the floor in a blanket of festivity. It's the happiest kind of chaos.

The past three months have been wonderful. Drew and I have gotten to know each other so well, and we even take the girls on dates with us all the time. There's a taco truck the four of us frequent near the Wichita River. We've settled into a comfortable routine, enjoying the happiness that comes from being surrounded by those you love, even if it's just mundane everyday life. We're a family, albeit a unique one. But a family nonetheless.

I wouldn't change a thing.

Okay, that's a lie. I'd love to sleep next to Drew each night instead of saying goodbye to him, then stalking back down to the basement. But we both agreed we'd wait until we're married for that step.

I'm cuddled up next to my man on the sectional while we watch the girls play together with their new American Girl dolls. Emily is between them, helping them dress their dolls in the new doll clothes "Santa" brought. Sam plops down into Emily's lap, and Emily kisses the top of her head. She's so sweet with the girls. Sam has fallen in love with her just like she did Drew. She even calls her Aunt Em now.

Glancing at the clock on the dining room wall, I groan and wrap my arms around Drew. "Sorry, but I gotta go caroling soon."

He chuckles and rubs circles on my shoulder. "Better get ready to go. I know you've been looking forward to it."

"I *was* looking forward to it before I realized it would be twenty degrees outside today."

He smirks. "Just bundle up, and you'll have fun just like you always do with those rowdy ladies."

"You're probably right. Knowing Bernice and Gerda, they'll likely bring some kind of spiked hot beverage for us all to partake in," I say with a laugh.

Apparently, the Wonderful Widows group goes caroling every Christmas together, and this year they wrangled me into it.

He kisses my temple. "It's just a few hours. The girls will play with their presents, then we'll all load up and head to your parent's house for dinner."

With a sigh, I stand from my comfortable warm spot on the couch. I look at Drew with a pout and he laughs at my dramatics. I head downstairs to my bedroom and pull on my thickest socks and some knee-high boots. There's a chance of snow today and I need to be prepared. In the bottom drawer of my dresser, I have all my winter items tucked away. I pull out a matching hat and scarf set that looks Christmassy. It's red and green plaid, lined with brown fur. Lastly, I grab my black puffer coat that hits me at the knees and slide my arms into it.

I walk back upstairs and Drew meets me at the top of the stairway. He gives me one of those sexy smirks before grabbing the zipper at the bottom of my coat and slowly zipping my coat all the way up.

"This would be a lot better if I was removing clothing and not adding clothing," he says with a wink.

I swat his hands away with my fluffy gloved ones. "Don't be naughty."

"Why not? Santa already gave us our presents." He grins, then gives me a quick kiss on the lips. "I started your car so it should be nice and warmed up for you."

"Aw, thank you. You take such good care of me." I smile at him, then spin on my heel and walk toward the girls. "Alright, girls. Be good and I'll be back later."

Samantha hops up from her place in Emily's lap and runs towards me. "Bye, Momma!"

"Bye, Sophie!" Penny says as she chases after Sam, both plowing into my giant coat and hugging me.

"See you all in a few hours!"

ele

An hour into Christmas caroling with my fellow Wonderful Widows, we round the corner in the College Hill neighborhood. I'm basically frozen to death by this point, but Bernice and Gerda are still going strong.

"Oh, hey, my parents live on this street," I tell them and then take a swig of the thermos filled with very strong Irish coffee.

Bernice and Gerda give each other a look—one of those looks where they're obviously communicating with each other without words.

"Well, whad'ya know?" Gerda says before looping her arm through her sisters.

"Fancy that! What a coincidence," Bernice replies with a smile and then they continue walking.

I look over at Ashley and Lisa, who are on my right. They shrug their shoulders, looking equally guilty.

Evie is on my left, and she makes a strangled squeaking sound. I flip my head to look at her, but she's just looking at her feet. Hm, maybe I imagined it.

We continue caroling, singing the same two Christmas carols at each house on the opposite side of the street from my parent's home. Many of the residents recognize me since I grew up on this street, and a few even give us little treats like Christmas candies and cookies.

When we finish caroling to the home directly across from my parent's, Bernice and Gerda abruptly cross the street instead of continuing down the row to the rest of the houses. I can't carry a tune to save my life, and definitely wasn't wanting to sing for anyone who actually knows me. I run ahead to catch up with our fearless leaders.

"What are we doing? This is my parent's house. Can't we just skip to the next one?" I beg, trying to escape my inevitable embarrassment.

They just smile at me endearingly but continue walking up to my parent's front door and ring the doorbell.

Mom and Dad open the front door not even one second later, like they were expecting someone.

"Oh, hello! Oh my, are you Christmas carolers?" My mom asks with a beaming smile. She's a terrible actress.

"How delightful!" Dad claps his hands together.

Madden, Odette, David, and Brooks all step out onto the front stoop with huge smiles lighting up their faces. They all have coats and gloves on already, so it's pretty obvious they knew we were coming.

Bernice and Gerda take a few steps back to stand with the rest of our group and they start us off singing, "We Wish You a Merry Christmas."

This is so freaking weird. Why wouldn't anyone have told me we were caroling to my family today? And how did they even know the correct address?

Our song ends, and instead of the second classic Christmas carol we've sung to literally every other house, Bernice and Gerda begin to sing Mariah Carey's, "All I Want For Christmas is You." When everyone else jumps in to sing with them—my family included—my mind is still reeling at how strange this is becoming.

The front door opens behind my family, and Drew comes into view. His mouth slowly pulls up in a grin. Emily, Penny and Samantha, who are all bundled up, rush outside with him to stand with my family. Drew walks towards our group, but everyone disperses, leaving just the two of us standing in the middle of the front yard. Right before Drew gets to me, he bends at the waist and grabs the ends of two extension cords laying in the grass and plugs them together. The top of my parent's house lights up and my jaw drops.

Tears rush to my eyes when I see the words "Will you marry me?" spelled out on the roof with Christmas lights.

When I bring my attention back to Drew, he's down on one knee in front of me. Everyone is still singing in the background as he takes my hand in his. He removes my left glove and kisses my palm before turning my hand over.

With his free hand, he takes a small velvet box out of his pocket and opens it. "Sophie, will you please marry me and move out of my basement and into my room?"

He opens the box to reveal a gorgeous emerald-cut diamond on a thin gold band.

I laugh as tears stream down my cold cheeks. "Yes, Drew. I'll marry you."

Without waiting for him to get back up on his feet, I kneel, put my hands on his cheeks and kiss him good, not caring who's watching. The group of friends and family surrounding us whistle and cheer, but we just keep kissing each other. Penny and Samantha storm out to meet us in the yard, so we finally pull apart and hug them. Drew places the lovely ring on my finger and the girls ooh and ahh over it.

"Alright, it's freezing, let's get inside!" Dad shouts and opens the front door.

Mom nods. "Yes, there's plenty of hot soup for everyone!"

Everyone shuffles inside, but Drew, Penny, Samantha and I hang back for a minute, enjoying this moment together. The four of us eventually walk inside, hand in hand. All together as a family.

Sophie

One Year later

As I walk toward the stage, my hands shake nervously. I steady myself, which isn't easy in these stilettos. My navy blue formal gown sways at my feet as I make my way up the stairs and across the stage to the podium. There are at least five hundred in attendance this evening, which is great, but that's a lot of people to speak in front of.

Ugh, I wish I had Madden's knack for public speaking.

The grand ballroom in the Broadway Hotel downtown feels incredibly glamorous, perfect for tonight's event. Everyone is seated at the various round tables around the ballroom, decked out in formal wear. The tables are donned in white linens and have lovely centerpieces of red and orange flowers. My mom helped me plan the event tonight, thank goodness. I couldn't have done it without her.

I take a steadying breath before I start my speech and lock eyes with Drew, sitting at the very front of the room. He smiles and nods his head toward me, an encouraging gesture. His faith in me gives me the courage to be up here in front of all these people.

"Good evening, everyone," I speak into the microphone with a smile. The room quiets down and waits for me to continue.

"Thank you all for being here tonight to help us raise money for something very close to my heart."

After marrying Drew in an intimate backyard ceremony in my parent's backyard, we honeymooned in Hawaii. During our honeymoon, we had *so* much time to talk ... uninterrupted. Which allowed us to have several long conversations about things we'd never discussed before. Such as my trust fund. I knew what I wanted to do with my trust fund and Sam's life insurance money, but the fact that Drew wholeheartedly agreed with my plan made it even better.

"Together, with my husband Drew, we are very excited to announce that with your help, we have fully funded the Samuel Miller Scholarship fund."

Cheers and applause fill the large room, and I take a moment to clap along with the crowd. Drew beams at me from his seat, looking so dashing in his tuxedo and freshly shaven face. I grin back at him.

The applause dissipates, and I continue, "This scholarship will help so many children in our community to attend Heartland Academy. Our school has so many great resources that, for so long, couldn't be afforded to families who could benefit from them the most. Especially families with special needs children. With this scholarship fund, we are providing the link for these families to access the resources they need to help their children."

I pause to look down at the notecards I brought up on stage with me, not because I don't know the words, but more to build up some courage.

"My late husband, Samuel Miller, would've been so proud of what we're accomplishing here for our community. Your generous donations have not only allowed us to provide several scholarships, but we've also partnered with Heartland Academy to hire another special education teacher, and created a sensory room."

Glancing around the room, I can see my family at one of the tables near the front. They're all here showing their support tonight, my parents and all of my siblings. The pride in my father's eyes means so much to me, especially knowing that we haven't always agreed on how I should use my trust fund. I lock eyes with my dad and he winks at me, like a silent acknowledgment of his support.

"Thank you all so much for coming out tonight for our very first Samuel Miller Scholarship Gala. We couldn't have made this happen without you! I'll stop talking now so everyone can start dancing."

I smile toward the crowd and earn some laughs before retreating from the stage. Another round of applause goes around the room as I walk back toward our table. Music from the live band begins, and Drew stands from his seat and comes forward to take my hand.

"Mrs. Reed, may I have this dance?" He pulls my hand up to his lips and kisses the back of it.

A smirk pulls at the corner of my lips at his endearment. He never misses a chance to call me Mrs. Reed, and I love it.

"I thought you'd never ask, Mr. Reed."

He meets my gaze as we walk toward the dance floor, a devilish twinkle in his eye. "That's *Dr.* Reed, thank you very much."

"Oh? I thought you were a phlebotomist. My apologies," I reply before biting my bottom lip to keep from laughing.

He chuckles as we reach the dance floor and pulls me into his arms.

"You think you're really funny, don't you?" He asks just as we start to sway to the music.

Instead of answering, I just wink at him.

The dance floor has filled with couples, everyone obviously enjoying the big band music. Madden and Odette pass by us.

"Great speech, sis!" Madden says before spinning Odette.

"I learned from the best!" I respond, and he grins.

"You really did great up there," Drew says, drawing my attention back to him. "I couldn't be more proud to be your husband. I love your generous heart."

This man never ceases to melt me. I slide my hands around his neck and stand on my toes to kiss him. Drew leans into the kiss, tightening his hold around my waist.

"Geez, you two, get a room." We pull apart and look over to see Brooks standing next to us with his pretty blonde date.

Drew grins at him. "Sounds good to me." He glances back at me. "How soon can we get out of here, Soph?"

"Gross, I do *not* want to know about any of that." Brooks grimaces and steers his date in the opposite direction.

Drew ignores him and releases me into a spin. I can feel his eyes roam over my formal gown, the heat of his gaze sending a tingle down my spine. My dress is navy blue chiffon with a sweetheart neckline. It cinches at the waist and flares out at the hips. But the best part is the—tasteful—slit that goes up to the middle of my thigh. The gown is classy *and* sexy. I knew Drew would love it.

"But seriously, though, how soon can we get out of here? Because the slit in your dress is beckoning me." He pulls me back into his arms as the music from the band slows down.

I push my bottom lip out in a pout. "As much as I'd like to get you out of that tux, we should probably be the last ones to leave tonight. Seeing as we're the hosts and all."

He heaves a sigh and rolls his eyes sarcastically. "I was afraid you would say that."

Two hours later, we're happy but exhausted from dancing and chatting with the guests. Drew and I are the last ones here along with the hotel staff who have begun to take down the tables. My feet are killing me from wearing heels all evening. I don't know how I'll even make it to our vehicle in the parking garage.

I lean into Drew's side for support. "You're going to have to carry me to the car."

One side of his mouth pulls up into a smirk. He reaches into the breast pocket of his tuxedo jacket and pulls out a key card.

"Thankfully, we're staying in a suite upstairs for the night."

My jaw drops slightly, and then I smile. "Well, aren't you full of surprises!"

"It was actually Emily's idea, but I thought it would be perfect. She said she'd stay with the girls until noon tomorrow so we can sleep in." He slips his arm around my waist and snuggles me closer to him.

"Remind me to get her an extra nice Christmas present this year," I tease as we walk out of the ballroom.

I nuzzle into Drew's large form, thankful he's supporting my weight since my feet feel like they're about to fall off. We reach the elevator to go up to our room and step inside. The hotel is historic, but it's all been remodeled into a glamorous but modern design. The elevator doors and fixtures are brass, giving them an old-world feel. Just as I'm admiring the marble floors of the elevator, I realize I didn't pack an overnight bag.

"Oh, no ..." I look at my husband, who's standing by my side, and bring my hand to my chest. "I don't have anything to change into."

He turns to face me, a seductive smile on his face. "That's alright, you can sleep naked." He waggles his eyebrows.

"Drew! I'll look ridiculous when we check out tomorrow morning and I'm still in a formal gown!"

He bursts out laughing, the sound filling the small elevator. I shake my head in mock dismay, but can't hide the smile on my face.

Once he stops laughing long enough to talk, he says, "Soph, I packed overnight bags for us. They're already in the room."

"You're horrible. Here I thought I'd be doing the walk of shame in the morning." The elevator dings once it reaches the top floor and we exit.

Drew is still chuckling when he links his arm through mine and kisses the top of my head. "You should've seen the look on your face."

We reach the door to our room and he slides the keycard into the slot to unlock it. He holds the door open for me to enter, but I cross my arms and pretend to be annoyed with him.

"You're on thin ice, mister. Teasing me after such a long day."

He grabs my arm and yanks me against him, walking us back into the suite and letting the door close behind him.

"I can think of a few ways to get back in your good graces, my love."

I sigh as he places hot kisses along the side of my neck. "I could never stay mad at you for long."

"Good." I can feel him smiling against my neck. His mouth moves to my ear and he whispers, "I love you, Sophie Reed."

"I love you too, Mr. Muscles."

The End

Thank you for reading!

If you enjoyed this book, could you do me a favor?

I would be so grateful if you took a few moments to leave me a review.

Positive reviews on Amazon and Goodreads will help others to find and read my book!

As an indie author, your support and feedback are vital! It also helps me give readers what they want in future books!

Many thanks in advance! <3

Other Books by Leah

Have you read Madden and Odette's story, *Running Mate*? Find it on Amazon!

Stay in the loop!

For updates on future releases, head to my website and subscribe to my newsletter!

David Windell's book, *Check Mate*, is now available for preorder!

Acknowledgments

Writing a book is not a one-person show. There are so many amazing people behind the scenes helping me out, or brainstorming with me!

Thank you to Amy Guan for editing, your input helped me add so much depth to my story.

Thank you to my incredible sister-in-law, who always reads my very early manuscripts before they've developed and turned into a beautiful butterflies!

Thank you to my BETA team, Amanda @my.bookish.heart and Madi @apageofpeace ! You ladies are awesome. Your suggestions were so helpful in turning this manuscript into a great story!

Lastly, thank you to my ARC team! I love how excited you guys have been for Drew and Sophie's story! Can't wait to hear what you all think!

About the Author

Leah is a military spouse and currently resides in Northern California with her husband and three children. Kansas is her home state, and holds a special place in her heart.

Her parents always told her she lived in her own little world and was oblivious to reality. The real world was simply too boring. Writing is how she enjoys sharing her little world with others.

Printed in Great Britain
by Amazon

THE SECRET OF EMU FIELD

ELIZABETH TYNAN is an associate professor in the Graduate Research School at James Cook University Townsville. A former journalist, her book *Atomic Thunder: The Maralinga Story* (NewSouth, 2016) won the Prime Minister's Literary Award (Australian History) and the CHASS Australia Book Prize in 2017.

In this sensitive and insightful account of the impact of the atomic testing in Australia, Elizabeth Tynan reminds us of the human and cultural cost of a most aggressive form of imperial colonisation, ensuring a shameful episode is remembered not just for the horror it inflicted but the strength of spirit of those who survived it and have lived with its legacy. *The Secret of Emu Field* is meticulously researched and a must-read to understand a cold war history, an arrogant officialdom and an unfathomable desecration of Aboriginal land.

LARISSA BEHRENDT

This is an important and well-written book. It brings back from the far edges of living memory the extraordinary story of Britain's atomic bomb tests in Australia. Emu Field was the site of the first two explosions on the Australian mainland in October 1953. Elizabeth Tynan uncovers much of the story which is still surrounded by walls of secrecy. She uncovers a saga of British recklessness and an indifference to the long-term consequences of the tests. The reader is left with a revealing glimpse of the Australian government's lazy complicity and deference to Britain. The difficulty we had then in dealing with our 'great and powerful friends' is still with us.

HENRY REYNOLDS

The question 'why weren't we told?' is heard far too frequently in relation to Australian history, particularly in reference to Aboriginal histories. Tales of dispossession, death, destruction, and disadvantage are regularly greeted with a refrain of 'we didn't know'. In this meticulously researched book, the award-winning author of *Atomic Thunder: The Maralinga Story*, Elizabeth Tynan presents us with the shocking story of the two atomic tests and five minor trials performed at Emu Field, South Australia, in the 1950s. The black mist released from the cruelly named 'Operation Totem' can now be seen by all. Tynan's razor-sharp prose and forensic level historical research jolt the reader from any comfort or certainty and ensure that going forward Emu Field will be remembered alongside Maralinga as sites of treachery, suffering and anxiety on the long road towards healing.

LYNETTE RUSSELL